Praise for
the Novels of Cecilia Tan

SLOW SE[...]

"Tan returns to incredibly h[...]
the light to ex-flame James's d[...] for a bit of fun, he
presses Karina to give up on James. The sex scenes here are
once again as hot as they are imaginative."

—*RT Book Reviews*

"5 Stars! *Slow Seduction* was a tasty treat to say the least. I
cannot wait to get my hands on book three. If you are looking for erotica, stop whatever you are doing and get this
book." —DivasDailyBookblog.wordpress.com

SLOW SURRENDER

"4½ stars! This is the BDSM novel all the other millionaire
dom heroes want to star in. Tan takes an overused trope and
turns it into a dreamy, erotic fantasy that draws the reader
down the rabbit hole along with Karina. The sex scenes are
lush and erotic...Readers will be clamoring for the next book
in the series." —*RT Book Reviews*

"Move over, E L James. Cecilia Tan's *Slow Surrender* is sin-
fully sweet and sublimely erotic. As with sipping a superb
single-malt scotch served neat, you'll savor the slow burn as
it builds to a deliciously unanticipated...climax."

—Hope Tarr, award-winning author

"Loved, loved *Slow Surrender* and am waiting on pins and needles for book two...Another brilliant outing from Cecilia Tan...Her characters are full of life and emotion, and so believable. Definitely a keeper!"

—NightOwlReviews.com

"If you are a fan of the billionaire dom, you should not miss *Slow Surrender*. Cecilia Tan weaves a compelling and red-hot tale that will have readers eager for more."

—RomanceNovelNews.com

Slow
Satisfaction

SLOW SATISFACTION

CECILIA TAN

FOREVER

NEW YORK   BOSTON

Copyright © 2014 by Cecilia Tan
Excerpt from *Slow Surrender* copyright © 2013 by Cecilia Tan
All rights reserved. In accordance with the U.S. Copyright Act of 1976, the scanning, uploading, and electronic sharing of any part of this book without the permission of the publisher is unlawful piracy and theft of the author's intellectual property. If you would like to use material from the book (other than for review purposes), prior written permission must be obtained by contacting the publisher at permissions@hbgusa.com. Thank you for your support of the author's rights.

Forever
Hachette Book Group
237 Park Avenue
New York, NY 10017

www.HachetteBookGroup.com

Printed in the United States of America

RRD-C

First Edition: August 2014
10 9 8 7 6 5 4 3 2 1

Forever is an imprint of Grand Central Publishing.
The Forever name and logo are trademarks of Hachette Book Group, Inc.

The Hachette Speakers Bureau provides a wide range of authors for speaking events. To find out more, go to www.hachettespeakersbureau.com or call (866) 376-6591.

The publisher is not responsible for websites (or their content) that are not owned by the publisher.

Library of Congress Control Number: 2013949886

ISBN: 978-1-4555-2928-5

For everyone who had to wait for satisfaction while I finished writing this novel. All of you.

Contents

Acknowledgments

Many people helped bring me to this point in my career and it is impossible to name them all, even if it were not tricky to name people in a work of erotic fiction. But corwin, my corwin, deserves first mention. My dreams would have been so much harder—if not impossible—to achieve without that last twenty-three years of love and support from him.

This book wouldn't have happened without my indefatigable agent, Lori Perkins. Thanks, Lori, for never telling me I was too kinky.

Huge thanks go to my colleagues over the years at the New England Leather Alliance, whose mission of outreach and support for the leather, BDSM, and fetish communities has made a real difference in people's lives: Vivienne, Danny, Scott, Rae, Percy, Jack, Bendy, and everyone else who has busted their hump to volunteer for the community and fight for BDSM acceptance and education.

To my parents for always telling me yes when it came to expressing my creativity, whether it was music or writing or

acting or what, and never judging me for my choice of partners or my sexuality.

And to my fandom friends, who truly understand that
love is what binds us all together and makes being human
worthwhile.

Love is the music that makes the soul sing.

SLOW
SATISFACTION

One

Your Mother in a Whirl

Dearest Karina,

I have no idea if you'll read this. I hope you will. I decided to sit down and write because whenever I try to explain myself to you in person, either my passions get the best of me or my fears do. Perhaps sitting down in a quiet place to compose this, without the distraction of your presence, I can put my feelings into words.

First, an apology. I regret many things, but none more than how much I hurt you. I have no excuse. My past is my past. My baggage is heavy, and perhaps now you can see why I wanted a fresh start with you, as if I had no past, no attachments, no burdens. And you gave me the freedom to be myself and to love you without reservations. I wish I had been able to keep my past and my demons at bay for one more day back in April, and I wish it again now. I'm sorry. I let my fears get the better of me that night at the ball, my suspicions and my paranoias blinding me to what I had right in front of me.

The love of my life.

I'm a fool. Maybe that means I don't deserve you. Stefan, who has never said a word out of line in all the time he has worked for me, even told me I had made a mistake.

I hope you will let me apologize in person. I have so much more to tell you, so much that I dare not put in a letter. I want to tell you everything. Everything you want to know, anyway. It might take years. But I want to spend years with you. I want to share my life with you. Whatever life I will have going forward from this moment, I can't imagine it without you.

But I cannot lie: that life is about to get very complicated again.

I thought I had put a whole chapter behind me when we met. I thought my contractual obligations had been fulfilled and I thought the false obligations had been dissipated, but it was not so. I cannot say more in a letter, but please let me tell you in person.

I do not know what will happen from this point. I would disappear completely, into anonymity in some distant country, perhaps, except for you. There is no other woman like you in the world and I was a fool not to love you as you deserve.

Please let me try.

Yours, heart, body, and soul,
James Byron LeStrange

My hands trembled a little as I read the e-mail from James on my phone, while the taxi picked up speed on the highway, hurrying me toward the hospital. Why did I read it then? Why? I should have at least waited until I was alone, but there had been three texts from him on my phone when I had landed, all saying some variation of "I'm sorry" and promising to explain more. And if there was one thing I wanted most from James it was an explanation. When I'd looked into my e-mail to pull up the name of the hospital my sister had sent me, I saw the message from James there, and I'd been unable to resist.

Unable to resist. That was my second beef with James. He seemed to be able to manipulate me too easily. How else could you explain how much I missed him, how much I wanted him, even though I was trembling with rage at him?

He probably thought his message was as apologetic and conciliatory as possible, but it only made me angrier. Any apology was meaningless without an explanation after all the secrets he had kept from me, so an apology that still kept all his secrets intact was as fake as the aliases he used. Did he truly not understand that? After failing to tell me who he was during our affair in New York until I forced it out of him, failing to tell me about the secret BDSM society in England he was a member of, failing to tell me he pushed Damon, a member of that society, to "test" me, and then failing to tell me that he *might be married*? Failing to tell me anything about what the hell was going on while throwing out phrases like "love of my life" and "love you as you deserve" was insulting.

Part of me wanted to believe him. Part of me wanted to forgive him immediately and kneel at his feet and wait for him to tell me all about it. Surely he would...If he really loved me...But damn it, he didn't deserve my devotion or my submission the way things were right now. He was going to have to earn it back.

If I let him.

I considered deleting the e-mail.

But I didn't. I had other troubles coming at me at the moment. I didn't know what I was going to find when I got to the hospital. I barely saw the office parks and housing developments roll past as I stared out the window. My mother had fallen down a flight of stairs. The last time Jill and I had talked, they hadn't yet known the full extent of her injuries, especially the blow to her head. All I knew from Jill's e-mail was that she had come out of surgery okay and that Jill was worried Mom's boyfriend might have had something to do with it.

I hoped she was wrong. I hoped that was merely Jill being freaked out over the accident and needing someone to blame. But I couldn't do anything from thousands of miles away in England, which was why I was here now.

I read James's e-mail again. If there was one thing James was good at, it was holding back: emotion, information, even his orgasm. Here, he wasn't holding back the emotion. I could tell he was trying to be sincere. *Love of my life.* James wouldn't say, or type, those words if he didn't absolutely mean them. James had never lied to me directly; he insisted on honesty in everything we said.

But that didn't cover what was not said. I saw the words "I would disappear completely, into anonymity in some distant country" and felt a spike of anxiety and rage. *I know you would, James, because you've done it to me once already.* How did I know he wouldn't do it again?

He did say he would explain. In person. But in person he had a way of making me forget myself, of drawing me into his aura of power and desire. Even in public.

I turned off my phone as the taxi exited the highway, the blue signs pointing to the hospital showing it was near.

Pulling my fully stuffed suitcases up to the hospital reception desk was awkward. Thankfully, the nurses on my mother's ward were very sympathetic that I had come directly from the airport. They took the bags behind the duty desk where they'd be out of the way, and a nurse with a cardigan sweater over her scrubs led me to my mother's room.

Jill was sitting in a chair outside the room, reading the newspaper. She stood up when she saw me, giving me a bear hug.

"Can we go in? How is she?" I asked.

"She was asleep last I looked." Jill folded the paper as if trying to keep it from making crinkling noises and then tucked it into the tote bag on the floor next to her chair.

The nurse motioned for us to wait and slipped into the room. When she came out she said, "Yeah, she's asleep. It's probably best to let her try to rest as much as possible. It'll be time for her next meds in an hour. I'll be back then."

Jill pulled another chair over from farther down the hall and we sat down together. I finally let out the breath I had been holding. "Well, I made it."

"I'm glad. It's been rough here by myself."

"Have you seen her boyfriend? You said something on the phone about him and in your e-mail."

She scrubbed her face with her hands. "I haven't seen him. But I'm suspicious as hell."

"So you said! You also mentioned some of Mom's stuff going missing?"

"It's hard to be sure. It's nothing so obvious as the place looking ransacked, you know? But I couldn't find that velvet case with the good silver in it."

"The silverware she never let us use, you mean?" Some holidays my mother would take the silver out and polish it, but I never once saw her put it out on the dining room table for a holiday meal. I couldn't understand the point of having a special set of fancy silverware if you never used it, until one day Jill read me a book about dragons and then it started to make sense. The silver wasn't for using: It was guarded treasure. It was part of Mom's dragon hoard. "Her hoard?" I asked to see if Jill remembered.

She smiled. "Yeah. Speaking of which, I'm pretty sure some of her jewelry is gone, too. That's the thing though. It's only a few items, not all of it. Just most of what I remember us playing with as kids."

"Could she have pawned it herself?"

"Maybe. I called the bank because I was worried maybe he was emptying out her bank account, too. She doesn't seem to be hurting for money right now, but who knows? Maybe she sold it years ago and we just don't know."

"I take it that means there was no suspicious activity on her account."

"No. They assured me she doesn't have a cosigner and the only automatic withdrawals are for the minimum payments on her credit card and a monthly gym membership."

"Gym membership!"

"I know, right?" Jill couldn't help but smile at the thought of our mother, who thought sweating was unladylike, going to a gym. "There's a shiny new place downtown."

"Maybe it's the hot place to meet guys," I said, not joking at all. "Okay, but, Jill, back up for a second. You haven't actually told me anything that points at what's-his-name."

"Phil. Okay, I admit, the missing silver could have been Mom's own doing. But her engagement ring? The one Dad gave her? She's not wearing it and I couldn't find it anywhere. It used to be in a special ring box of its own."

"I don't remember that."

"Really? We used to play with it. Here, look at this. Do you remember this?" She dug into her bag to pull out a family photo album. She flipped a few pages, and there we were in dress-up clothes, clearly playing "wedding." From the look of the napkin on my head, I was the bride. Jill must have been playing the part of the priest, and the whole wedding party, including the groom, was made up of teddy bears and stuffed animals. Many of them were wearing bow ties.

"Am I wearing her engagement ring here?" I squinted at the picture. I couldn't have been older than four.

"I think you are. I remember the ring clearly, and it's definitely not in her stuff now. Neither is the string of pearls she told me Dad bought her on their honeymoon."

"And what are the chances that one day she got fed up with the stuff from Dad and sold it in a fit of pique?"

"It's possible, but not likely. I think she really liked those keepsakes of him." Jill sighed.

"You still haven't told me a good reason to suspect Phil. Not all men are jerks, Jill."

"You think I don't know that!" She started to raise her voice, then hushed herself before a nurse could come scold us.

"I'm just saying don't jump to conclusions. I don't exactly have great examples of men treating me well in my past, so trust me, I'm inclined to jump on the boy-bashing bandwagon right now. But let's try to be calm about it and think it through. I know we're both upset about Mom. I'm just saying let's not take that out on some poor guy who may be sitting at home worried half to death that his girlfriend is seriously injured."

Jill took a deep breath. "Okay, let me tell you the rest of

what I know, which will explain why I'm so suspicious of him. Did I tell you yet about her car?"

"No. What happened to her car?"

"When I got here yesterday, I went to the house thinking, stupidly, that I'd use her car. So I go into the garage and find it completely dead. Not a click. At first I think that's weird, I wonder if she left her lights on and totally drained the battery or what? I didn't have time to wait around for a jump start, so I took a taxi. Later, I went back to the house to sleep, and that's when I started to think things were missing."

"So you said."

"So it could have been the boyfriend, or it could have been someone who heard about her being out of commission who broke in. Either way, I didn't feel safe in the house, so I spent the night with the Rosemonts next door. And they told me the car's been out of commission for six months and that Phil drives her everywhere."

"Okay, that's weird."

"I think he convinced her not to get it fixed in order to make her depend on him. 'Oh, honey, it'll be so expensive. Why don't you just let me drive you?' Meanwhile, Mary Rosemont says she hasn't spoken to Mom in months, either. She's cut off all her friends and even stopped going to church."

"Well, is that because the real reason she went to church was to try to meet men?" I asked.

"Karina!" Jill's voice was sharp.

"Seriously, Jill. I'm not joking around. She found a guy and then she didn't have to go anymore."

"I think it's more likely he's the kind of abuser who cuts a woman off from her friends and family and makes sure she's completely dependent on him with nowhere else to turn."

The word *abuser* made my throat tighten up. "And you think he attacked her?"

"I don't know. Plenty of abusers don't use force, though. Sometimes the manipulation is more emotional and psychological. They just have to feel like they're in control all the time and like the woman doesn't have any autonomy." She rubbed her face and sighed. "When I did that domestic violence training course, I never thought I'd be applying what I learned to my own mother."

"What domestic violence training course?"

"You remember. When I was volunteering at that shelter. There was a whole orientation course. Chilling stuff."

"I can imagine." I swallowed, wondering what Jill would think if she knew I'd spent the summer messing around with a bunch of rich bondage nuts in England. Probably that I was nuts. And what would she think about a guy who made me agree to being spanked or fondled before he would do it? Wasn't that what my own abusive professor tried to do? Get me to agree to his terms before sexually using me? How was Renault different from Damon, or James? What if James wasn't any different from Phil?

My stomach made a queasy flip as I entertained the thought. What was the difference between James and a creep like Phil or the abusers Jill learned about? Maybe I was too sucked in and blind to be able to see that there wasn't one.

The truth was, I missed James. The whole flight from England, even though I was burning with anger, my arms had ached with emptiness. I missed his scent, and even now I kept thinking I could hear his voice coming from somewhere down the hall. Was I deluded? Was it like being addicted to a drug that felt good but was ultimately the worst possible thing for me?

I tried that thought on for size, but it didn't fit. James might be bad for me, but it wasn't abuse. I couldn't quite put together why at that moment, but I felt there was a difference. I still had massive issues with him, but abuse wasn't one of them.

I wondered if Jill would agree, but this felt like the wrong time to bring it up...I jerked upright, realizing that I had nodded off right there in front of her.

She glanced at her watch. "Let's go see if she's awake."

"Okay."

We tiptoed into the room in case she wasn't.

My first sight of her took my breath away. Her face was drawn and pale, making the bruise on her forehead look even darker and more lurid than it actually was. A bandage was wrapped around her head. There was an IV in her arm, and other tubes and monitor wires disappeared under the beige blanket. The bed was arranged so she was reclining sitting partway up, but her eyes were closed as if she were sleeping. Her left hand was bandaged and in a splint, too.

I crept closer, until I stood at the railing next to her outstretched IV arm.

Her eyes flew open then, and she whispered, "Karina!" Then she cleared her throat and said in a more normal tone of voice, "My baby girl, I'm so glad you came to see me!"

I leaned down to kiss her on the cheek, trying not to get tangled on any of the wires or tubes. "I'm so happy to see you, too."

"Oh, I've missed you missed you missed you *missed you*," she crooned. "Did it take you a long time to get here?"

"Well, I was working in London for the summer, so I had to fly back, but it's fine. My assignment was over anyway. Are you okay, though, Mom? The doctor said you had a fall."

"Oh, I'm sure I will be fine very soon, honey. Don't worry about that. London, you say? You mean England?"

"Um, yeah. At one of the big art museums. It was only an internship, though."

"Oh, when are you going back to Oberlin, dear?"

Oberlin? I had graduated from Oberlin five years ago. I tried to laugh it off. "Oh, Mom, I think you forgot. I'm in grad school now. In New York."

"Oh, oh, that's right. I have so much on my mind these days," she said, patting me on my arm with her free hand, but frowning. "There's so much to worry about with your brother being in trouble."

She went on to describe what Troy had been up to around the time I was graduating from college. I let her go on for a while, nodding and agreeing that he was really a pain in the rear.

Then she looked from me to Jill. "But, Karina, you're being so rude. Who's your friend?"

At that point Jill stormed out of the room. I couldn't say I blamed her. I didn't know what to say, either. I made up an excuse. "Um, I think I hear the nurses calling us! I'll go check, okay, Mom?"

"Okay, darling."

I hurried out into the hall and found Jill sitting in her chair against the wall, her forehead resting in the palm of her hand. The nurse we'd spoken to before swept past us into the room.

Jill looked up. "That was hard."

"Well, she's kind of out of it, but..."

"She doesn't recognize me, Kar."

I put my hand on her shoulder. "Jill, seriously. She's on painkillers and doesn't have her glasses..."

"So why did she recognize you right away?"

"Well, she mistook me for a younger version of myself. Five or six years ago? All that stuff about Oberlin?"

Jill sighed. "I don't know. She sounded more coherent than last time she was awake, but... wow."

I remembered something then. "Remember how you cut your hair for my graduation?"

"What?"

"It was just like it is now, super short and butch. Mom hated it."

"You think she doesn't recognize me because of my hair?"

"That or it's that thing she always does where she pretends something isn't the way it is, just because she doesn't like it. You know, like she still orders things in restaurants that they took off the menu ten years before, as if she doesn't know perfectly well they don't make it anymore."

"You're right. That is exactly what she does. It's a particularly annoying form of denial." Jill shook her head the way she did at aggravating customers in the restaurant when she knew they couldn't see her.

I didn't like feeling stuck between her and Mom, but there wasn't much of a choice at the moment. "I know it hurts being denied you're *you*, sis, but maybe that's all it is. Between the blow to the head, the medications, and being disoriented, she falls back to being that way."

Jill rubbed her forehead again. "Maybe. Thanks for saying it to make me feel better even if it's wacked, KayKay."

She hadn't used that nickname for me since back when we'd both lived here. For a second she looked worried I was offended by it. I gave her a hug. This was tough enough without me being a prima donna. "It's going to be all right," I said. "You'll see."

The nurse came out of the room then. "I gave her her pain meds. She's going right back to sleep now, girls. Why don't you two go down to the hospital cafeteria for a while?"

"Or we could grab a bite down the street," Jill suggested.

"All right. If we're going to drive, though, would it be too much trouble to drop my bags off at the house?"

"That's not a bad idea. Come on."

We had a quick bite to eat, and Jill finally filled me in on the rest of the medical details. The surgery had been for her broken left wrist. Her ankle was sprained but not broken. And there was the blow to the head, but there was only so much they could do for that.

I was droopy-eyed throughout the meal, so Jill suggested instead of dropping my luggage at home, she leave me there with it. When we pulled into the driveway, she opened the automatic garage door using the remote, but warned me as I got out of the car, "Be sure to lock the inside door. I'm sure Phil has the other door opener in his car."

"I will." I didn't point out that if he was Mom's boyfriend, he probably had a key also. No reason to make her worry more than she already was.

I dragged my bags through the back hall and then up the stairs to what had been my bedroom. In a lot of ways, it still was. My mother had redecorated after I'd gone to college, taking down my old teen idol posters and pictures, but the furniture was the same, and she'd left the bookshelf pretty much untouched. Books about horses mingled on the shelf with the ones about the magic punk girl in "Shangri-L.A." Silly teen books, but I'd loved them and read them again and again. I perused the titles.

A spiral-bound book was thrust in among them, its narrow white wire coil protruding from the rest of the spines. I pulled it out, wondering what it was.

I sat down on the bed when I recognized my week-by-week calendar from junior high. Someone had given it to me as a gift for my birthday or Christmas because I'd said I liked art. Each spread had a color photo of a different piece of famous art, faced with spaces for Monday, Tuesday, et cetera. I opened it and found the expected Michelangelo and Da Vinci and Picasso in the pages. But I had forgotten the rest. Two different pages held details from the paintings of Hieronymus Bosch. I must have looked at those pictures a lot, I realized, judging by the amount of doodling on the pages opposite. The Bosches showed tiny nude figures being tortured in hell. I remembered being fascinated, but I had no memory now of what I had thought of the images at twelve years old. Was I even thinking about sex yet?

I flipped through the book some more. Was it my imagination or was there a lot of kinky imagery? A painting of Saint Sebastian being martyred where the rope bondage looked surprisingly sophisticated. A Pompeian fresco of a woman showing her bare back to another who appeared to be raising a flogger. A very dominant Jupiter with a very submissive-looking Thetis, nude, on her knees in front of him. Was the curator who picked all this art into kink? Or was there simply so much out there that I hadn't noticed until now? When I was twelve and poring over the details in the paintings, especially the kinky ones, I don't think I was even aware of what fascinated me so much. The adults in my life had all approved. "Art is smart," one of my mother's boyfriends had said, possibly the one who gave me the calendar. And suitable for a girl to study, my mother had thought.

I startled at the sound of the garage door going up again, and quickly stashed the book under my pillow. Had Jill forgotten something? No. Out the window I could see a Cadillac I didn't recognize pulling into the driveway.

I hadn't locked the downstairs door from the garage yet. Stupid.

I fired off a quick text to Jill: *I think Phil just showed up.*

Moments later I heard a male voice call from downstairs, "Hello? Is someone here?"

I kept my phone in my hand as I treaded lightly down the stairs. "Hello?" I called in response, trying to sound innocent and clueless.

He was taking his Windbreaker off in the entryway to the kitchen. Except for the bags under his eyes, Phil Betancourt was a young-looking fifty-something, and I wondered if the color of his hair had come out of a bottle. He was respectably dressed, like he'd just walked out of a country club, a gold watch on his wrist and his polo shirt tucked in.

"Hi. Can I help you?" I asked, as if he were a door-to-door salesman who had wandered into the house by accident.

"Karina! You must be Karina, right? Your mother showed me so many photographs of you!" He hung his jacket on a peg and then moved as if he were going to hug me. "I've been looking forward to meeting you for so long."

"Uh, hi." I dodged back, and he settled for patting me on the shoulder.

"Good girl," he said, like I was a pet poodle. "How is she?"

"Good," I said, still trying to think of what to say or do. Jill didn't trust him. That much was clear. But if this guy was the love of my mom's life, was it really fair for me to treat him like dirt without knowing more? Was it because I was having relationship issues myself that made me disinclined to cut him much slack? He'd caught me off guard. I wondered if it was a coincidence that he had come in right after Jill had dropped me off, or if he had been… *What, Karina, lying in wait? That's a pretty big conspiracy theory.*

"Did they tell you when she'll be out? She's gonna be okay, right?"

I decided to stick with the safe truths like this one: "I haven't talked to a doctor yet. I just flew in myself."

"Ah, good girl, come to see your mother in her time of need." He moved to the refrigerator and took out a can of beer.

I wanted to stop him. I wanted to say, "What the hell are you doing?" But he clearly felt at home here. Who was I to throw him out?

"You want one?" he asked, as he cracked open the beer.

"No, thank you." I tried not to fidget. I desperately wanted to go to bed and get some sleep, but there was no way I was doing that with a strange man in the house. Even if he was my mother's boyfriend. Maybe especially because he was my mother's boyfriend. Being sleepy was making me slow-witted. "Um, what are you doing here?"

He gave me a look like I'd spoken to him in Chinese, confused and a little offended. Then his face softened. "We better talk. Come in here."

He grabbed his jacket from the peg and then went into the dining room and sat down at the table. "Come *here*," he said again, like I was a reluctant horse. Jill had really prejudiced me against him, but he wasn't doing much to overcome my distrust either, talking to me like he was.

I went and sat down in spite of myself.

He took a deep breath and nodded approvingly. I wondered if he had daughters of his own. Would he have come across as a bossy slime-wad to me if I had met him without talking to Jill first? Or if I'd grown up with a dad to compare him to? He wasn't the first of Mom's boyfriends to lose my respect by putting on a patronizing, paternalistic act.

"I have something you should see," he said. I was ready to bolt if he reached for his belt, but no, he dug his hand into the pocket of his Windbreaker. "Are you ready?"

What kind of question was that? "Since I don't know what you're about to show me, I have no way of knowing if I'm ready."

"Ah, ah, Charlotte said you were smart. College girl." He clucked his tongue like he was scolding himself—or me. I couldn't tell. "Well, here you go, college girl. What do you think of this?"

He put a black velvet ring box on the dining room table in front of me and gave me a self-satisfied, smug look, as if daring me to open it.

"What's that?" I asked, as if I'd never seen anything like it.

"That's the proof of how serious I am about your mother," he said. "Go on. Open it."

I folded my arms. I didn't like him ordering me around. I knew why he wanted me to open the box. When I saw what was inside, my X chromosome was supposed to kick in and make me go *ooh* and *aah*, right?

I pulled a strategy from the safety lectures my mother used

to give me about talking to strangers: if you're nervous about being alone with a person, pretend someone else is about to arrive. "Why don't we wait until Jill gets back from the hospital?"

He suppressed a sigh, cracking the box open himself to reveal a diamond engagement ring. "I love her," he said. "Your mother, I mean. I've been working up to proposing."

Once upon a time, I might have been intimidated by an older man, or any man, trying to push me around. I would have at least felt the need to be polite, to come up with some way to assuage him while trying to get rid of him. But after all I had been through, with Professor Renault creeping on me, Damon George trying to get me to fall for him, and James...being James, Phil had no chance of getting me to play nice girl for him. "Am I supposed to be impressed by a big piece of glass?"

"Piece of *glass*—!" You'd have thought I said "piece of crap." His voice turned hard and his face red before he mastered himself and put his nice guy mask back on. He tried to smile at me and rouse my sympathy, but I'd seen that flare of temper and was glad I was giving him a hard time. "I saved up three months to afford this. Your mother? She's the best. She deserves the best."

She deserves a hell of a lot better than you, I thought. There was no question in my mind at that point that he was a creep. "Are you planning to propose to her in the hospital?"

"If that's what it takes."

"What if she turns out to have brain damage? Will true love conquer all?"

He snapped the box closed. "I don't know what happened

to turn you into such a cynic, young lady. You and that sister of yours." He shook his head.

"Which reminds me. I should call for an update on Mom." I pulled out my phone and dialed Jill's number. I didn't think I would reach her because they made her turn her phone off inside the hospital, but I needed an excuse to get away from him for a while. As it rang, I got up from the table and went into the kitchen. Phil Smarm-and-Charm followed me, tossed his now-empty beer can into the recycling bin and poured himself a glass of iced tea from the pitcher in the fridge.

I didn't like how at home he acted. Or the fact that he kept following me around every time I tried to add space between us. I suddenly realized I didn't like him, period. I stepped through the sliding glass door onto the back porch and slid it closed behind me, figuring if that didn't give him the hint to quit following me, my next move would be to tell him flat-out to leave. The night air was humid and oppressive, but a few fireflies glowed at the edge of the yard.

Her voice mail picked up. "So I was stupid and didn't lock the door right away. He came in while I was still taking my bags upstairs, and now he's here and I don't know how to get rid of him! I don't want to be in the house alone with him, but I'm afraid to leave him unsupervised, too! Ack, call me, I guess." As I was hanging up, though, I felt a surge of relief as the sound of the garage door going up reached my ears. Jill was home.

When I went back into the house, Phil was nowhere to be seen, but I could hear the TV from the living room. Jill came in through the door from the garage and met me in the kitchen.

Mr. Charm came sailing in. "Jill, dear, how are you? Can I get you anything?"

Jill, thank goodness, was on the same page as me. She was having none of his solicitousness or his acting like he was the host and we were the guests. "Yes, you can get out and leave us alone," she said. She crossed her beefy arms. My sister was pretty butch as these things go, but her recent extra-short cut gave her sort of a beat-cop look.

"There's no call for that—"

"The hell there isn't! Don't you have somewhere else to be? Right now, my mother isn't mentally fit to take care of herself. That means this house is mine until further notice, and I'd like you to leave."

"Don't be ridiculous, girls. We should get to know one another in times of strife—"

"*Now.*"

"The game isn't even over. We could sit down and at least watch to the end—"

"What are you, five years old trying to stay up past your bedtime? I'm not your mother and this is not open for bargaining. You leave now or I call the police."

"Jesus." He got his Windbreaker off the back of the dining room chair where he had left it. There was no sign of the ring box. "I can see you gals aren't going to be reasonable. There's no reason for me to stick around if you're going to act like that."

He kept muttering nonsense of that sort until he had shut the front door. Jill stood there, watching through the small, high window until he had backed his car out of the driveway and drove away. Then she banged on the door. "Can you believe there's no dead bolt on this thing?"

"There isn't?" I stared.

"Unbelievable. And the door from the garage has that flimsy latch. And no crossbar on the sliding glass door, either..."

I couldn't help it. I giggled a little. "Listen to what a pair of New Yorkers we've become."

She shook her head and tried to smile. "Yeah, I know."

"Do you really think he's going to come back and try something?"

She sighed and turned off the TV. "No. I'd just feel safer if the house wasn't so weakly defended. I'm calling a locksmith tomorrow and that'll have to be enough." She looked at me then. "I got your message. I see you agree with me."

"I can't even tell you what it is exactly, but he creeps me the hell out!"

"Sure you can, KayKay. Could it be his smarmy manner? His total lack of boundaries? His 'come on be a good girl fetch me a beer and light my cigarette' attitude?"

I shivered. "Okay, yeah. I thought maybe it was my imagination because..." I decided now wasn't the time to go into all that stuff. "Glad it wasn't my imagination."

"Thing is, I think Mom likes that kind of guy."

"Or she doesn't know any better and at least that's the kind of guy she understands." The thought was depressing. I sagged.

"Get some sleep, Karina," Jill said. "We'll talk to Mom's doctor tomorrow."

"All right."

I dragged myself back upstairs. The art book was where I had left it under the pillow. I set it aside as I got ready for bed. I was almost too tired to brush my teeth, but somehow, in my mother's house, I felt morally obligated to.

When I climbed into bed, my phone chimed again with a text from James.

Karina, please forgive me.

I stared at it for a few moments. Then I turned the phone off and went to sleep.

Two

Believing the Strangest Things

The hospital loomed, gray and white, as the taxi pulled up. Hospitals are kind of frightening. Maybe from watching medical dramas on TV when I was a kid, I found them scary. There are things that go on there that I don't know or understand, and people get a lot of bad news in hospitals.

The nurse who met me at the ward desk was friendly but very matter-of-fact about everything. Her name was Rita. "Your mom's got the room to herself right now. Her roomie was discharged this morning. So you've got a little space to spread out in there if you want. At least for a while."

"Great, thanks."

"Everything's looking good right now," Rita added in a low voice. "She just needs to clear up *here*." She waved her hand in a circle over her face, signaling mental confusion. "She had her lunch already, and your sister is in there, too. Go on in."

I hadn't even taken notice of the other occupant in the room last night. The curtain that separated the two beds was drawn back now, though, and the sun came through the window onto the empty bed. Mom was in the bed closer to the door. Jill was in a chair against the wall. It looked like she had fallen asleep while sitting up.

The bed was set so that Mom was reclined at an angle, sitting most of the way upright but with her head back on a pillow. She was asleep, too.

I wondered if I should tiptoe back out and let them both rest. Jill had let me sleep in that morning, and I had been so tired I hadn't even noticed her leaving. The least I could do was return the favor, I thought.

Before I could sneak out, though, Mom's eyes fluttered open. She stared at me a moment, then said, as if she were continuing our conversation from last night, "You know, I was watching the television last night and they were showing these women in the latest dresses and they were so cute! I thought you would look really wonderful in one of them. As soon as I get out of here, I'll take you shopping. How does that sound?"

"That sounds great, Mom." I sat down in the chair closest to the bed and she adjusted the angle so she could see me easily. Jill hadn't moved, her head still back and her mouth partway open. I racked my brain for something I could talk to my mother about. "I bought a dress recently you might like."

"Did you? Tell me about it."

"Oh, I can do better. I have a photo." I took out my phone and flipped to one of the photos of me trying the blue ball gown on. One of the "clean" photos, of course.

"Oh, darling! It's lovely! What was the dress for, though?" A sly smile spread across her face. "You met someone, didn't you?"

That was the problem with talking. It led to more talking and more talking. I was out of the habit of lying, and, well, if we were going to bring her into the present, she needed to be told the truth about as much as possible, I supposed.

"I did meet a man," I said.

"Ooh, a *man*. You must be serious about this one, KayKay. Usually you tell me you met a *guy*."

"He's different from the others."

"What's his name?"

"James. I met him in New York."

"What is he like?"

"He's tall, well dressed..."

"Well heeled?"

"Um, yes."

She gave a little squeal of delight. "How wonderful! What's the point of going to a big city like that unless you can meet someone?"

"Well, Mom, the city has a lot to offer. Art museums, culture, restaurants..."

She clucked her tongue. "All those things are better enjoyed with a partner, dear."

"I...suppose that's true."

"So he's cultured? He takes you places?"

I couldn't help but blush. "Yes. In a private car. He has his own chauffeur."

"Goodness, Karina. Are you worried he's out of your league, though?"

"No, Mom, I'm not worried about that." I wasn't about to tell her I was contemplating cutting him off for good. The red haze of rage I felt when thinking about how he'd hidden things from me couldn't be healthy for a relationship, could it? Besides, she looked so happy for me right now. Sticking to good news seemed the right plan for the moment.

"So when can I meet him?" My mother's hands flew to her hair then. "Oh goodness, but not looking like this. When are they going to let me go home where I can do my hair properly? I have to make a better impression than this." She clucked her tongue again. "My ankle feels much better. They have to let me go soon."

"They want to make sure everything is healed up so you don't end up right back here again," I said. "I should...Oh, here's a doctor now."

A dark-skinned man in blue scrubs came in. "Are you Karina? Jill told me to be expecting you. I'm Dr. Mukherjee." I stood up and he shook my hand. Jill shook herself and stood up, too, and exchanged handshakes with the doctor as well. He then said to my mother, "Mrs. Casper, how are you today? I'm going to borrow your daughters for a minute and we'll be right back."

His hair was thinning a little, but he didn't look that old, maybe forty.

We followed him into the hallway. He turned to Jill. "How's her memory today?"

Jill shrugged. "She's been asleep most of the day and I really haven't been pushing the issue."

"She seemed pretty together just now," I said, "though for all I know she still thinks I'm in college. Doctor, yesterday she acted like she didn't even know who Jill was. Is that normal?"

"Well, as she reorients herself, it may be quite literally as if she is moving herself forward in time. She will probably never recover the memory of the trauma itself, but she may be working her way forward in her memories up until then."

Jill nodded. "She thought I was Aunt Tera when I first got here."

"She might have thought you were her sister," he said, "then when Karina appeared, that triggered her to jump forward a bit more. Is there anyone from her current life who's important to her who might trigger memories that are more recent?"

"Um." I exchanged a glance with Jill.

"We're concerned that her boyfriend might be the one who pushed her down the stairs," Jill said.

"Yes, you had mentioned that to me before." Dr. Mukherjee shifted back and forth from his toes to his heels. "All I can say is we've documented her injuries in case it should come up, and while she's here, she's in our care. But I don't think we should keep her longer than necessary. If she seems competent to leave tomorrow, I think she should go home. Her wrist should heal normally. Her ankle will be a little tender, and her ribs, too, but by noon tomorrow she really should be fit to go home. Mentally she may be behind the times, but she seems competent enough to be able to function in her own home."

"At least going home will make her happy," I said.

"But it'll make it harder to keep Phil away from her," Jill said. "Doctor, you have to understand, I think this guy is trying to pull a snow job. If she's susceptible, or suggestible, I worry he could convince her of things that aren't even true."

"I understand. But without a compelling medical reason to keep her in the hospital, we don't have many options. We also need the space for other patients."

"I see. Is there anything else we can do to...bring her up to date?"

"She is gradually building her view of the world, incorporating details from things you say, trying to fill in the missing pieces. So anything you can tell her that can help with that, about the current lives of family or friends, would be great. If she resists, if she refuses to believe something? Right now, let the subject drop. It'll sink in eventually and—"

He broke off as Jill's phone chimed and she pulled it from her pocket to silence it, a bit red-faced. Signs asking people to turn their phones off were hung several places nearby.

"Um, I have to go make a call," she said. She hurried toward the exit.

As soon as she was out of sight, I pressed Dr. Mukherjee on the issue. "Will Mom eventually start believing that Jill's Jill, though? I mean, it's one thing to act like I haven't broken up with the boyfriend she liked and keep asking about him six months later, and entirely another thing to not recognize your own daughter."

"Well, I am a neurologist, not a psychiatrist," he said. "I think she may know that Jill is your sister, but something doesn't seem right to her so she's coping by sort of faking her way through. Do you see what I mean? Because of her confusion, there are various things about her world she hasn't incorporated or doesn't accept. Give it time. Try to be patient. Do you have any other questions for me before we go back in?"

I didn't. I went back into the room with him and sat on the other side of the room watching while he examined my mother.

I looked up suddenly as a snippet of a familiar song played from the television mounted on the wall above my head. I turned to see a Lord Lightning video on the screen. My breath caught. He was wearing a mask over his eyes, but the curve of his ear and his long, graceful neck were recognizable as James. I wanted to nibble the muscles of that neck, lick the sweat glistening there.

I cursed myself for reacting that way to a mere glimpse of him. What would happen when we were in the same room, together? Was I going to roll over and beg if he told me to? It was like he had me trained.

Yes, Karina, *trained,* I reminded myself. But I was the one who walked away this time. I wasn't going to come if he called.

The image cut to a female news anchor or talk show host. I wasn't sure which.

"Rumor has it that Lord Lightning may not be done after all," she said. "Word from our sources is that the mysterious rocker might perform again, despite previous claims of retirement."

The screen then showed Chandra, the willowy African American woman I recognized from the time I had met her at James's doctor's office, who as far as I knew was a member of James's staff. The camera crew had ambushed her on the street outside Rockefeller Center. "No, no," she was saying. "At this time our only plan is for the release of the greatest hits album. Lord Lightning is retired."

"But what about reports that LL Productions has secured a Las Vegas theater? The same one where *Bride of the Blue* was perfor—"

"I don't know anything about that," Chandra said coldly. "Now if you'll excuse me—"

They cut to another excerpt from a video while the host talked about *Bride of the Blue.* This one had him stalking directly toward the camera, through a large group of dancers miraculously parting as he went, then falling to the ground behind him, into moves done in pairs that were artful imitations of sex. As he reached the front of the stage, his face filling the screen, he tugged down the gold-lensed sunglasses he was wearing and stared into the camera.

I felt that stare go straight down my spine. Meanwhile, in the back of my head, I wondered who his choreographer was. *Bride of the Blue?* In the rush to leave England to get here, I hadn't had time to talk to Becky. I needed to get her take on the whole Ferrara Huntington/LeStrange thing. This had to be part of what James had alluded to in his letter, about thinking his business was done, but it wasn't.

All I knew for sure was that there was a woman claiming to be James's wife chasing him through the streets of London, and that Stefan hadn't hesitated to get James away from her as quickly as possible. Paulina and Michel had been skeptical of the marriage claim, but there hadn't been time to find out everything they knew or suspected before I had to rush here.

I wished I could talk to Stefan. He would surely know the entire story.

Wait. Hadn't James said that Stefan still kept his old phone? I pulled out my own and texted:

Stefan? Are you there?

My heart sped up when almost immediately the phone vibrated in my hand.

Yes, Karina. I am here. Call me if you need anything.

Dr. Mukherjee didn't seem to notice I was using my cell phone. They probably didn't mean to keep people from texting, I rationalized. Perhaps it was only in relation to people talking on the phone, disturbing the patients.

I texted back. *I'm in Ohio. My mother had an accident and I had to fly straight here. Are you still in England?*

No. We arrived in New York this morning.

I hit him with one more question. *Are you alone? Can you talk?*

Stefan knew exactly what I meant by my questions. *He is not here. He is in a meeting and I am in the car.*

I slipped out of the room. I went down the hall and out the door. Apparently, Jill had gone out a different exit to make her phone call because she was nowhere to be seen. Maybe she was in the car.

I dialed Stefan.

He picked up on the first ring. "Karina. Are you all right? Is your mother all right?"

"I'm fine. My mother is recovering, at least. Hey, you must be jet-lagged."

"Coffee is my friend," he said. "But you didn't call to discuss my lack of sleep."

"No. I called to discuss Ferrara Huntington."

There was silence on his end of the line.

"Come on, Stefan. You took off like a bat out of hell when you saw her outside the gallery in London. What's her deal? Why is James so afraid of her?" *Please tell me it's not the same reason he was afraid of me,* I prayed suddenly. Why could I see now so clearly that I had asked him the one thing that was guaranteed to make him run away? When at the time it had seemed like the only reasonable thing to do?

Because if he wouldn't tell you who he was, then it was time for you to walk away, said a little voice in my head. *But you know now...*

"That woman is a snake and a terror," Stefan said, almost whispering. "She's the wife of...well, the ex-wife, I mean, of the record company executive who signed him to his first recording contract. They were a sort of notorious couple. She was supposedly the one with the eye for talent. Her husband was the one with the business acumen."

"So she's the one who made James famous?"

"That's one way to put it, yes."

"Then, what's up with her claiming they're married?"

"That...is a problem."

"So they *are* married?" My voice went up a notch.

Stefan sounded offended. "He certainly claims that they are not! And I will give you one guess which one of them I believe!"

"All right. But he said he was hiding from her. If her claims are spurious, why hasn't he come out and said so?"

"You know how he is, Karina. Can you imagine if they had to go to court? His face would be everywhere and all kinds of private details would come out. Depositions enter public record. I think she's blackmailing him, plain and simple."

"What does she want?"

Again there was silence from Stefan.

"Stefan," I pressed. "What does she want? Money?"

He snorted. "I think if money could make the problem go away, it would already be gone. No, Karina. I think she, uh, she wants him." I could hear Stefan blushing through the phone, I swear.

"Well, she can't have him." I sat down on the concrete bench next to some bushes with a thump.

"Karina? What did you say? I couldn't make that out."

Damn it. If I was going to fight Ferrara Huntington, I needed to forgive James.

Stefan made a sudden noise. "Karina—"

"Stefan?"

I heard a brief rustling, then a voice I longed to hear, even if I was angry at him all over again. "Karina." James sounded out of breath.

"Mr. LeStrange," I said, as calmly and coldly as I could. "Don't you know it's rude to interrupt a conversation?"

"I know. I know. I'm sorry. God, Karina, I have no excuse other than my desperation to hear your voice. Are you all right? Paulina said your mother—?"

"Don't change the subject. You don't deserve to know about my mother. You don't deserve to know *anything* after everything you've done!" I stood up again and I was shouting. Some people walking to the parking lot glanced at me nervously. I didn't care.

"You're right. You're right. Please let me make it up to you, Karina. Please let me explain."

"Fine. Explain."

"In person. Somewhere secure—"

"Oh, bullshit, James!" I could picture how it would go. He'd invite me to a penthouse somewhere, and fill the place with long-stemmed roses with *I'm sorry* handwritten in gold ink on every one, and I'd roll over and let him have me before I knew what I was doing. "You don't get to set the terms anymore. Do you understand? If you can't get that, then we have nothing to talk about."

He was silent, but I could hear his breathing. It sounded like he was still out of breath. I wondered if he was shocked. I wondered if he was crying.

When he spoke, his voice was gravelly and subdued. "I'm sorry. I...I'll wait. I'll come there if you want. Whatever you want. You're in control, Karina."

I sank down to the bench again. My knees had gone weak. I never thought I'd hear him say something like that.

An idea came to me then. "Find out everything you can about a Phil Betancourt from Xenia, Ohio. Then maybe we can talk again."

I hung up before he could respond. As I hit the "end call" button, it felt like a knife going through my chest, but there was also something deeply satisfying about it. I stared at the phone in my hand for a long moment before I got up and went back inside.

We hung around the hospital for another hour or two. After Mom dozed off again, Jill drove us into town to the luncheonette that I was surprised was still there. "Let's eat quickly," Jill suggested, as we sat down. "Then I'll drop you back at the hospital and I'll go meet the locksmith at the house."

"Sounds like a plan."

"You want to split a grilled cheese sandwich and a bowl of soup?"

"We could each get the half sandwich and cup of soup combo," I pointed out.

"It's cheaper if we just share a whole one, plus the soup's bigger."

"Get tomato in the grilled cheese and I'm there."

"Deal."

It was after the lunch crowd and before dinner so there were only a few other customers in the place.

"She seems pretty cheerful today," Jill said.

"Well, that's good, right?"

"When have you ever known Mom to be cheerful? That worries me."

"Jill, of course she's being cheerful. All she's ever wanted is for everyone to treat her like a queen. In the hospital they do."

"Hmm, true." She looked around. Most of the seats at the Formica-topped counter were empty. "Karina, I'm going to have to go back soon."

"How soon? Can't the bar deal without you?"

"From what I can tell, all hell is breaking loose without me there."

"They'll survive."

"That's what I have to tell you. 'They' is 'we' now."

"What do you mean?"

"I bought into part-ownership. The chef's been wanting his own place for a while. He got a rich friend to pony up some cash, and me and the head bartender each bought in for a quarter. So the old owner is gone and I'm the full-time house manager now. We're in the middle of the changeover." Her eyes were very round and exposed under her super-short haircut.

"Jill! That's great! How did I miss this?"

"Um, you were in England all summer?"

Right. "That's fantastic, though."

"It is if we can make it fly. I mean, the money could be a lot better, but that's if the place is successful enough to keep up with our salaries."

"That place was always packed."

"No, it wasn't. You mostly worked the weekend nights." She paused while the waiter, a kid who couldn't be more than eighteen, put the food down in front of us. "But we'll make it work. We're upscaling. Chef's snazzing up the menu. Small plates are all the rage, and a new cocktail menu's coming, too, but all the changes mean retraining the waitstaff. We're trying to take it up a notch and get on the hip foodie map. A gastro-pub."

"And you need to be there to train the staff."

"Yeah. This is killing me. My partners are depending on me. But, you know, this is *Mom* we're talking about."

"I know." We ate for a bit while I mulled over my options. "I still haven't checked in with the university to see what I have to do next. I might not need to be there at all if they haven't reinstated me..."

"I thought you were going to fight for reinstatement?"

"Well, I am, but maybe I could shoot for January." I shrugged. My case might look weak if I stayed away too long, but... "This is Mom we're talking about." I repeated her words.

She ran her fingers over her hair. "And I really don't like the idea of you home alone if Phil comes creeping around again."

"Me either. Even with the locks changed. I mean, if he isn't a criminal, he—" I was interrupted by a text. Stefan had sent a photograph.

On the screen was a mug shot of Phil Betancourt. He had a black eye and disheveled hair, but it was unmistakably him. The sign he was holding showed he'd been arrested in St. Paul, Minnesota. I showed it to Jill. "So much for the idea he might not be a criminal."

"Who's that from?"

"A friend," I said, which was true.

"A friend?" Jill said, suspicious.

Another text came: *If this is your man, he appears to operate under the alias Ernest Klugman. Or perhaps Betancourt is the alias. This arrest was for robbery, aggravated assault, and sexual misconduct. The injuries were sustained in a scuffle with police. Still researching, but I would advise you not to get mixed up with this fellow.* I showed it to her, too.

"A friend," she pressed.

"He's...a security professional," I said.

"That sounds a whole lot like a euphemism."

"Okay, he's a bodyguard and a limo driver."

"How did you meet him?" Her hackles were up.

"Oh, for fuck's sake, Jill. He works for a guy I met while waitressing for you!"

"Keep your voice down!" Jill yell-whispered at me. "What guy? What guy!"

I yell-whispered back. "The guy I went all the way to England to track down!"

She rolled her eyes and then forced herself to take a deep breath. "Okay. Could he come here to be with you while I go back to New York?"

"You're assuming I would want him here."

"Karina. Whoever he is, he's obviously someone you trusted enough to tell about Mom's abuser."

"Um, yeah." This was the problem with all the secrets, all the hiding. It made my relationship with James—and with Stefan—impossible to explain.

Jill sighed. "If you've got some kind of drama with him, fine, but a 'security expert' might be just what we need if Betancourt is as sketchy as this makes him out to be."

I wondered if James was serious about doing anything I said to try to get back in my good graces. If I wanted him to keep watch from a distance, would he? For that matter, would he send Stefan alone if I asked? Was there some other way James could solve this problem? "I'll...ask if it's possible," I said, hating that I wasn't ready to explain everything to Jill yet.

Gee, like James wasn't ready to explain everything to me? Look how waiting too long had hurt us.

Jill was clearly waiting for me to say more. I resolved I wouldn't let keeping secrets be what drove us apart. I forced myself to look her right in the eye. "I need to tell you something."

She looked at me right back. "Is this going to be one of those family secrets kind of moments?"

"I hope not. Listen. I was seeing this guy in the city for a while. Then we had a kind of...falling out, and I went to London to try to get him back. Only we had another big blowup, and now I'm not sure I want him back after all."

"Oh, KayKay, I'm sorry."

"Don't be. He...He wants a chance to make it up to me. I don't know whether to hope it works out or to hope he blows it terribly so I can move on. I'm still really...attracted to him. But I don't want to let him into my life until I'm sure I'm taking him back. Do you know what I mean?"

"You mean you don't want another Brad situation. Where Mom liked him better than you did."

"Exactly. This guy is nothing like Brad, though."

"An art-world type?"

"A rich art-world type and that doesn't even begin to describe him," I said. "Can we not talk about him right now? If I make up with him, I want you to like him. But right now all I want to do is rant about him."

"I understand," she said. "Love's complicated, KayKay. But we better figure something out and soon, because I need to get back to the city."

A funny thing happened after we left the luncheonette. The young waiter who had served us came running out behind us as we were unlocking the car. "Ma'am? Miss?" He seemed unsure how to address Jill. "I think you made a mistake. You left way too big a tip."

He had a twenty in his hand and some loose change.

Jill cuffed him on the shoulder with her hand. "That's for you. For good service."

"But—"

"But nothing. I waited tables a long time. I know. Someday when you're making more money, remember what it was like and you'll tip big, too."

His smile showed a crooked tooth and his sandy bangs fell into his eyes. "Aw, thanks!"

She took her wallet out of her back pocket and for a second I thought she was going to give him more. Instead, she handed him a business card. "When you get out of school, if you want a job waiting tables in New York, call me."

"Awesome! Thank you! I better get back now, though!" He ran toward the luncheonette.

Once we were in the car, I asked, "I wasn't paying attention. Was he that good?"

"Come on, Karina. You know the drill as well as I do. He brought water, refilled it before we asked, brought all the correct food, stayed out of the way, asked if we needed anything, didn't spill anything. The fact that you didn't notice him is a sign of a great waiter."

"I don't think I was ever that good. You'd really hire him?"

"Look at how honest the kid is. Besides, if he's anything like me, he wants to get out of here and move to a big city." She started the engine and pulled out.

"You think he's gay?"

"I'm sure of it."

"How could you tell?"

"What other kind of boy has a tiny safety pin with rainbow beads pinned to his shoelace?"

"I didn't even notice that."

"Well, I did." She smiled to herself. "We have to look out for each other."

"Does that mean I could have my old job back?"

"I thought you hated waiting tables."

"I did. But maybe I'd like it better now that you're upscaling. And I sure as heck will like it better than starving if I can't find a job when I finish."

"You'll find something better than waiting tables, Karina, especially with your art-world connections."

"I was thinking worst case scenario, that's all…"

"I'm sure I could find something for you to do if you were desperate," Jill said. "Let's worry about one thing at a time."

Three

The Key We Must Turn

Jill dropped me back at the hospital and went to meet the locksmith.

Mom seemed happy to see me again, and I kept up the chatter with her for a while. She volunteered nothing about her own life or the neighbors, which I took to mean her memory was still foggy and she knew it. Instead, she asked me questions. I ended up telling her a lot of things I'd never really bothered to before, like about my roommate Becky in New York, and about art history.

Of course she asked me one or two more things about James, but after what I'd told her before, she had settled in her mind that I was with a suitable man and therefore she no longer needed to grill me about him.

By all outward appearances, the conversation was very pleasant and the least contentious one we'd had since I was in college. But I felt weird knowing that her contentment was partly brought on by a blow to the head. She hadn't been this accepting of me in years and she hadn't been this uncritical since I was small.

When I figured Jill would be coming back soon, I couldn't help myself. I started trying to prepare her. "Oh, Mom," I said. "Jill got a really short haircut."

"Did she? Whatever did she do that for? She's the only one of us who could hold a real pin curl!"

"Well, you know, working in the restaurant like she does? Long hair is a health hazard."

"Is it, now? The things you learn."

When Jill came in, I repeated my act of earlier. "Jill!" I hugged her. That was far more demonstrative than we usually got, but Mom took the hint, nodding to Jill and saying "hello, dear" instead of completely ignoring her like she had been.

"Jill's going to drive me back to the house now, Mom," I told her, and kissed her on the cheek. "We'll come check on you again tomorrow."

"The doctor said if everything checks out okay, then you'll be taking me with you," Mom said.

"I hope so." I kissed her again and then hurried out with Jill.

"How's she doing?" Jill asked once we were in the parking lot. But before I could answer, her phone rang. She cursed and put it up to her ear. "Hey. Yeah, I know. I told you I'd let you know. She might be getting out tomorrow, but I won't know for sure until morning. Yes, my sister's here, but... Darby, listen, shut up for a second, will you? I get that you need me. But I can't wave a magic wand and make it all better, okay?"

She unlocked the door and I got into the passenger seat of the unnaturally clean rental car, trying not to listen, but that was difficult to do when she was so vehement I could hear her right through the glass.

"Hold your horses and I'll try to be back as soon as I can! I don't know about tomorrow. Inspector? What inspector? The kitchen is your job, pal."

She opened the door and got in. "Wait, what? Accessibility ramps? We have those! Okay, listen, I'll have to call you later. I'm getting in the car now. Bye."

She hung up while I could hear the person on the other end still trying to talk. She let out a long breath, then started the engine.

"They kind of need you there, don't they?" I said.

"They'll figure it out. It's good for 'em," she grumbled as she backed out of the parking space. "Anyway, how did she seem?"

"You know how you thought it was weird she was so cheerful? I think it's weird she's not haranguing me to bag some marriageable bachelor like a fourteen-point buck in deer season."

"Did you tell her about the guy in New York?"

"I did. But I didn't tell her we're kind of on the outs right now. She's like 'when can I meet him?' " I sighed.

"I want to meet this mystery man, too."

"Why? What if I dump him?"

"KayKay, I've never seen you this intense about a guy. I've never seen you this intense about *anything.* You better believe I'm curious about what's changed. I mean, maybe it's grad school and you're getting ready to move on, but..." She shrugged like she didn't want to say something that might offend me. Then she said it anyway. "You seem like you're finally growing up."

I stuck my tongue out at her to prove that I wasn't, but that made us both laugh.

*   *   *

When we got to the house, Jill gave me a new set of keys. Dead bolts had been added to all the doors, and a new garage door opener had been installed. This one had a button remote as well as a keypad. I set a code for myself and then we went inside.

"Okay. I'm going to go up to my room and call him," I announced, psyching myself up for it.

"Are you going to tell him to come here?"

"I don't know. I might end up telling him to go to hell."

"Well, if you need a shoulder to cry on after, I'll be watching the game," Jill said. "Don't feel like you have to make up with him just to solve my problem."

"I won't," I said.

I went up to my room and sat down on the bed. The drowsiness of jet lag that had stayed at bay all day suddenly swept through me. "Oof."

I texted Stefan. *Is he around? I want to talk.*

The phone rang seconds later. James. I picked up without saying anything.

"Karina." He cleared his throat.

"How did you find out about Betancourt?"

"A combination of knowing where to look and using the Internet. Most people are not good at hiding their aliases."

"Aha. And you are." I felt a flash of anger. I couldn't help it.

"Yes, Karina, I am. I've got a bit more at stake than a two-bit con man who targets widows and divorcées."

I tamped down my anger while I tried to focus on what he was telling me. "Is that what he is?"

"It appears so. Under his alias I found one restraining order against him, and at least two joint bank accounts with women's names. All three women are widows or divorcées. I'd say that looks like a pattern, and I haven't even dug much deeper."

"Maybe he just likes older women," I said, to be contrary.

"Or women appropriate for his age are better targets and better camouflage than younger ones," he said. "Please don't get mixed up with him, Karina."

"Is he dangerous?"

"The woman who took out the restraining order certainly thought he was."

We were silent a moment while I mulled that over.

"Karina," he said suddenly, "I worry you're not safe if he's there."

"You weren't so concerned for my safety when you sent Damon George to try to get into my pants." So much for tamping down my anger. "Where was your protective instinct then, James?"

He said nothing, and I wondered if he was trying to think up a justification or an apology. If he came out with a justification, I thought I might throw the phone across the room.

"I'm sorry," he said, almost a whisper. "That was one of the stupidest things I've done in my life. I...I don't even know what I was thinking."

You weren't thinking, I almost said, but I realized it was more than a snappy comeback. It was true. He had acted scared and hurt. He had tried to reassert control even while running from me.

"I'm sorry," he said again.

"You don't make the best decisions when you're afraid," I said.

"No, I don't."

"And you're scared for me now, aren't you?"

"Yes."

"Don't get any bright ideas," I warned.

He had clearly been thinking about it, because he immediately said, "At least let me send Stefan to protect you."

"I don't need a limo driver."

He bristled. "Stefan is far more than a driver—!"

"I know. I know. Just busting your chops," I said, calming down now that the wave of anger had ebbed. "You'd really do that? Send him here?"

"Your mother has been severely hurt, possibly by a con man intent on getting her money. I don't even want to contemplate whether he's desperate enough to hurt you, too. If Stefan's mere presence is not enough to deter him, he is more than capable of defending you, as well."

I couldn't help it. Hearing how James's way of speaking grew more and more precise the more emotional he got made me miss him terribly. I wanted to give him a chance to explain, but I wanted to be sure I was ready for it. *You didn't chase him all the way to England so you could slam the door in his face,* I reminded myself.

I stood and looked out the window at the front yard. "You said you wanted to explain yourself to me in person."

"Yes. I...I feel that's best."

"So you can put your dom aura on and make me believe you?"

"No, Karina. I don't trust any other kind of communication. Not only for secrecy, but if we're going to trust each other, we need to be in the same room. You need to see my face, hear my voice. You need to read me as much as I need to read you."

Well, that was probably true. "And you aren't afraid I'm going to strip-mine your soul?"

"Of course I am. That's what I've been trying to tell you, Karina. You're the one with my heart in your hands. I let that fear drive me away from you and let it spur me to some terrible decisions. I'm done with letting fear rule me, though. I want..."

I could hear him struggling to compose himself.

"I would rather be ruled by love than fear," he finally said. "And even if you turn me away, at least I will have conquered fear."

Knowing that he was as afraid of his feelings as I was of mine made me feel calmer. And determined. "When can you be here?" I said.

"We'll drive all night if you want us there by morning."

"No. Stefan is as jet-lagged as you. I don't want him driving off the road into a ditch." I did the math in my head. Ten-hour drive, eight hours' sleep, some time to pack or stop to eat. "How about tomorrow night?"

"We can be there by seven. We'll set up a security—"

"No." I cut him off before he could get that ambitious. "Get a hotel. Stefan can stay here, but you..." I felt my heart squeeze in my chest as I gathered the nerve to say it and stand firm. "You get one shot at being honest with me. No dom bullshit. No holding back. If that goes well, then maybe I'll consider seeing you again."

"I understand."

You better do your damnedest to fix this, James Byron LeStrange.

"Give me a chance, Karina," he said then, as if he read my mind. "I'll make things right between us."

"Tomorrow," I said.

"Tomorrow," he agreed.

I hung up before I could lose my nerve and sank back down on the bed. It was too early to go to sleep for the night, but maybe if I just closed my eyes for a little while...

I let a wave of drowsiness submerge me as I lay my head down on the pillow.

We were dancing. I could feel his hand at my waist as we swayed across the ballroom floor and when I looked, we were at a ball. The ball that changed everything between us.

The music shifted to something warm and slow, and I pressed close to him like it was a slow dance at the prom. The heat of his body seemed to seep into me, desire kindling. As our hips gently rocked in time with the music I could feel the reaction he was having at being pressed so close.

It was a dream, but I hadn't realized it yet. I was caught up in the moment, part memory, part imagination. He had brought me to a kinky party where all the rich people used aliases—my BDSM debutante ball!—where we had sex for the first time. I had coerced his name out of him, though, the price for getting between my legs. To James it must have been like his fairy-tale princess turned into the troll under the bridge.

But in my dream world that hadn't happened yet. Everything was still storybook perfect.

"Are we going upstairs soon?" I whispered into his ear.

"Why would we do that, sweetness?" he murmured back, sliding his hands down my rump to press me against the iron of his erection.

"I thought we came here to have sex for the first time."

"Everything we do is sex, sweetness," he chided.

"You know what I mean. What you've been building me up to all this time."

"I know." He spun us in a circle, making me slightly dizzy. "But we don't have to go upstairs for that."

He lifted me up so that I was straddling him, my legs locked behind his back. In real life the ball gown would have made that impossible. In the dream, though, it magically parted so that my pussy was rubbing his fly...then his cock. I held tight around his neck while he ground against me, the length of him growing slick from my juices and running up and down over my clit.

I knew we were on a dance floor with tons of other people. I knew that didn't matter. I wiggled, trying to get him inside me. That only made him tease me more, backing his hips off and pressing my clit with short thrusts of the tip.

"Put it in. Put it in!" I demanded.

"Hush. Who's in charge here?"

"*Please* put it in," I tried.

"Nice try, but that's not the magic word."

I racked my brain, trying to think of what the magic word could be. Sorry? No. I had nothing to apologize for. Fuck? Doubtful. Wait. I had an idea. This had to be it. I kissed him first while I worked up the nerve to say it.

"I love you."

That was it. He thrust inside me, searing me with the sudden intrusion and burst of ecstasy that filled me as he drove all the way in. I clung to him, squeezing him inside and out, unable to speak, barely able to breathe from the bliss and pleasure and intensity of it all. And relief, a huge sense of relief that we were together again...

That was when it hit me that it was a dream and the relief was fake. We weren't together. This wasn't happening.

I woke with a start to a rumble of summer thunder and the sound of water pouring off the roof as the rain overwhelmed the gutters. One of my hands was in my panties. Despite the strangeness of the dream, I was as wet as the weather. The clock read three a.m., and I guessed Jill had let me sleep through dinner.

A brilliant flash lit up the pull shade in the window, followed by a closer crack of thunder, and I slid my fingers into myself with a stifled moan. My only chance to get back to sleep and get onto a regular schedule was to hope that if I came, I'd drift off again. The rain pelted down outside and I let my fingers slide back and forth as I rocked my hips, unable to stop myself from imagining James watching, whispering to me, teasing me...and telling me to come.

I woke in the morning to a frantic e-mail from Becky, wanting to know what was going on. I ended up calling her and trying to bring her up to date on my mother, her skeevy boyfriend, and James, but I had to cut it short when Jill was ready to leave for the hospital.

We had a brief meeting with Dr. Mukherjee who had already examined Mom, and then got drilled on home care instructions by the staff. They seemed most concerned that we not let her do too much walking on her tender ankle, and told us how to keep the wrist splint dry while she bathed. I was more concerned with the warning signs to look for in case something more serious developed with the blow to her head. Fortunately, they'd already scheduled a follow-up appointment with Dr. Mukherjee for that. Now, if only I could be sure, with her memory problems, that she would remember to go.

We went into the room to find Mom had gotten dressed in clothes Jill had brought yesterday. She was out of bed and sitting in a chair, ready to go. When we came in, she hopped to her feet. "Karina! I'm so glad you're still here." She kissed my cheek, then looked past me at Jill. "Jill. Have you been taking care of your little sister?"

Jill looked surprised; this was the first time in days our mother had addressed her by name. "Of course I have."

Mom reached up and rubbed Jill's hair. "A shame they had to cut your hair so short, though, when you fell and hit your head."

Jill and I looked at each other.

"Doctors have to do that sometimes," Jill said carefully. "But hair grows back."

"I know it does." Mom's hand fluttered by her own ear, and she forced it down. "It just takes time."

Jill nodded, poker-faced. "I kind of like my hair this way, though, Mom. I think I'll keep it."

"Really? Well, to each her own. Come on, now, girls. Let's get moving."

The nurses were there with a wheelchair. Mom said that she could walk, but they insisted that leaving the hospital by wheelchair was how it was done. My mother, never wanting to seem like she was bucking tradition, relented and sat in the wheelchair.

I pushed it down the hall myself. Now I could see Mom had a large shorn patch of hair on the back of her head where they put in stitches after her fall.

Jill drove, Mom sat in the passenger seat, and I rode in

back. Mom put on the radio and hummed along with the song that came on. At least she was cheerful, I thought. She was easier to deal with, though being cheerful didn't make her any less critical or judgmental.

"Oh, look at that ugly new building," she said, as we passed what might have been new construction. I couldn't tell. "Why the city felt the need to put that monstrosity in, I'm sure I'll never know." Once she got going, her monologue turned into a steady stream of judgments about the way people kept their lawns, the clothes they were wearing, the cars they drove. I hadn't sat in a car with my mother in a long time, and hearing it this time shocked me a little. This was normal, I realized. Whenever she drove us anywhere—school, the store, dance lessons—she had kept up a running commentary. Once upon a time I'd been so used to it I could tune it out, but I no longer had that immunity.

A Lord Lightning song came on the radio and I braced myself for her to say something cutting about it. But she didn't seem to notice the music now and was more interested in telling us about the landscaping the Rosemonts were doing to their property and how scandalously expensive it was. "A thousand dollars for that sad little tree in the front alone! Couldn't you find something better to do with a thousand dollars? Goodness. Give it to a charity if all you're going to get out of it is a pathetic thing like that."

"I'm sure they're hoping it'll grow up to be a beautiful tree someday," Jill murmured.

"The Ugly Duckling of trees?" Mom sniffed. "I suppose it could happen, but I won't hold my breath."

When we drove past the house, I could see what she meant about the tree, though. Did that mean her memories were up to date now? Once we were inside the house, Jill put the central AC on and the three of us made lunch. After we ate, we sat down in the living room to talk.

"Mom," Jill began, "you know you had a fall and hit your head, right?"

"Oh, I know. They told me at the hospital. But I'm fine now, dear. How are you doing?"

Jill sighed, defeated. "Look, Mom, there's one thing we haven't talked about yet, and I want to make sure we do before I head back to the city."

"What's that, dear?"

"We're concerned that your boyfriend may have stolen from you."

Mom sat very still for a moment, then merely said, "Oh?"

She doesn't even remember him, I thought.

Jill plowed ahead. "Yes. In fact, we're concerned he might have been the one who pushed you down the stairs in the first place."

"That would have been absolutely terrible!" Mom put a hand to her cheek.

"Yes, it would. The fact that you can't remember anything about the fall, well, that's one reason we're worried." Jill must have been thinking the same thing I was. "Mom, do you remember your boyfriend?"

"Oh, of course I do. I could never forget someone I cared about," she said, but something about the prissy way she said it made me think she was bluffing.

"Do you remember his name?" I asked.

She looked at me, then at Jill, then back at me. "Names are very important, Karina, honey. People make judgments based on names."

"I'll take that as a 'no' then?" Jill said. "It doesn't matter anyway, Mom. We think the name he gave you was a false one anyway."

"Really!" Mom looked and sounded scandalized.

"Yes. We think he conned you into thinking he was in love with you, sold your good silver and your jewelry, and that he might come back. If he does, we're worried you could be in danger."

"Well, no need to go to extremes, but..." My mother put her hand to her cheek, then folded her hands in her lap, her spine very straight. "I do know how to handle men, you know, girls."

"Just be careful, Mom," I said. "We're worried about you."

"It's nice to know you care." She leaned over and gave me a little hug. "It's been so long since we had girl time, the three of us like this."

Jill couldn't keep her sarcasm inside. "What, sitting around talking about boyfriends?"

"Exactly! Karina, you were just telling me about the man in your life, weren't you?"

"Well, a little, yesterday." Time to drop the bomb, I guess. "You said you wanted to meet him, so he's coming to Ohio—"

"Is that so? Oh, we definitely have to go shopping and get you that dress I was talking about! All of us should go."

"Mom, are you sure you aren't tired out? Do you need a nap?" Jill asked.

"Jill Elizabeth Casper. I have done nothing but lie in bed for days. I could not be more ready to get out of the house than I am now. Come on. Let's go to the mall. You can rent me one of those scooters."

There was really no arguing with my mother when she

got like this. That was how I ended up with not one but two new dresses and a pair of sandals, which I wore home along with one of the dresses because doing so made her happy. Jill didn't completely escape either, though Mom seemed to know not to push things too far. Jill got a Windbreaker. Mom bought herself some new skin cream at one of the makeup counters in a department store and commented that she had already made herself a hair appointment for the morning.

"When did you do that?" Jill asked.

"From the hospital, dear. You remember your old friend from school? She has her own salon now." She fluffed her hair next to the patch where they had shaved it in back.

"What friend?"

"Velma. Only everyone calls her Velvet now."

"Oh!" Jill blushed deeply then, but my mother was too busy looking at herself in the makeup counter mirror to notice.

"I made it for first thing in the morning so I'll look nice to meet Karina's new beau."

"Um, Mom, he's coming tonight…"

"Tsk. I'm sure I'll be asleep by the time he arrives. Perhaps we can meet him for lunch."

I took that as a hint that she was tired, so we took her home. Jill meanwhile found out she was on standby on a flight tomorrow evening, and at the least they could get her onto the last flight out for sure. So that was it. Tonight would be the only night with the three Casper women in the house together.

When we arrived home, Mom went into her room for a nap and Jill and I went down to the garage to check out my mother's car. Within five minutes Jill had figured out the battery had been disconnected. "You see this here?" She pointed down inside the engine where I couldn't really see. "It's cut. That way, even if you put a new battery in, it'll still act dead. Sneaky fucker. Well, we might as well call for a tow truck to take it to the shop."

"Wow. I can't believe he did that."

"The worst part is he probably seemed like a really good guy to Mom—you know, driving her everywhere, her knight in shining armor, when he was the one who did this in the first place. Unbelievable."

"Well, at least she's doing better."

"I know. Her memory seems to have finally caught up. Of all the things to remember, me and Velma!"

"Okay, I don't remember you and Velma, though…"

"I didn't bring her around here much," Jill said with a grimace as she shut the car hood. "She was one of my first girlfriends."

"Oh." Now I understood why she blushed. "Do you think Mom remembers *that*?"

"I don't know and I'm not going to ask. I sure as hell tried to keep it a secret at the time. I was still in the closet. Plus there were people who disapproved of me being friends with an African American girl in the first place. Not that I care what those fuckers thought anyway, but you know, I was already trying to fly under the radar. Last thing I wanted was some loudmouth from church or wherever saying something to Mom and setting off a rant about appearances or something."

"You don't seriously think Mom would have cared about race."

"Mom herself wouldn't bat an eye. But if she thought

people were being judgmental about it? Come on, KayKay. You know how appearance-conscious she is. She might cave. I didn't even want to go down that road to find out what she'd say."

"Well, she seems to like her perfectly well now," I pointed out.

"She likes my current girlfriend Pauline, too. Speaking of which, you promised to feel her out on the marriage issue."

"I haven't forgotten, but this hasn't exactly been the right time."

"I know. I know. But I'm leaving tomorrow. Maybe you'll get a chance after that."

"Maybe."

We went back into the house so Jill could call a tow truck, and I went upstairs to finally get on the phone to Becky.

"Karina, oh my God, the Lord Lightning fan sites are blowing up with news right now, and did you get your mother today? You know the landlord needs to know if I'm keeping the place."

I closed my bedroom door. "One thing at a time, Becks! One thing at a time. I thought you were going to keep the apartment whether I came back or not."

"Well, that's the thing. It's been really lonely here without you all summer. If you're not coming back, I should try to find a place I can share with a roommate. But you're the only one crazy enough to use the living room as a bedroom like you do."

My apartment really wasn't meant for two. I'd taken Becks as a roommate because I'd needed the money, and to convince her to move in, I'd given her the bedroom while I used the folding futon in the living room as my bed. "Okay, but it's

really late to be finding a new apartment and a new roommate by September first."

"I know," she said dejectedly. "Which is why I'm really
hoping you're coming back."

"Seems likely one way or another," I said. "Meanwhile, my
mother's doing pretty well. She's going to have some physical
therapy for her wrist and ankle and some follow-ups for her
head injury. But she's definitely on the mend."

"Oh, thank goodness."

"So what's the latest on LL?"

"Since I talked to you this morning, there's been definite
proof that his production company reserved the same theater
in Las Vegas where they put on *Bride of the Blue*. But no one
has been able to find out if it's going to be a reprise of that
show or what."

Becky was a huge Lord Lightning fan. And I should have
been the ultimate insider for that information, but until I
talked to James, I didn't know a thing.

I thought about his e-mail though, how he'd hinted at the
fact that he had business obligations that were cropping up
unexpectedly. He'd hoped to retire from the music business,
but now Ferrara Huntington was chasing him down.

"I might know more after I talk to him," I said. "He's coming here."

"Ohio?"

"Yeah. Here's the thing, though, Becks. I don't know if it's
going to work out between him and me."

She gasped. "Don't say that! You spent all summer searching for him and you found him!"

"And then I found out he was pulling the strings, trying to
manipulate me," I said. "Although he did just send me this

e-mail apologizing." Practically groveling. "He called me the 'love of his life.'"

"Oh my God."

"I know. But you know what? An e-mail and saying it face-to-face are different."

"Saying I love you?"

"Saying *I'm sorry.*"

"Ah, gotcha."

"So he's coming here and I'm giving him a chance to make up with me."

"What if he doesn't?" Becky asked, clearly alarmed by the thought.

Before I could answer, I heard raised voices coming from across the hall. Jill and Mom were having some kind of argument. "I've got to go, Becks. I'll call you once I know when I'm coming back."

I opened my door a crack and listened. It sounded like they were arguing about the missing jewelry.

"I told you some of it was missing!" Jill said. "It was the first thing I noticed after the silver! Phil, the guy conning you, must have taken it!"

"Well, why wouldn't he have taken all of it, then?" my mother said with a huff. "Why just these pieces? Are you sure you or Karina didn't take the pieces for yourself?"

At that point I couldn't stay out of it anymore. I stepped into the hallway. "Honestly, Mother! Jill and I don't even wear jewelry! Why would one of us have taken it?"

"That's exactly what I mean!" Mom was sitting on the bed, a small silk jewelry bag in her hands. "Neither of you appreciates the sentimental value of a gift a man gives you."

"That's not true at all," I said. "First of all, for a gift to have sentimental value, it doesn't have to come from a man in particular. Secondly, my generation demands honesty instead of jewelry from our partners. That's way more valuable to me."

Mom sat up very straight, looking at me. "Well," she said.

I braced myself for a fight, but that was all she said. I suppose that was her way of conceding, or at least ending the argument.

And just in time, too. My phone chimed with a text from Stefan. He and James had arrived at a hotel a few miles away.

Four

Love to Be Loved

Jill made a dinner of mostly comfort foods and then Mom went to take what she called a nap, but we suspected she might be down for the count. Thinking about James and the imminent conversation with him had put butterflies in my stomach and I could only nibble some macaroni and cheese. After Mom was settled, while we were cleaning up, I told Jill he had arrived.

"So the security expert and his boss are in town." I opened the dishwasher and started putting glasses in.

"Aha. And the boss? That's your boyfriend, right?"

Boyfriend sounded wrong, but I didn't quibble. "The one I'm mad at, yes."

She paused in wiping down the stove to look at me. "You sound nervous."

"Well, I kind of am. I might be about to have the epic breakup fight of my life."

"But you might not."

"I did say I'd give him a chance to make it up to me."

"And you don't think he will?"

"I don't know if he *can*."

Jill took the glass out of my hand and put it in the dishwasher herself. "You're about to find out, though."

"I guess I am."

"Go meet him. It's not even seven yet."

I dithered a moment more.

"You can take the rental," Jill prodded. "The keys are on the hook by the door."

"Better sooner than later," I said resignedly. "I'll go find out if he's free."

Of course he was. My text to Stefan was answered within seconds with the hotel address and room number.

I got my purse and the keys. "I'll try not to stay out too late," I told Jill. "I'll keep my phone on, so if anything happens or you need the car, call me."

"I will. But, hey, KayKay," Jill said as I opened the door to leave. "One of the ways you know you found the right one is not that you don't argue. It's that after you argue, things get better instead of worse."

"I'll keep that in mind."

While I drove, it was nice feeling like there was someone on my side. For the longest time, no one had known about James except Becky. It was as if he was someone I'd made up.

But he was real. He was here. My mother even wanted to meet him. It struck me then that he was even willing to meet her.

James was ready to take off the mask I'd been trying to pry off him all this time. Was I really going to tell him, *Never mind. Go back to England. Go back to your cave of anonymity. I'm done with you?*

Only if he kept up the bullshit. I made a resolution. If he tried to dom me into listening, if he held back anything, if he demurred or guarded himself, I was done.

When I arrived in the lobby of the hotel, there wasn't anyone at the front desk, so I breezed past to the elevator, checking the room number Stefan had given me.

The room was all the way at the end of the hall, and I wondered if that made it special, or larger.

I didn't know whether to laugh or cry when I saw there was an envelope on the door. I tore it open, thinking if this turned out to be some cheesy "strip and kneel" set of instructions, I was going to cry, rip it to shreds, and leave.

It wasn't a cheesy set of instructions. Inside the envelope was the door key, as well as a handwritten note in firm, elegant script.

Forgive me.
Forgive me for my anger. You rouse such passion in me. Forgive me for my irrationality. You distract me and make me forget logic. Forgive me for ever questioning whether I love myself more, or you.
I am truly naked before you.

James

I stood there a moment, my breath shaky. That was what he had said at the ball, when I'd insisted he tell me his real name. He'd thrown the condom away and said it was time I learned that he was *truly naked before me.*

I'd thought he was merely making a play on words of some kind, his way of poetically saying that he wanted to come inside me, to be as close as possible. I had been so high on endorphins, pleasure, and the newness and intensity of it all that I hadn't heard the edge in his voice, hadn't realized that the entire time he had been fucking me he was in a downward spiral of panic and fear.

Something clicked. That woman, Ferrara, had been trying to blackmail him into marriage, or something, *all along.* That made him wary of sex or relationships with anyone who knew who he was. Add to that how vulnerable his feelings for me had made him...No wonder he bolted when I forced his name out of him!

That didn't justify his actions, but at least I felt I was starting to understand them.

I slid the key into the lock and opened the door. The room was dim. "James?" He was sitting on the corner of the bed, facing the window. The curtains were drawn and only one light on the far side of him was on.

My breath caught as I realized what I was seeing. He was naked. A blindfold covered his eyes and his hands were bound behind his back. His feet were flat on the floor, knees spread, his balls enticingly exposed. His cock appeared to be rising. He looked like a statue, one of those Greek sculptures with perfectly muscled chest and abs, his cheekbones emphasized by the edge of the cloth over his eyes and his lips barely parted.

I slid my sandals off and tiptoed until I was directly in front of him. "James," I said, louder.

He startled, his shoulders giving a tiny jerk, his spine stiffening.

"*James,*" I said more softly, drawing the "a" out longer. "I thought we were going to talk things over like real people."

He moistened his lips with his tongue before he began to

speak. "If this isn't real for you, Karina..." He swallowed and drew a shaky breath. Afraid. "Then I should go back to New York without you."

He's afraid of sex itself, I realized. Each time we'd had it—full intercourse, I mean—he'd gotten angry at me and tried to run away. Because he was afraid of being so exposed? Or so connected?

That he was presenting himself to me this way, vulnerable and bound, made my breath catch in my throat. "You're saying I'm in control?"

He swallowed. "I'm showing you."

"And if all I want to do is talk to you?"

"Then I'll listen."

"And if I want to interrogate you?" The idea, I admit, had appeal.

"Then I'll talk."

"Hmm."

I reached out and cupped his balls, then drew my fingers upward along his shaft, which quivered expectantly. A dewy droplet gathered at the tip. I ran one finger over it, drawing a slow spiral on the head of his cock, and this time as his breath stuttered in and out of him, it was with equal parts lust and fear.

"Naked before me," I said softly.

"Utterly," he said.

"You did say you'd do anything to gain my forgiveness."

"I did."

I ran my fingertips up his shaft again. "Anything?"

"Anything. Because I trust..." He swallowed again, struggling to speak. "I trust you."

The feeling of power that surged through me made me

dizzy. Having seen what sorts of things went on at the "society" parties in London, I knew I could make him suffer for having made me suffer. If I wanted to, I could violate him, even humiliate him.

But I didn't see the point in doing that. So what if making him prance naked down the hallway with a carnation in his teeth saying "I'm sorry" two hundred times was well within my rights? That wouldn't fix things between us. I could singe the hair off his balls with a cigarette lighter if I wanted to, but that wouldn't heal the pain I'd felt.

And being whipped or humiliated wasn't what he feared anyway. He feared giving up control. He feared exposure. And at some very deep level, he was afraid of sex itself.

Well, thanks to him, I wasn't. I slid my panties off. "I'm wearing a dress, James. Would you like me to describe it to you since you can't see it?"

"I would like that."

"It's blue. Not as dark a blue as that other dress; you know the one. A much lighter blue. This one is also shorter. It's a casual dress, but it's pretty, and I look pretty in it. At least, my mother thinks so. She thinks it's a nice dress."

"I'm sure your mother is quite right."

I slid my fingers between my legs. Beyond the tuft of hair on my mons, I wasn't surprised to find my shaven labia slick. James naked and at my mercy was one of the hottest things I had ever seen.

I straddled him then, and he drew his legs together slightly to give me better support. I scooted forward until my lower lips were touching his cock. I rocked my hips, spreading my slickness onto him.

I stood where I was, still astride him, and took his chin in one hand. I bent my neck to kiss him, eating at his mouth until he opened to me, not breaking away until both of us were whimpering. I lowered my body until the head of his cock was bumping against the inside of my thigh.

"You would never lie to me when you're inside me, would you, James?" I whispered, as I reached down to steady him with my hand.

"I would never lie to you at all, Kar—" He sucked in a gasp as I impaled myself on him.

"Hush," I murmured in his ear. "I'll want to hear it all, later." I concentrated on relaxing enough to take him in as I slid lower and lower. Once I settled with him completely inside me, I reached down to circle my clit with two fingers. We both gasped as I tightened around him.

"I've missed you," he whispered.

"I said hush," I whispered back, and he bit his lip, chastened.

I lifted myself up, drawing him out of me slowly, then lowered just as slowly. All the practicing I had done for the dance at the ArtiWorks had given me quads of steel.

I fucked him that way, as slowly as he had once fucked me, forcing the penetration to be so gradual it was agonizing for both of us. I shifted so I could rub my clit against the rigid muscles of his abdomen as I went up and down.

"So. Here's your chance, James. You have until I come to make your case. To convince me I should give you another chance. And in case it's not clear, you better not come first."

"Of course," he rasped, breathless already. "First things first. I should have told you my name. But my name was only one of the secrets I was keeping from you."

"Oh, you mean like the fact that you're an internationally renowned entertainment figure?"

He swallowed. "Who told you that? Paul and Misha? Mandinka?"

I slapped him lightly across the face, but even a light slap, delivered unexpectedly, shocked him when he couldn't see it coming. He jerked inside me. "I figured it out on my own! Accusing my friends of betraying you is doing nothing to help your case, you know."

"I'm sorry. I'm sorry!" He tipped his head back and gulped air. "Old habits die hard."

"If you're very good, maybe I'll tell you how I figured it out. *Later.* Continue."

"Right. You're right. I should have told you sooner. I intended to tell you—I truly did. But I wanted to wait until after the party. I wanted to...to seduce you so thoroughly, love you so well, and master you so completely, that even if you had been in league with Ferrara or anyone else trying to get to me, that you'd come over to my side."

"Do you always have to have an ulterior motive for everything?" I blurted.

"Not ulterior," he said, as I rubbed against him. "Just multiple. I figured I wanted you to fall for me as hard as I had fallen for you. That it would quell my suspicions or foil any plots was a bonus. I'm sorry I didn't trust you then, and I'm sorry I didn't trust you this summer, as well. You surprised me."

"Was it really your idea for the Tate to hire me?"

"Not exactly."

"Not exactly? That doesn't sound like raw honesty to me," I said, lifting up high enough that I was threatening to disengage entirely.

"The truth is not always simple!" He sounded desperate. "Remember that first time you met Reginald? At the Carlyle

Hotel? I told him that day I thought he should consider hiring you for something. He laughed it off at the time. Then he read your dissertation. He had no budget, no intention of hiring anyone, but after reading it, he very much wanted to bring you over, so he asked me if I would fund your trip and your salary."

"He hired Tristan," I pointed out.

"Was Tristan receiving a stipend?"

"Oh. I don't know."

"I doubt he was. Or if he did, the funding came through his university. No, you were special, and Reg did not want to let you get away. So he asked for the money to fund your position, since you had been my suggestion. I said yes, if he'd do me a favor and keep an eye on you for me."

"Keep an eye on me?"

"I don't mean it in the 'spy on you' sense. I meant in the 'make sure you were all right in London' sense. I didn't know you'd be moving in with old friends of mine, too!"

"All right."

"So hiring you was my suggestion, but Reg was the one who decided to actually do it. My patronage helped it happen. But it was you, Karina, your knowledge, your skills that impressed him and made him want you there. He had no idea that I had my own agenda."

"Even when you sent a kinky playboy to fuck his submissives in the gallery in front of me?"

James swallowed. "Did Damon George—?"

"No, but he gave me the impression he might've. 'Special, after-hours donor tour,' *hah*. I should have known some kind of kink was involved. Which reminds me. When I got to London, Martindale showed me some photos you sent him.

Was that all a sham? Or were you hiding from him, too, at that point?"

"Was that how you made the York connection?"

"Hey! I'm asking the questions here! Do you need to be punished to remember who's in charge right now?"

He clenched his teeth. "Sorry. I'm sorry. I...won't do it again. What was the question?"

"When you sent the photos to Martindale, were you hiding from him?"

"Ah. Yes. Once I had his promise to take care of you, I cut off contact with him."

"Then why send the photos at all?"

He drew a shaky breath. After a few moments, I ground against him. "Mmm, I'm starting to get close. You may be running out of time..."

"I was out of my mind, Karina. Thinking about you, dreaming about you...Terrified that under it all you were in league with Ferrara but hoping, hoping desperately that you weren't and that there would be some way to...to...connect with you. I sent him the photos under the guise of letting him know I was working on the commission, hoping maybe you'd see them, hoping maybe...I don't know. I was desperate and unsure of myself."

"I knew the second I saw them that you were thinking about me."

"Obsessed with you."

"So obsessed with me that you sent Damon to test me?"

"I admit that was one of my stupider ideas. The thought of him touching you, Karina, of him laying a finger on you..." He broke off, jaw clenched, his cock stabbing upward inside me.

I remembered how he'd acted so very affronted to find

me there at the club, how he'd stalked off, as if offended.
To know that his own actions had put me there...My anger
spiked again. He had stalked off not because he had been
disgusted with me, but because he had been disgusted with
himself. I shifted so that my knees were gripping his hips, the
instep of my feet hooked inside his thighs. Now I could really
grind my clit against him and drive myself onto his cock. I
held on to his shoulders. "You know what I learned from
Damon Georgiades?"

"What?"

"I learned that kink isn't enough. I said this in front of you
and Vanette in London, but I don't know if you remember,
what with how we were rudely interrupted." I was drawing
close. Anger was heating me up as much as James inside me.
"I don't particularly like it unless it means something. Unless
I'm in love. Guess who I'm in love with, James? One hint. It
isn't Damon."

He was silent. The one drawback to the blindfold was that
I couldn't see his expression.

"That wasn't a rhetorical question," I said. "Do you believe
me, James? If you do, say so. Who am I in love with?"

He wetted his lips again. "You're in love with me."

"Are you sure?"

"Yes. Yes goddammit, Karina, I'm sure!" His hips jerked
under me, meeting my thrusts. "You wouldn't be doing all
this if you weren't!"

I ground against him with each question I asked. "And
who understands you?"

"You do."

"And who understands your art?"

"You, Karina, you."

"Mmm, I think I'm getting used to this call and response thing we have going on here, James. You know that every time I give you my body, I give you a piece of my heart, right?"

"Yes."

"I think it's only fair if you give me a piece of yourself in return. Doesn't that sound like a good idea?"

"Yes, yes."

"A piece of information, a piece of your past. That's a fair exchange rate, don't you think?"

"Definitely! I want to hide nothing from you."

"Good. That'll do for now," I said. "Now hush and hold still while I make myself come."

I didn't make it easy for him to hold back. I ran my hands down his chest and toyed with his nipples, feeling his cock twitch hungrily inside me when I did. I half wondered what I'd do if he failed to keep from coming until told. The other half wondered what wicked things he would do to me to make me pay for this. Holding back for that long against the steady onslaught of my pussy couldn't have been easy, either. I was very close myself, soaring along on a high, tense peak before I finally broke through.

I screamed when I did, my hands clenching his shoulders, knocking him backward onto the bed, thrusting my pelvis against him again and again, suddenly close to a second orgasm and hungrily seeking it with desperate cries and spasms. The second explosion followed the first, hot and bright, making me see colors behind my eyelids before my tension subsided. I went limp atop him, the dual sound of both our harsh breathing making a fading rhythm.

Five

Mother Said Get Things Done

I was a little surprised James hadn't done any of the things I thought he would. He didn't try to dom me into listening, he hadn't hidden anything, and he hadn't guarded himself in the slightest.

It was as if he knew what it was going to take to get me back. I was amazed at the thought that he knew me that well and that he could go against his own fears and instincts to convince me of it. Amazed and appreciative. Maybe this was going to work.

"Karina," he whispered.

"Yes, James."

"My arm is somewhat wrenched under me."

"Oh. Sorry." I lifted my head, but it took me a moment to reconnect feeling to all my limbs and control them. I eased myself off, then helped him roll to his side. I pushed the blindfold off his head before untwisting the cloth that had been binding his wrists together, and he brought his arm forward with a groan.

"Are you all right?" I worried I'd actually hurt him.

"Fine." He wiggled his fingers. "I'll be fine." He turned over to face me. "Well?"

"Well, what?"

His eyes were serious, even as his face and body were relaxed and languid post-orgasm. "Did I convince you to give me another chance?"

"You at least earned the ability to tell me even more of what I don't know."

He took my hand in his, like he had so many times before. This time he kissed my fingertips, his eyes closing as he did. "I have a lot to tell you. More than any single interrogation might reveal."

I squeezed his hand. "Speaking of interrogation, this was nice, and I understand why you did it. But I shouldn't have to interrogate you for the answers."

He sucked in a breath. "No. Of course you shouldn't. There's so much I need to tell you if you're really going to get to know me." He reached up and traced the curve of my cheek with his fingertip. "Yet I feel like you know me better than anyone."

"I do know you," I said. "I just don't know the *facts* about you."

His gaze shied away from mine. "Many of the facts are sordid."

"Says the man who put a six-inch dildo into me and walked me around the Metropolitan Museum of Art."

"I mean much more sordid than that." Now his face had completely clouded over.

"I want to know, James. I need to know. I have a right to, if we're going to be together."

He nodded, though his eyes were closed. "I know. I agree. That still doesn't make it easy for me to open up."

I raised an eyebrow. "Except during sex."

"As you well know. Were you serious about what you said before? I would sincerely give you a piece of my past for every time you give me…" He kissed my fingertips again. "Anything. Sex. Your body. Your submission."

Even though we'd just had sex, I felt a thrill go through my loins. "I wasn't suggesting it lightly."

"I want to be sure. Sometimes we say things in the heat of passion that seem less than wise afterward."

"But sometimes we get inspired." This could be the perfect solution, I realized. "I know the time you're the most open is when we have sex. That's the time your answers will be the best. Of course, if we do this, I could still revoke my forgiveness at any time."

"Of course. Just as you can revoke your consent at any time. I understand, Karina. It's *One Thousand and One Nights*, only this time I'm Scheherazade, telling the stories."

I touched his face with my fingers, feeling like a weight was slowly lifting from my back. Maybe we were going to make this work after all. The fact that he was willing to try so hard made a huge difference in how I felt. And I wanted him. The part of me that had been needing him and pining for him all summer was quelled by the knowledge we could do this.

I sat up and discovered I'd been lying on something. I held up what he had used to bind his wrists. In the dim light I could still recognize what it was. "These look a lot like a pair of panties I used to have."

"That's because they are."

"You've been carrying around my underwear?" I turned to look at him.

Lying beside me on the pillow, he wore a familiar expression: serene and a bit bemused. "You left them in the car. Did you think I'd throw them away?"

"I never really thought about it before."

"If I left a pair of my underwear behind with you, what would you do?"

"Yeah, I see your point. I've got a handkerchief of yours I keep in the—"

His expression changed suddenly, his eyes widening and his lips parting in slight surprise. "That's it, isn't it?"

I felt myself blush even though I wasn't keeping anything a secret. "Um, partly anyway. My roommate—"

"I know. I met her at the spa that day. Becky. She knew the Lord's Ladies."

"Yeah. And she got one of the handkerchiefs you threw from the stage at Madison Square Garden. It matched one I got from you." Well, from Stefan, strictly speaking.

To my surprise, James smiled. He sat up and kissed me softly. "If I believed in fate, I'd say that was a sign. What are the odds?"

"And are they better or worse than the odds of being struck by lightning?"

His smile turned into a laugh. "Was that a pun?" In a flash he pulled my legs onto his lap, spanking me playfully several times. I couldn't help it. It was like being ambushed by tickling. I kicked and giggled and shrieked.

I wriggled free, hug-tackled him, and ended up on top of him in the center of the bed, kissing him all over his face. "I'm still mad at you, you know."

"If you say so," he said. "By the way, I agree with your mother. This *is* a nice dress."

"She bought it for me today. She wants to meet you."

"What have you told her about me?"

"That you're rich and good-looking, which is what she cares about most. My sister wants to meet you, too. They know you're an art-world type but that's all." I was coming to my senses a little, now that the intense pleasure of the orgasm was receding and the play-spanking had woken me up. "And if you'd really put the rock star stuff behind you, that'd be all they need to know. But that sounds like a big *if*."

"A very big *if*." He nodded slowly, his face sobering again into his usual mask.

That would not do. The biggest question he still hadn't answered for me was the story of Ferrara Huntington. It was the biggest thing that I thought could still be a deal-breaker and send me out of here a single woman. I leaned down and nuzzled his neck, as if the subject were closed for now. He smelled delicious, igniting all my cravings again. I nibbled behind his ear. He arched under me, his cock not yet ready to harden again, but the rest of him responding just fine. He pulled me down beside him, kissing me back and exploring my neck with his mouth.

Hadn't we just finished having sex? I felt my insides melting again though, my desire rising like a tide. Maybe my body felt we should make up for lost time.

Making out was nice and I enjoyed the feeling that we were in no hurry. When had we ever done this, kissed for the sake of kissing? I lost track of time. Minutes ticked by in my haze of affection, pleasure, and relief. Yes. We needed this kind of connection, too. Affection, exploring each other, letting chemistry take over.

My hands roamed his back, his sides, his hips, until one of them strayed between his legs, and I sucked in a breath as I met the scorching hot stiffness there.

There was no reason to wait. There was so much we had to talk about. "You're ready for more?" I teased.

"With you, Karina, I always am."

"But you know what it means, don't you? If we're going to continue, you'll have to spill the beans about Ferrara."

"I will be unburdening myself when I do," he said, pumping his shaft into my hand as I tightened my fingers around it. "You don't know how much it means to me that I can trust you, Karina."

"Even if you had to set spies on me to be sure of it?" I squeezed a little too hard.

"I never should have done that. Never. But I do not regret the trust I have now, no matter how I came to it," James said, his eyes fluttering under the pressure of my hand. "I need your forgiveness, Karina."

"Need it? Why do you need it?"

"Because you're the person who means the most to me. The person whose esteem means the most. You understand me. You understand my art. I...I will never forget the way you drove that point home to me in London."

I stroked him lightly, then, quickening his arousal. I'd said those things to him. To hear him say them back was deeply gratifying.

He went on. "There's no one I'd rather share my secrets with. No one else I can imagine sharing my secrets with. No one else who gets this close."

Meaning not even Stefan, or Chandra, or Lucinda, or any of the other people in his life I had met. It struck me suddenly that our positions had reversed in another way: Once upon a time I knew nothing about him and he had seemingly known everything about me. Now I was the one who had met his friends, patrons, and ex-lovers, while he had yet to meet the people in my life other than Becky.

His cock pulsed in my hand. "How much do you want me, James?"

"Enough that I can't put a number on the answer."

"And how do you want me?"

"So many ways, Karina. So many ways."

"Such as?"

"All the ways I've already had you, and more."

"Oh? Tell me what you're imagining."

"My mind is full of images. Of you, bent over, blindfolded, tied. Of me taking you in public, in private, with my fingers, with my glass, with my cock, in my bed, in my car, on the roof of a building..."

"Hmm. I don't remember the roof of a building."

"That's part of the 'and more.'"

His desire was palpable. "Go on. What are you going to do to me, James?" I ran my thumb over the head of his cock, spreading slickness. "It's not enough to just fuck me, is it?"

"Man does not subsist on meat alone," he murmured, nibbling my neck. "Or woman. Admit it, Karina. You like what I do. You like what I demand."

"I do."

"Which is why you'll let me tie your legs apart and spank your pussy."

"Yes, James." Another deep thrill ran through me as I felt

the power shifting, as I felt his dominant side coming forth after being in check all evening.

"In public."

"Yes, James."

"With my cock in your ass."

My butt cheeks clenched at the suggestion. "Yes, James." That wasn't something we'd done yet, or even discussed. I supposed we were discussing it now. "But remember what we talked about."

"You give me your heart, your body, I give you a piece of my past."

"Tell me about Ferrara," I said, leaning down to lick the head of the cock in my fist like an ice cream cone.

His grimace was feral. "Tell me everything you know about her and I'll pick up where you leave off," he said, "*after* I get this dress off you, before I ruin it."

Yes, I decided, this trading sex for knowledge rule was working out very well. "Well, let's see. I know she's the ex-wife of your record company guy." I helped him by wriggling free of the top of the dress. "And that she's claiming you're married. That's all."

He kissed his way down my naked torso and then breathed softly into the pubic hair I'd kept. He parted my lips with sure fingers and licked in a careful circle around my clit until I wriggled to put him right on target. Then I yelped because he nibbled at my clit, not hard, only to warn me, to remind me who was in charge now. With it trapped between his teeth, he could flick his tongue mercilessly across it and I dug my fingers into the bedspread.

I noticed, of course, that while his mouth was busy, he couldn't answer my questions. I supposed if the delay was buying him time to think about his answer, at least I approved highly of the method. He let go and returned to gentle licks then, making me whimper, but I held perfectly still this time.

"Good girl," he whispered when he lifted his head. "Now. Things you should know about Ferrara. She's been lusting after me for more than ten years. Since before I signed with the record company, in fact."

One of his fingers played lightly up and down my seam, distracting me slightly, but only slightly. "How old is she?"

"She was Huntington's trophy wife. I think she is now thirty-nine."

"Okay, but was she chasing you before or after they were married?"

"After. But she and Huntington weren't traditionally monogamous." He chuckled as he slid a finger into me. "She's the one who introduced me to the society."

"Ah, right. Vanette told me she knew her but wouldn't tell me anything else." I sucked in a breath as he drew his finger gently in and out of me.

"The other thing you should know about Ferrara, which hardly anyone else does, is that she took over the record company from her husband about two years ago when they divorced. She's a very hands-on executive, and she served as producer when I did a residency in Las Vegas called *Bride of the Blue*. A rock opera spectacle."

"I imagine it was."

"She grew increasingly difficult to work with over the course of the show. That was the last straw for me, why I decided to quit entirely." He paused in his speaking to slip two fingers into me and lick my clit at the same time. He kept that up until I started to tighten up, nearing orgasm, and then he backed off. "Her husband and I had made a deal that an earlier double album counted as two, and then the farewell tour album would be the final one on my contract. Unfortunately for me, it was a verbal deal, and the week before the Madison Square Garden concert, she began leaving me phone messages insinuating that would not satisfy her."

"Satisfy her? You mean the record company."

"She is the company now. She keeps her ex-husband around as a figurehead, and he continues to do whatever she says. Probably hoping she'll take him back if he's a good boy." He clucked his tongue. "So, quite literally, she owns me."

"I had no idea being a rock star was akin to indentured servitude," I joked.

"Oh, but it is," he said seriously. "Did you ever see George Michael's videos from the nineties?"

"I had a friend when I was like eleven who was in love with him, yeah."

"He sued his record company in England, saying they had essentially turned him into a 'professional slave.' He lost the case, but it wasn't a frivolous one. At a certain point it doesn't matter what they pay you. When they can force you to do whatever they want, you're beholden to them."

"I don't imagine you take well to being forced into anything."

"No." He dragged his fingers over my G-spot and my toes curled. "Is that enough for now? There is more to tell you about my battle of wills with Ferrara."

"You owe me the rest...later." I tried to wrap my legs around him, but he put his hands on my knees, flattening my bent legs against the bed.

"You've gotten more flexible," he observed.

"Some of my flexibility returned when I was training for the ArtiWorks performance," I corrected.

"I approve. Anything that lets me do this." He ran his cock up my wet seam, levering himself up on his hands. "Are you ready for me?"

"Yes, James." I held my breath for a second, thinking he was going to plunge in. But no, he teased me with the tip, pushing in an inch or two and pulling out, again and again. "Oh fuck!"

"Mmm. Most sensitive part of my cock and the most sensitive part of your opening. What's not to like?"

I groaned. The shallow penetration felt so good I was melting, but at the same time I wanted more. So much more. "You're fucking me the way you give information, a little bit at a time!"

He laughed then and drove deep, exhaling and closing his eyes as he did. "You don't know how hard it was waiting to do this."

"I think I have some idea!"

"From the very first time we met, I mean." He fucked me slowly now, savoring every inch as much as he savored being back in control. "That very first night. Ten years earlier, I would have had you six ways before we got to your apartment, and then I never would have seen you again."

"Then I'm glad it's now."

"Me, too." He tucked his hands under my butt and levered me up to meet each slow thrust.

"So what would the six ways have been?"

"It's just an expression."

"Nothing is just an expression with you, James."

He chuckled. "Very well. Let's see. Six ways. Well, your

mouth, your pussy, your ass, with both my fingers and my cock, that would count as six. But let's not count my fingers. Let's count my cock alone. I could have also fucked you between your breasts, against your tailbone, and between your legs but not inside you. That would be six, too."

A year ago I wouldn't have counted being fucked between the legs as "sex," but after what I'd been through in London, I definitely counted it now.

"Oh, and, Karina, in case I wasn't clear, one of the reasons I want to leave the music industry is that I take my promises seriously."

"I know you do." I reared up enough to kiss him.

"And one of the things that I love most about you is that you do, too." He moved his hands now to press my palms flat against the pillow on either side of my head, his hips speeding up as I wrapped my legs around him at last. "We worked long and hard to reach this point, to be able to join like this." He punctuated his point with a sharp thrust. "To deserve each other like this."

I nodded, feeling like liquid pleasure was pouring out of his body into mine.

"So here's the promise I want to ask for, and that I want to give. Explicitly." He paused, though, as the sensations washed over him, too, making him shudder.

"Is that why they call it explicit sex?" I asked.

He half laughed, half growled and kissed me to shut me up. When he raised his head he went on. "This is for us alone. My cock, your pussy, exclusively."

"Meaning you won't fuck Ferrara even though she owns you?"

"Yes!" He raised himself up a little. "And you won't let anything enter you but this. Well, and other things that I put there."

"I promise," I breathed.

"I promise," he answered, solemnly, and then began fucking me so hard the bed shook against the wall.

This time after we were done we took a quick shower and he told me more about Ferrara's efforts to micro-manage the *Bride of the Blue* production the last time they were in Las Vegas. James's sense of outrage thrummed through the small room.

"Seriously, who does she think she is? I'm the artist. It's my vision. What does she know?" He toweled his hair dry and then shook his head, leaving short black spikes going every which way.

"Well," I said, merely to play devil's advocate. "What *does* she know? I thought she was a talent scout?"

"I suppose." He calmed down slightly. "She used to dance and do some choreography before she married Huntington, so she thinks she knows that side of it. But her knowledge only gives her license to meddle."

"Does she sing?" I wrapped a towel around myself.

"Thank goodness, no. But honestly. I got quite tired of her trying to tell the dancers or my choreographer what to do, and they eventually learned to do what she said while she was watching and then go back to doing it my way the second she was gone. No company needs that kind of stress." He pulled on a bathrobe. "For the farewell tour, thankfully, she stayed put, and I have a much better relationship with the dancers than she does. And the band? They won't even speak to her unless they're forced to." The smile on his face as he thought about his bandmates was relaxed and genial.

Then he sobered as he watched me getting dressed.

"Karina," he said in a soft voice. "Are you satisfied? I mean, information-wise."

"For now," I said, squeezing his shoulder as I pulled on my sandals. "I should get back."

"Stefan will follow you and check out the neighborhood." He pushed a button on his phone, and I realized he must've had Stefan on some kind of speed-dial. Speed text? "With any luck, your mother's con man will have moved on to another target, but better to be safe."

"All right." I wished Stefan could drive me so we could continue to catch up, but I had a car of my own to drive. We could talk on the phone, but it was nicer to sit in the front seat with him. "My sister's leaving tomorrow."

"To go back to the restaurant?"

"Yes."

"They must really be missing her there," he said, rubbing his chin thoughtfully.

Something about the way he said it caught my attention. "That's right," I said with a frown. "Do you know why?" I didn't remember telling him this.

"Yes. They're launching the new menu on Thursday," he said, looking at me quizzically, then with alarm as my frown turned to an angry glare. "Karina, what's wrong?"

"How did you know about the restaurant changing?"

"Shouldn't I know about it?"

I yanked the phone out of my purse and shook it at him. "Do you have some kind of tap on my phone? Some other kind of spy crap? Didn't you just get through saying you should have trusted me? What the hell, James!"

He had his hands up as if I were shaking a gun at him, not a smartphone, and tried to defend himself verbally. "No! Nothing like that! Karina, don't jump to hasty conclusions!"

"What the hell kind of conclusion am I supposed to make, then? How do you know about the restaurant?"

"I'm Xavier's angel investor," he said.

"How the fuck do you know Xavier!" I shouted.

The alarm on his face only grew. "Karina, it's not what it looks like..."

"A patent attempt to own all the people around me so you control everything?" I spat.

A soft knock came at the door. Stefan, most likely.

"No, Karina. It's nothing like that."

"The hell it's not," I said, and yanked open the door. Stefan was standing there looking sheepish. "Come on. Let's go."

I marched into the hallway as Stefan looked back and forth between us before hurrying after me, catching up after a few steps.

"Everything all right?" he asked hesitantly.

"Argh! Your boss is the freakiest control freak who ever lived!" I said, jabbing the elevator button.

We stepped in. After the door closed, Stefan said, "I cannot dispute that, though I have very few points of comparison." He looked quite distressed.

"Don't give me that look."

"I'm upset that you're upset. That's all, Karina."

"I thought it was going to work. I thought we could get past the bullshit. But now I'm not so sure."

"Give him a chance, Karina, please."

"Why? Why should I give him a chance?"

The elevator doors opened, but Stefan stood blocking them, his hands pressed together like he was praying. "Because he loves you so very very much. And I have never seen him in this much pain."

"Not even with Lucinda?"

"Not even close. Karina, please. Because I care about him and you as well—"

I pushed past him into the lobby and headed for my car. For a moment, though, I couldn't remember which one it was, and he caught up while I was staring at three or four rentals that were all almost the same.

"I'll give him one more chance tomorrow," I said. "One more." I pushed the key fob and one of the cars in front of me flashed its lights. "Do you know my address?"

"I do," Stefan admitted. "It wasn't hard to find."

"Fine." If I had been smart, I would have told him the make and model of Phil's car. But I couldn't remember. I'd only gotten a glimpse of the car and had been too focused on Phil himself, and getting rid of him, to think about it. "Let's go."

I fumed the whole way home. Stefan followed at a discreet distance, as if giving me space to vent.

When I got home, I saw the limo circle the block at least once, and then I stopped paying attention. I sat down with Jill to watch the late news.

She took one look at me, though, and said, "You don't look so happy."

I shook my head. "One step forward, two steps back," I said. I really didn't want to say anything about the restaurant, though. The last thing I wanted to do was throw a monkey wrench into Jill's dreams.

"What happened?"

"Oh, we talked a lot. He answered all my questions. I really thought everything was going great. But then... right at the end he let something slip that made me stop trusting him all over again."

"That sucks," Jill said.

And then a third voice I didn't expect, added, "Trust is hard."

I looked to see my mother standing at the bottom of the stairs. "Oh, Mom, did we wake you?"

She shook her head and came to sit on the couch next to me. She took the remote off the coffee table and turned down the volume partway. "The medicine wore off is all," she said with a shrug. "I think I'm going to try to switch to ibuprofen."

"Okay, if you're sure."

"There's no pill for a broken heart, though, dear." She patted me on the knee. "All we can give you is sympathy."

"Thanks."

"Well, and ice cream," Jill said. "Who wants some?"

I raised my hand weakly and my mother nodded her agreement.

"I'll go dish it. I'll heat up hot fudge, too." Jill hurried into the kitchen.

"Mom," I said, putting my hand over hers. "You were saying something about trust."

"It's difficult, I know, because you can't read people's minds. Men, you think you can tell what they're thinking, but if they are really in it for something else? What can you do?"

"Are all relationships doomed to fail?"

"No, dear, but it takes either a lot of love or a lot of compromise. And sometimes, when you have a man who dotes on you, who provides, for some people, that's enough."

"But if I don't trust him, it doesn't matter how much he loves me or how much money he has," I said.

"Isn't that what I just said?" She blinked at me and then turned the TV down even lower, though not off. "Well, perhaps I didn't quite finish my thought. As you get older your priorities might change. But since you can never be sure, since trust always has an element of faith to it since you can't read their minds, then love is the only worthwhile reason to put yourself in someone's hands."

She had never talked to me like this before. Her previous relationship advice had always been about how to be attractive to a man, or how to keep his interest.

"His love or mine?" I asked, feeling bewildered.

"Both, dear, both. He loves you, you love him…If you're sure about that, then you have to figure the rest out somehow. If it turns out you really can't trust him, then maybe he doesn't love you after all. Or he doesn't love you enough to change."

Did you think you could change Phil? I wondered. *Or did you settle for a guy you didn't trust because he gave you attention and you needed that more than actual love?*

"I've made some terrible choices in men, Karina," my mother finally said. "I don't want to see you repeat the same mistakes. Don't settle for the 'safe' choice over love. It's not worth it. Especially when they're not as safe as you think."

"Oh, Mom." I wondered if I was any better at picking men than she was. Then again, *safe* wasn't exactly a word I'd use for James. "We've all made bad choices. Well, except Jill."

I could hear my sister getting the bowls out of the cabinet, and the microwave humming as she heated up the fudge sauce. I got a sudden idea.

"You know, Mom, she and Pauline have been going steady for almost three years."

"Oh, I know," she said, as if to make it clear she hadn't lost her memory of that.

I leaned close. "They're thinking about making it... permanent."

I didn't use the word "marriage" on purpose. With my mother, I figured, if she wanted to pretend the possibility of gay marriage didn't exist, she'd play dumb, but if she was open to the idea...

I nearly panicked as I saw her eyes well with tears and she sucked a breath in through her nose to steel herself. But then she said, "Oh, if only I still had my engagement ring. I always..." She paused to compose herself again. "I always wanted one of you girls to have it."

I took her hand. "Maybe it'll turn up."

She shook her head. "I think you're right. I think that creep made off with it. Phil. Fool, more like."

I squeezed her hand. "Your blessing would mean a lot more to Jill than the ring would." I could see Jill emerging from the kitchen with the bowls in her hands. "She wasn't sure you'd be...okay with the whole concept."

"Karina. If there's one thing I've learned, it's that if someone finds the right person, they should hang on with all they've got. And *everyone* deserves someone right for them."

When she said that, I got a little misty-eyed.

Jill raised an eyebrow as she took her seat again, setting the bowls onto the coffee table. Each one had a spoon tucked under the scoop of ice cream. "You gals okay out here?"

"Have you set a date yet?" Mom asked. "For you and Pauline?"

"Oh! Jeez, not yet. Haven't even popped the question, Mom!" Jill eyed me with a surprised look. I grinned. "Um, horse and carriage. Central Park." Apparently my mother's sudden, enthusiastic embrace of her plans knocked loose Jill's ability to form full sentences.

"Sounds lovely! That is really the right way to do it." She picked up her ice cream and toasted Jill with her spoon. "I knew I raised you right."

I took up my own bowl and ate quietly, happy for Jill, and happy that our mother approved of her choice. Would she be as enthusiastic about mine? Or as supportive if I decided to break it off with him?

I didn't want to think about James even if only for a little while. Instead I distracted Jill into discussing what she and Pauline were going to do if they bought their condo, and talked a little about what I had done to help Paulina and Michel renovate the ArtiWorks in London. We had a laugh about the similarity between Paulina and Pauline and how I might end up doing demolition for both.

Taking a wrecking ball to something right then would have felt really good.

Six

Like Blackened Sunshine

The next morning, before I awoke, Jill had called to cheek on mom's car at the shop and then she took Mom to get her hair done. While I was eating breakfast the shop called back to say the car needed new spark plugs. When I asked for more details, they explained the thing that was wrong with the old plugs was that they were...missing. Jill had told them about the cut battery cable she had found so they were on the lookout for anything more. Thankfully it looked like nothing major beyond that. The mechanic assured me they would check everything and test-drive it, too.

Hey, I wanted to say. *Great. What can you do for a sabotaged relationship?* I hadn't called James yet. I wasn't ready to. Sitting here in the kitchen where I'd grown up, his dom aura seemed very far away. What kind of a controlling bastard was he, really?

Jill brought Mom back shortly after, then started packing her bag to try to get on that afternoon flight.

"Oh, Jill, honey, I have some clothes you might want," my

mother said. "Karina, come help me dig in the closet. With this wrist it's tricky."

"Okay." We went up to Mom's bedroom, and the next thing I knew, I was pulling nearly everything out of a whole section of the closet and spreading it out on the bed.

"Here's a skirt that would be great for you, Karina. I bought it on sale and I don't think I've ever worn it." She handed me a sort of Gypsy-dancer skirt, long, loose, and colorful. To humor her I put it on and was surprised it fit. "Jill, come look. There must be something for you, too."

Jill shook her head. "We're really not built the same, Mom. I'm much bigger than you are."

"Oh, but I have these sweaters that are too big for me. And these necklaces. If you're going to be playing hostess in a white-tablecloth restaurant now, you'll need some classy looks."

"I . . ." Jill started, then shared a look with me as she decided not to argue.

Mom pulled open the same jewelry box they had been looking through yesterday when they had been arguing. "Here. What about these?"

"The one with the shell, that one I like," Jill said, and took it from her. "It'll make people think of seafood."

"Is there a lot of seafood on the new menu?" I asked.

"I'll see when I get there. Chef made a lot of decisions while I was gone."

"Well, he had to if the new menu goes live in two days," I said, as I pulled another armload of clothes from the closet.

"Two days? Who said two days?" She looked at me in puzzlement.

Dammit. James was the one who had said they were going to launch on Thursday. I didn't want to get into telling them why I was angry at him right now, so I changed the subject. "Hey, you said Xavier got an angel investor to put up his half, right?"

"Yeah."

"Did he tell you who it was?"

"We don't know his name."

That sure sounded like James's style. "How'd Xavi meet him?"

"He said it was some guy he knew from the music industry. Xavi used to do backstage catering and got to know a lot of record reps and stuff."

I felt a sudden sinking in my stomach at the same time my head felt giddy and light. "Oh, really. How interesting."

Maybe James had been telling the truth. Maybe it had nothing to do with me.

"Um, when did this investor first get involved?"

"Over the winter. Maybe January? Around the time you quit."

Three months before James and I met.

I suddenly remembered James knowing my name, my real name, when we'd talked on the phone after meeting that very first time. And I suddenly felt very stupid.

He hadn't walked into the bar randomly the night we met. He'd gone there because of Xavier. James never went anywhere he didn't have an in! Of course he didn't! And after he'd left, the first thing he did, probably, was call Xavier and find out who I was and whether I was crazeballs or not.

I wondered what Xavi said.

"Well, I'm sure it's going to go great," I said, sounding a little dazed or distracted I'm sure. "Have a good flight, sis."

She kissed me and Mom on the cheek. "Thanks for the necklace, Mom. I'll let you know if Pauline says yes."

"Oh goodness, I nearly forgot. Here, you have to take some of my eighteen-karat gold for Pauline, too." She put a few things into a small velvet bag from the jewelry box and handed it to her.

"Thanks, Mom. I really appreciate it." Jill kissed her one more time. "See you in the Big Apple, KayKay."

"Fly safe," I said weakly.

After Jill was gone I turned my attention back to helping Mom sift through her closet. She didn't look like she'd ever gotten rid of very much, as outfits I had never seen her wear emerged from the depths. Bit by bit she winnowed down what she wanted to keep. "I figure if I haven't worn something in more than ten years, at this point it probably doesn't even fit," she said, "and it certainly isn't something I need."

She set me to making piles, then folding the clothes and putting them into trash bags. "You're not going to throw this all away, are you?"

"Oh, goodness no. There's a battered women's shelter in town that takes donations. I happened to pick up their flyer when we were at the hospital," Mom said breezily.

Happened to. Mom never did anything by accident, though she often made it look as if things were a coincidence. I took it to mean she either remembered more about Phil or she was taking our warnings very seriously. Either way, it was good for her.

I ended up taking a cardigan sweater that was a little too small for her and a skirt that I thought Becky would like. I didn't have room for a lot else in my suitcase. Plus my mom's stuff wasn't really my style. My mother had a sensibility that seemed mostly based on glamour actresses from before her time, from the Hollywood starlets of the 1940s and 1950s. Then again, my style was "poor grad student."

I hadn't thought about my thesis in limbo or the furor with Renault in days. I supposed I was going to have to start thinking about it again as soon as I went back to the city, though.

One thing at a time. First, I had an apology to make to James.

Once we got all the bags of clothes down to the living room, Mom took a nap on her once-again clear bed, and I took to texting: *I think I owe you an apology.*

There was no answer for several minutes, and I agonized, wondering if I had gone too far with my outburst last night. He'd told the truth and I'd flat-out refused to believe him. If I was going to be like that, then it didn't matter how deep into his soul he dug for the truth. This wasn't going to work.

I was distracted momentarily by the mechanics dropping by with my mom's car. They'd not only fixed it up. They'd also vacuumed the carpets and washed the windows. I thanked them and they wished my mother good health.

When I got back to my phone, there was a reply from James: *Would you like to deliver your apology in person?*

I texted back immediately: *Yes, please.*

Followed by: *But my sister is gone and I'm worried to leave my mother entirely alone.*

Not because she can't take care of herself. She's doing fine in that regard. But because Betancourt might come back.

A full two minutes went by before the reply came: *Then I'll see you in the car. Stefan can keep watch.*

I sucked in a breath. That made sense. *When?*

Tonight after your mother goes to sleep.

I nearly texted *OK* but then remembered, and sent *Yes, James* instead.

Mom and I cooked dinner together. I tried to convince her she shouldn't be on her ankle so much, and she placated me by sitting at the counter to chop an onion. With her wrist brace on, she couldn't lift anything heavy with that hand, but she could still hold on to things enough to do a lot. Thank goodness it was her left wrist, and she was right-handed. We sautéed onions and peppers and browned beef to go into pasta sauce, then baked ziti in the oven with cheese. It was everything we loved about lasagna but half the work.

I ate sparingly, though, my stomach nervous about meeting James later.

We had nearly finished dinner when the phone rang. My first thought was it could be Phil. It wasn't. It was Aunt Tera calling to get an update. "Jill said she's doing a lot better, but way to give me a heart attack, girls! How is she today?"

"Why don't you talk to her yourself?" I suggested. "Here, you chat while I clean up."

I handed the cordless phone to my mother and she moved into the living room. She and her sister were off to the races, each one talking a mile a minute. I washed the pot and loaded the dishwasher.

I finished and they were still talking, so I went up to my room to read a book.

A little while later my mother stuck her head in. "Tera says hello," she said, as if I hadn't talked to her myself, or perhaps apologizing for the fact that she was only now off the phone. "She's going to come visit for two weeks."

"Oh? When?"

"She's getting ready to quit her job, but to stick it to her boss she wants to make sure she's used up all her vacation time first!" She beamed, energized by talking to her sister and happy about seeing her. "So she's going to drive up tomorrow."

"That sounds great! Here. I'll go put clean sheets on Jill's bed."

"Thank you, dear."

The evening crawled by. I made up the bed, did another load of laundry. Mom watched a movie. When that was done, she finally declared she was going to sleep.

I waited until she had been asleep an hour and I could hear the raspy sounds of her snoring before I texted James to say all was clear.

He replied with where the car was parked, at the cross street a few houses down.

No other instructions. Despite that, I couldn't help but think about the time he'd had me report for punishment. The mysterious doctor's office. The delicious torture that followed.

But that time the "correction" had been for a manufactured flaw, hadn't it? It had been a game we played.

This wasn't a game. This time our whole relationship was precarious and I didn't want to make the misstep that would send us over the edge. We'd each made mistakes now. The question was, could we fix it? If only it could be as simple as submitting to a spanking. If only that could make all our problems go away.

I used my new keys to lock the door behind me and then walked up the street. The neighborhood was quiet, as usual on a weeknight by eleven, most of the houses dark. I caught sight of the car just beyond the tall privacy hedge the neighbors on the corner had grown to enclose their property.

Stefan gave me a small wave with the binoculars in his hand. I heard the doors unlock.

I opened the back door and slipped in before I lost my nerve.

James was sitting inside looking grave and inscrutable. Thank goodness I was sitting down. I felt weak in the knees. He was in full suit and tie, but it was his dark expression that affected me most.

"James…" I said, and it came out a whisper because my throat was so tight.

"Karina," he said, coolly, but in that way that I knew meant he was very tightly wound. "I'm listening."

"I'm sorry. I lost my head. I jumped to the conclusion the only reason you bought my sister's restaurant was to control everything in my life." I pressed my hands together. "And then I didn't listen when you tried to explain. I was wrong. I'm sorry."

He gave a short nod. "I'm sorry, too. If I had not given you reason to doubt me, I am sure you would not have. But, Karina, have I ever lied to you?"

I made sure to take a calming breath before answering. "No. You haven't. You left out some things, but you've never lied."

"Will it reassure you if I make a promise never to lie to you?"

"It'll at least reinforce it in my mind," I said. "Because I know this whole deal we have going, trading sex for information? It isn't going to work if I don't believe what you say. I really am trying to give us a chance, James."

"And I am trying to be both truthful and complete."

An idea struck me then. "Let's make it a mutual promise. I...I'll renew my promise to you, too. How's that?"

I saw the relief on his face, a sudden easing of the lines around his eyes. "I'd like that." His tongue darted out as he considered. "How would you like to go about making this vow?"

The electricity in the air between us ramped up. I couldn't quite explain it. It was as if once the tension of the apology had dissipated, it was replaced with sexual tension. We were doing this together. The relationship might still fall apart, but we were going to at least try to fix it. Together. And for all the trouble and angst we'd had, the one thing we never lost completely was that physical, chemical connection. It might have been tamped down temporarily, but as soon as we got on the same wavelength again, *boom.*

"We should hold hands," I said, "to make the promise. And I'll go first, since mine's a renewal, and then you can go."

"All right."

I got onto my knees on the seat so I faced him directly, and I saw his eyebrow twitch at that. I was still wearing that Gypsy-dancer skirt. I held out my hands, palms down, and he gently brought his under mine until they were clasped. Mine were trembling until his steadied them.

"I promised you once, a long time ago, in this car, that I would not lie. I kept up that promise all the time we were separated in the summer. I'm now renewing that promise to you, James. No lie shall pass my lips...Or if I have to, I'll tell you, so you can...correct me."

It was as if electricity crackled on the word *correct.* Or maybe that was because I bowed my head without even realizing it.

His voice was low and smooth. "And how shall I correct you?"

"Any way you see fit," I whispered.

"Very good. Shall I now make my promise to you?"

"Yes." I swallowed.

"Look me in the eye, then," he said. "Karina Casper, I, James Byron LeStrange, shall let no lie travel from my mouth to your ear. Under penalty of losing you."

His eyes were moist with tears. So were mine. *Are we going to make this work, James? Are we?*

"All right. We should…seal the promises now," I said.

"How should we do that?"

"Traditionally." I swallowed. "With a kiss."

"Very well." He pulled me gently toward him by my hands then and brushed my lips with his.

My breath caught, but he wasn't finished. His breath was like ozone, charged, as he pressed his mouth more firmly against mine, his tongue swiping the seam of my lips until they parted.

And then I was crushed against him, lips and body and all, as he pulled me into his arms, lying back against the door and pulling me on top of him. Every fiber of my being thrilled at being so close, his firm muscle under me, his arms around me. I was filled with a sense of belonging and rightness I had never felt with another person before.

When he let my mouth free at last, I asked, "So do you forgive me?"

"I thought the kiss was to seal the promise of honesty."

"It was. But, you know, I'd like to be sure you really forgive me."

"Aha." He looked into my eyes. "Does that mean I should be sure you were really sorry?"

I suppressed the urge to grin like a fool, because that would wreck the mood. "Yes, James. Please."

"Hmm. And how do you propose I do that?"

"Isn't spanking the traditional way?"

"Well, it is, but we're not always so traditional."

"Please, James? Please spank me?" Lying on top of him the way I was, I felt the thrum of desire shoot through his cock when I begged. He was already hard, but my words set him aquiver.

"Straddle me." His voice was rough with desire. "Then I'll spank you."

"Yes, James." I slipped my shoes and panties off while he repositioned himself with his feet on the floor, his cock protruding eagerly from his fly. He unbuttoned his shirt partway from the bottom, revealing the firm abs I loved and the tuft of his pubic hair that proved he was a natural blond.

"Leave the skirt on," he ordered.

"Yes, James." I straddled him, then bent my knees on the seat on either side of him.

He reached under the skirt and rubbed his cock up and down my wet pussy a few times. "Down," he said.

I sank onto his cock slowly. Even though I'd done almost the same exact thing yesterday, at this angle he felt even bigger.

Before I could get all the way down, he had pulled the skirt up and given me the first hard swat. I yelped and pulled up without realizing it.

"Down," he repeated, and this time I didn't go slowly. I shoved myself down onto him, gasping at the sudden fullness, then again at the smack that followed.

"H-how…how many?" I asked.

"Oh, now you ask? Karina, I think it's a bit late for that, don't you?" he chided gently. "I am going to spank you until I am satisfied. However many that takes."

I bit my lip. "Well, it's no less than I deserve." Then I sucked in another breath. Under my skirt his fingers had found my clit. Two of them pressed gently from either side, making it protrude, and his thumb slipped quickly up and down the little bulge.

I shook. He could make me come in under two minutes that way. I clung to his neck, unable to do anything but accept the sensation, trembling.

Of course he stopped just before I was ready to come, though. Of course he did.

And then he pulled the skirt all the way up over my back, and spanked me hard, five, six, seven times, each hit driving my clit against him.

"Squeeze me," he said. "Inside you. Faster."

I couldn't stay still as I did what he asked, my hips rocking slightly as I contracted my muscles, and his fingers returned to their grasp on my clit, this time rubbing in the same rhythm as my squeezes.

I broke out in a sudden sweat and he switched from pleasuring me to beating me again, the heavy flat of his palms raining down on my ass, driving me to scream, driving me to come. I clung to him helplessly as the spasms shook me all the way down to my toes, and then I hung on as he drove his cock upward into me, four, five, six times, deep sudden thrusts that signaled to me that he was coming, too.

As we lay there, still entwined but now limp, he tugged my skirt down and said breathlessly, "I...hope...you're... sorry now."

"Oh, very. Very sorry." This time I couldn't hold back a giggle.

"Good. I would say I am done forgiving you for the moment."

He guided my face to his with his fingers, still damp from touching me, and kissed me, tenderly exploring my lips this time.

"James," I said. "We're going to figure this out, aren't we?"

"I certainly think it's within our abilities to do so."

"I hope so. Because it seems like no matter what I try to tell myself, my body won't accept anything but being right here." I squeezed him once more, but now he was softening, and he slipped free.

"So long as we are continuing to rebuild our trust, I think we are headed in the right direction."

"All right."

"Now tell me, what do you wish to know?"

"Oh!" I blushed. "I didn't come prepared with a question. I didn't think we were going to have sex."

"Neither did I until you got on your knees to make the promise."

I grinned and nuzzled his neck. "That was a good idea, wasn't it?"

"A very good idea. But don't think I've forgotten that I have a lot to make up for. How upset you were yesterday is proof of that. Even if your reason for being angry at me turned out to be insubstantial, your overall reason for being sensitive is still very much on my mind."

"I'll try not to fly off the handle. Why don't you tell me more about being an international rock star?"

"Why don't you get a little cleaned up and into a more comfortable position, and then I'll try to figure out where to start with that," he suggested. He handed me a kerchief to wipe up with.

Once we were settled again, with my head on his chest and his arm around me, he started again.

"It's much as you read about in the popular press," he said. "You record an album; the record company mucks about with it; sometimes they make you change things. They solicit orders from the retail stores. They collect the money. If you are lucky, you even receive some of it."

"What? Surely you get a percentage, right?"

"Well, they pay you an exorbitant sum at the beginning of the contract, as a kind of down payment on what they are going to owe you later. It's not uncommon to receive ten million dollars but then be required to deliver ten albums over the next ten years."

"Was that what you got?"

"Ten years ago, yes. The thing is that the royalty percentage is not very large, and various costs and fees on the part of the record company cut into it. Essentially, for every fifteen-dollar CD sold, I make about a dollar. Let's assume a platinum sale, which means a million copies sold. That's considered very good. However, they already paid me that million dollars ten years ago, so I don't receive anything additional on those sales."

"But all your albums have done better than platinum."

"True. But sometimes not right away. Much of the money I've made has come from merchandising rights and from touring. Normally a record company makes almost nothing from what an artist brings in from ticket sales."

"Normally. Why do I hear a 'but' coming?"

"Because I have not always toured in the traditional

manner. *Bride of the Blue*, for instance, was an installation production in Las Vegas. It required a bit more investment than merely putting a rock band on the road. The theater had to be rebuilt with a custom stage and effects, for one thing. I allowed Ferrara and the record company to act as producers the way one would with a Hollywood film production. She invested money up front for a share of the profits later."

"But she turned into a royal pain."

"Yes."

A moment passed between us.

"Okay, so in your e-mail to me you said you were going to explain why the business you thought was concluded... wasn't."

"Yes. Some time ago, when Huntington was still in charge of the company, before the divorce, he and I had planned that the final three albums I owed him on the contract would be a double album of *Bride of the Blue*, and then the farewell tour album. At the time he was afraid I would be wooed away by another record company and was preparing to renew me for another multimillion-dollar deal. This was before I decided to quit."

"Aha."

"Then he split with Ferrara, she took him for all he was worth, and suddenly I was sure I wanted to get out. She's now claiming that the double album only counts as one. She is not entirely wrong, but it was my mistake not to get that agreement in writing!" He twitched angrily, but calmed himself. "At any rate, she has been making various demands ranging from the sensible, like I fulfill the contract with a greatest hits album that includes one new song, to the nonsensical, like the one that I move in with her, because I married her."

"But you didn't marry her. Did you?"

"I did not. It's a very strange claim." He shook his head. "I think perhaps she is a bit unhinged. All the more reason to have as little to do with her as possible. She is also demanding that I tour in support of the album. I refused but agreed to do a new residency in Vegas, which will be simulcast into movie theaters, pay-per-view, and livestream on the web."

"And that will satisfy Ferrara?" I sat up to look at him.

"I hope so. The thing to understand about Ferrara is that she is quite motivated by the upkeep of appearances. Everything she has tried to force me to do has always been within the confines of a contract, an obligation. She's learning that I have limits, though, and when she pushes too far, she may push me to say to hell with the contract, which would be bad for everyone."

I brushed his damp hair back with my fingers and it fell in soft, straight sections as it dried. "But the marriage thing…it sounds like she wants more than money."

"She's a complex creature." James pulled a water bottle from a compartment in the door and offered it to me. "I mostly have to convince her that she wants the money and the continued rights to my record catalog more than she wants to fuck me."

I almost choked on the water when he said that. I'd been tiptoeing around the actual issue and not saying it out loud. "Do you think you can?"

"I believe so. I've held her off for years, Karina. I just have to do it a little longer." He took the water bottle from me and drank a few gulps himself. "I have a proposal for you."

"I'm all ears."

"I don't want to only tell you about my life, Karina. I want you to join it. Be a part of it. That means being a part of what's happening in Las Vegas."

"What do you mean by 'be a part of it'?"

"Answer me a question first. What's happening with your university now?"

"I have to speak to the dean. Best case scenario, they accept my thesis as is, rubber stamp me with a PhD, and tell me to get the hell out. Worst case scenario, they make me start over with a new advisor, writing a new thesis. Honestly, if that's what they want...I don't know if it'll be worth jumping through those hoops. If other opportunities are beckoning me, I don't have a lot of incentive to go back. Other than pride and not wanting to have wasted five years of my life." Not to mention the student loan money.

"I see. Well, I am hoping you might be able to defer whatever might occur there for another semester so you can join me in the performance."

"You mean—"

"As a dancer."

I shook my head instantly. "I can't measure up to a troupe of professionals. I'll look ridiculous."

"I assure you you're wrong about that. Well, if the performance were tomorrow, maybe. But we have a few months, Karina, and I'll be expecting you to work with a trainer every day. I need to get back in shape myself." He stretched one arm toward the far window and unfurled his hand elegantly, probably thinking about dance exercises. "I haven't danced or sung since the night we met."

"Have you missed it?"

"I have, a little. I don't miss the grind, though. I don't miss having to keep up the facade all the time. I never realized how exhausting it was until I stopped." He leaned over to kiss me on the cheek. "I'm an incredibly lucky bastard."

"Are you?"

"Yes, because if I had let my guard down for anyone but you, it would have ended in a ball of flames."

"It nearly did anyway."

"But it didn't, because of you. Because of the wonderfulness of you. You're special, Karina." He offered me the bottle again and I took another sip. "How much longer do you think you'll be in Ohio?"

"I'm not sure. My aunt Tera called today to announce she's showing up tomorrow to stay for two weeks. If that's true, I won't have to stay." I did have to get back to the city. To deal with my landlord and the university and who knew what else.

James was looking at me thoughtfully.

"What? What is it?"

He smiled. "I'm just noticing how many strong, independent women you seem to have in your life."

"Well, I don't know if I'd count my mother as strong... though it seems like she picked up a backbone in the hospital!"

"She raised you and your siblings on her own. I'd say she can probably lay claim to independence if she wants."

"True. And her opinions are never weak. Those are always quite strong." I glanced in the direction of the house. "I guess I should be getting back."

"Well, if you think you'll be staying more than a few days, I'll contract a dance trainer for you here, to start getting ready for the performances." He folded one of my hands into his. "That is, if you agree to my proposal. You still haven't said yes."

Of course he would notice that. "I think it's questionable I'm good enough to get on stage with you. Maybe you ought to have someone besides yourself look at me. I don't think you're exactly an impartial judge."

"And you're far more talented than you think. How about this? We'll hold an audition for principal dancer. I won't tell the judges who you are. We'll let them give their opinions. The final decision will still be up to me, of course, but you can get an honest evaluation of where you stand in relation to others. If they think you look ridiculous, they'll say so without hesitation."

I slipped my shoes on. "All right. When?"

"Let's say in a month. That'll give you time to prepare."

"Okay. I mean, yes. That sounds like a plan." I slipped my arms around his neck and kissed him. "Now, are you and Stefan planning to sit out here all night?"

"I defer to Stefan on our security plans. If there is any hint of trouble, though, promise me, Karina, that you'll contact us immediately."

"Yes, of course."

"Good. Then you should probably sneak back into the house."

I kissed him on the forehead and grinned. "You know, I never did this when I was a teenager."

"Did what?"

"Sneak out of the house after my mother was asleep to have sex in a guy's car." I kissed him on the mouth then. "Something tells me it was worth the wait."

Seven

Look Out, World

Aunt Tera blew into town the next day like a summer storm, flattening everything in her path, though in a good way. It was great to see her, but within an hour of her arrival she had us cleaning out the entire pantry, getting rid of canned goods that had been there more than a few years, vacuuming under the couch cushions, you name it. Tera had gotten rid of a few leech boyfriends in her time, she said, and the best therapy was a thorough turning out of the house. I think my mom's purge of her closets and jewelry boxes had been the same idea, but Tera extended it to the whole house.

By dinnertime we were all too tired to cook, so Tera took us out to eat. I brought up the e-mail I'd gotten from the head of the art history department about needing to schedule a meeting with me. They agreed that I should get back as soon as possible. I'd invested too much in my education not to fight for reinstatement.

I told them I could go back the next day. With James.

"Do you think that's a good idea?" my mother asked. "I

mean, if you're not getting along, to be stuck in a car together for ten or twelve hours?"

Tera snorted. "Sounds like the perfect arrangement to me. He can't weasel away."

"But will you be safe with him?" My mother was suddenly an expert on domestic violence. For once I didn't mind that she decided she had all the answers, even if it meant I had to listen to a lecture on the warning signs.

Maybe it was good to hear them, actually. I could truthfully say I felt safe with James, physically anyway. Emotionally there was still the fear that he could disappear again.

That's why he wants you to dance in this show, I thought. *He's trying to prove to you there's more to him than sex in the back of a limo.*

"Yes, Mom, I'm sure I'm safe with him. Besides, we won't be alone. His chauffeur does the driving."

Tera's eyebrows went up at that, and she looked back and forth between us for an explanation.

"Karina has a rich art dealer from the city at her beck and call," my mother said.

"Sounds like you have him by the balls!" Tera laughed.

"It's not like that," I said, but I couldn't really explain.

"Well, am I going to get to meet him?" my mother asked.

"Why don't we wait until I'm sure I'm keeping him? I don't want another Brad situation where you end up liking him better than I do."

My mother sighed. "Very well."

It had been so long since I'd felt like she approved of anything I'd done that it was a little disorienting to hear her agree so readily. But a relief, too. Not feeling like I had to argue with every sentence out of her mouth was incredibly liberating. For once, the only reason I was eager to leave home had nothing to do with her at all.

To reassure myself it really was all right to leave, I went with my mother to her doctor's appointment in the morning. She remembered everything now, it seemed, except the accident itself. That was fairly common, they said. Her wrist was healing quickly and so was her ankle. She pressed Dr. Mukherjee on when she could return to the gym.

Tera and I spent the afternoon mowing the lawn and neatening up the flowerbeds, and after dinner it was time for me to hit the road. To keep the drama to a minimum, just in case, I had Stefan come and pick me up without James.

My mother was very reassured by Stefan. As usual, he exuded an air of friendly competence, and he gracefully accepted a case of bottled water and box of granola bars from my mother when she insisted we take them as necessities on a long drive.

James had some work to finish up at the hotel and by the time we got on the road it was nearly ten at night. He looked quizzically at the case of bottled water as Stefan hurriedly moved it to the trunk, putting a few bottles into the cup holders throughout the car.

"A gift from my mother," I explained as we settled into the backseat. "She's definitely getting back to normal: driving me crazy about that sort of thing. Does she think we can't just buy water if we need it? She didn't need to spend the money."

James cracked open a bottle and took a sip as the car began to move. "Did you ever consider that maybe it's not about that?"

"What do you mean?"

"Maybe it's just a way to show she loves you. It isn't that she doesn't think you can take care of yourself. It could be her way of caring about you."

"Hmm. I never really thought about it that way. Does your mother give you things you don't need?"

"Every time I see her! I try not to be guilty of the same thing."

"You try?"

He held out his arm, beckoning me to sit closer to him. "I try to say what I mean instead of using gifts in place of what I'm unable to express. But I don't always succeed. There's also the case that with my mother, she doesn't listen to me. So I give her things. To cover all the bases, you know."

I accepted his invitation, settling against him. There it was again, that feeling that this was right, that I belonged there at his side. Rather than fight it, I relaxed against him to enjoy the ride. There was no traffic, one of the reasons Stefan liked driving at night. Our plan was to go for a few hours and then stop for the night to break up the trip. "You know, sometimes you let your actions speak instead of words."

"That's true. But I try not to make too many assumptions. Especially with you." He rubbed my arm. "I let my assumptions get the best of me once. Not again."

I basked a little in the warm feeling that came with his apologies, though I wondered a little, as I sat there thinking it over, why he'd never called me on the fact that I'd basically coerced him to tell me his name. That wasn't exactly the loving, trusting thing to do. Yet he'd never come out and blamed me for it. "James?"

"Yes, sweetness?"

"I really am sorry I pushed you into telling me."

"I understand completely why my behavior led you to think you needed to go to such extremes," he said.

"Hey, don't make excuses for me when I'm apologizing!" I teased. "Seriously, I didn't realize at the time how out of line that was. I should have, I don't know, talked to you more seriously about it instead."

He kissed me on the hair. "Is it out of line when a man drops to his knee and proposes to his unsuspecting girlfriend in a public place?"

"Oooh, that's a trick question!"

"Is it? People think it's romantic..."

"What if he does it when he suspects she wants to break up, and he thinks he'll shame her or guilt her into staying with him?"

"Then he likely gets the miserable relationship he deserves for doing something so jackassed. On the other hand, if he knows she's likely to say yes, or he feels she's really waiting for him to pop the question?"

"That's different."

"Indeed. In many circumstances I would agree that coercing someone to tell a secret is not right. But you were quite right, Karina. You had every right to know before you let me take you. You had every right to demand it, and you knew me well enough to know it was the one way to ask that I wouldn't refuse. Had you merely asked me in the car on the way there...? I don't know that we'd have gone any further."

"What do you mean? Would you have lied to me?"

"I might have ended things rather than lying to you. Think of it this way. We were playing a game. All the time that you interacted only with my mystery identity was a game. You basically declared it was time to move from the realm of fantasy to reality or you weren't going to play anymore."

"Yeah. That's pretty much what I was demanding, I guess."

"I was already trying to figure out how to move us into the realm of reality. But I wasn't quite ready yet. You beat me to it."

"And you're saying that might have worked out fine...if you hadn't been paranoid about Ferrara being after you?"

"Exactly. Although now, Karina, I truly hope we've reached the point where we can talk to each other if we have any issue?"

I paid no attention to the highway speeding by outside. My focus was completely on James. "Me, too. Although I have to ask, does that mean we're starting over?"

"Or maybe it feels like we're actually starting, for real, for the first time. Because I think perhaps we are."

"Hmm. It certainly feels like since you arrived in Ohio, I've been talking with the real James for the first time." I lay my hand on his chest, listening to his heartbeat with one ear against him. "It feels so right to be here with you, to touch you this way. How can I be this comfortable with you when in the back of my mind I'm still telling myself you might do something crazy again? I thought it was your *dom aura*, but now I'm not so sure."

"Dom aura? You mean like a spell that magically seduces submissive women?"

"Yeah. Or, you know, you've trained me to feel this way."

"Karina, I don't think it's possible for me to train your emotions. I can train your body, your physical responses, with pain and pleasure, but I can't control how you feel about what I do, or about me."

"Good to know."

"Many doms' hearts are broken when they learn the hard way they can't make their subs fall in love. Spankings and bondage don't make a person fall in love any more than candlelight and roses do."

"Good point."

"Trust, on the other hand? Spanking and bondage definitely increase those feelings. That's not training exactly. That's something we built up gradually over time by pushing the envelope, by taking risks and having adventures together."

"I guess we built it up strong enough that a few big blows didn't knock it all the way down—only partway."

He nodded. "I want more than anything to regain your trust."

"How do you plan to do that?"

"By keeping my promises. By telling you everything you want to know. By doing exactly what we did before, only not as a game."

"What do you mean what we did before?"

"As I said, by pushing the envelope. You enjoy being challenged, and every time you met a challenge, your trust in me grew. So did your confidence in yourself. In fact, you grew so confident you walked into that lion's den with Damon George without hesitation."

He was right. I no longer had fear of being desired, by him or any other man. I wondered if thinking about me and Damon was making him jealous and horny now. It seemed likely, even if he said nothing.

And so what if he was contemplating taking me right now in the car? So what? If he wanted sex, I realized, I had no reason to fear that, no reason to fight it. The reflex to automatically resist must have been something left over from the crappy relationships in my past. I had no wish to resist James's desire.

It made me wonder, though, what would happen if I did.

"I can always say no, right?" I asked aloud.

"Hmm? Of course. That hasn't changed. Your right to refuse is the bedrock on which everything is founded. I will never force you."

"But everything's not a simple yes-or-no situation, is it?"

"Power dynamics can be complex. A safe word, even one as simple as 'no,' always bears with it the possibility of creating a rift. It's your responsibility to tell me what I can't know or might have missed, which is that you need to or truly want to stop, and it's my responsibility to never push you to the point that our trust breaks." He nuzzled my hair. "That night when you asked for my name, you took that risk because you knew you couldn't keep trusting me without it. It was my mistake thinking that you broke our trust when in truth you were cementing it."

"I guess when you put it that way, I'm not sorry I did it. But I really will just try to talk to you from now on."

"And from now on we'll have the basis to do so, if you'll be a real part of my life, and I'll be a real part of yours."

"You really think it's a good idea for me to dance with you?"

"I do." He nuzzled me. "You know, I got my first hint that I was wrong the night of the party when Stefan gave me an earful."

"Did he? When he went back to pick you up?"

"He waited two days. I'm not sure if he was waiting for me to calm down or if that was the point at which he couldn't stand it any longer. He wagered his position on it."

I lifted my head, glancing at the glass that separated Stefan from us. "What do you mean by that?"

"I mean, he said 'I'm about to tell you something you don't want to hear, but I feel so strongly about it I'm going to say it even if it gets me fired.' Well, that got my attention, I assure you. And after he told me, and we argued, he took it one step further and said he would bet on it. If I was right, I should fire him."

"But he was right. So what did he win? Besides keeping his job. That's hardly a fair wager then."

"True. I bought his mother a new house."

"Oh?"

"Yes. In France."

"That seems... like a lot."

"Sometimes one resorts to giving gifts to express how much one cares," he murmured softly.

"Mmm-hmm." I settled against him again. "So the whole thing with Damon was you trying to prove yourself right."

"To my shame, yes. You saw far more clearly than I did what was important to me, and maintained more faith in me than I deserved. I am still trying to live up to that." He stroked my hair. "Still trying to believe that I am so blessed. There will always be doubts haunting the back of my mind. But I try to use them as perspective, rather than letting them cloud my vision entirely."

"Doubts? About our ability to get along? To understand each other?"

"No, those doubts are being quelled day after day. I do... have doubts about your ability to actually withstand the full force of my desire."

I sat back, my hands on his chest. "You're kidding, right?

After how hard you fucked me at that party? Or what about the time you fucked me with a string of pearls so hard they broke?"

His gaze locked with mine. "I'm not talking about how many pounds per square inch of force my cock exerts. This isn't only on you. I have doubts about my ability to hold back."

"You didn't feel like you were holding back either of those times."

He said nothing for a few seconds. Then, "That sculpture of mine you saw in England. You saw what it represents. You saw the space in it for you."

I could picture the huge glass creation in my mind's eye, shiny and red and jagged. "I told you. I thought it was a representation of male desire, your desire, like an unstoppable wave, a force of nature. James, seriously, if you need to fuck me very, very hard, I'm willing."

His eyes softened. "I don't doubt your willingness. My doubts are about the possibility that someday I could break you. Someday I may shatter the bond of trust between us when I go too far."

"You just said you wanted to push the envelope so that we could rebuild our trust, though."

"I know. That's the catch-22. So I'm going to push...but I'm going to try not to push too far, too fast. There's always the possibility, though, of me getting it wrong. That sculpture, look at it again. It's also the virgin sacrifice being taken into the mouth of the dragon."

"I'm not afraid of dragons," I said.

He smiled wanly. "I know you're not. You don't need Perseus coming to your rescue. You will ride the serpent all on your own."

As he said that I slipped my hand into his lap, where the erection I expected to find was indeed tenting his slacks.

"Karina," he said, seriously, "the serpent isn't just my cock. It's my sadism. It's my need to see you submit to me, my need to see you screaming in pleasure and pain at my hand."

I nodded. "Tell me something I don't know, mister."

He relented with a chuckle. "Don't you have to do something you've never done for me to do that?"

"Sure." I rubbed him through his slacks, feeling him twitch. "What do you have in mind?"

"Why don't you suck my cock while I think about it?"

"Gladly." I undid his belt and fly, then freed that needy flesh. My fingers playing up and down it made him shudder.

I figured I'd give him a long time to think, so I didn't hurry, pulling his balls out of his underwear and starting there, nibbling and massaging them with my mouth. From the sound of the small groans coming from him, he wasn't getting much thinking done.

I worked my way up the shaft, licking, making him moan with sideways squeezes of my lips. By the time I reached the tip, there was a generous amount of precome gathered to reward me. I licked it and then worked my tongue all around the head.

When I took him into my mouth at last, he said, "Your mouth!" but couldn't manage a full sentence.

I set to sucking the head and taking as much of him in as I could, slowly bobbing my head up and down.

When he couldn't stand it anymore he grabbed me by my hair and pulled me up into a rough kiss. Then, without letting go: "Get on my cock now. *Now!*"

He let go so I could wriggle out of my jeans and underwear

and then I straddled him. I was sopping wet and took him in quickly, gasping a little as he widened me. Even though we'd had sex twice in the past three days, he was large enough that he always felt like a tight fit.

We fucked like that for a while, his eyes closed with an expression of blissful relief.

He opened them and looked at me, licking his lips. "We need something new, hmm?"

"Yes, James."

"Turn around and suck me again."

He slid down in the seat and we got into a 69 with me on top. It was a little awkward sucking him with his cock upside down, and I tried not to scrape my teeth against him. It was also extremely tricky to maintain my concentration when he was licking my ass.

And then, oh God, pushing his tongue into my rear hole. Then something long and hard: his finger. I tensed.

"This isn't even my cock yet, Karina. Are you sure you can withstand my desire?"

"Hey, even my vagina wasn't ready for you the first time and now there's no problem."

"So true. Well, since it worked so well the last time..." He cleared his throat. "I didn't say to stop sucking me, you know."

"You asked a question!"

"And you answered it. Back to it, please."

I took his cock into my mouth again, making mock grumbling noises as I did so. I felt him fumbling around with something and realized from the sound that he was sending a text message.

The next thing I knew, I felt the car pull over and come to a stop. His finger invading my ass again distracted me though, until I felt the breeze on my bare, damp flanks. I dared to stop sucking him long enough to see a gloved hand passing a small glass dildo through the open window on James's side.

Stefan must have retrieved it from the trunk at James's text order.

I resumed suckling and Stefan resumed driving, and the next thing I felt was the unforgiving hardness of the glass rubbing up and down my pussy, getting it good and slick. And then him pushing it into my rear.

"Now," he said. "Crawl forward and get on my cock again."

He kept a hand on the base of the dildo as I did so, and I quickly learned how this diabolical fucking would work. Every time I rocked forward and back on his cock, I fucked myself on the glass cock as well.

"Pace yourself, Karina," he said. "No orgasm for either of us until later. We're near the hotel where we intend to stop for the night."

"Okay. Ah, crap! I mean, yes!"

He clucked his tongue. "Did you forget I still have one hand free to spank you with? A summer away from me and you've slid right back to your old habits, despite your training at the society. That'll be twenty licks for forgetting your language."

"Twenty!"

"Forty, for protesting."

He couldn't see how widely I was grinning. I couldn't help it. This was too much fun. "Yes, James."

"Go on. You count. I'll deliver one stroke for each time you thrust yourself back against me."

That meant each time I gave myself the jolt of deep pleasure from driving both his cocks into me, it was served alongside the blossom of pain on my butt cheeks. And the longer it went on, the hotter and redder they got, and the more it hurt…and yet I wanted more.

I got so lost in wanting that I lost count at some point and didn't even notice I had trailed off. So it was somewhere around a hundred spanks that I whimpered, "I…I'm getting close."

"Thank you for warning me," he said. "Slow down, then. No more spanking, I think you like it too much."

Instead he ran his fingernails over my reddened flesh as I slowed the pace of my rocking to half what it had been.

I don't know how long it went on. I tranced out on the rhythm of our bodies.

The next thing I knew, I felt the car slowing as we went down an off ramp. Shortly after, we came to a stop.

James opened the compartment in the back of the front seat.

I heard something rip open and I thought it was a condom package, but no, it was a handy-wipe. It was cold against my flesh and I yelped as he cleaned my rump and between my legs. Then he toweled me dry but did not remove the dildo from my ass. "Put your clothes back on. We'll finish up once we've checked into the hotel."

I did so carefully, keeping the dildo in place, while he cleaned himself up and put his own clothes back together.

The car moved again as Stefan brought us around to another entrance. I heard the sound of the trunk as he took out our bags.

James opened a bottle of water and took a swig. I realized suddenly how thirsty I was. He handed me the bottle and I gulped it greedily.

"Be sure to thank your mother for the water," he teased. "Granola bar?"

Eight

We Kissed as Though
Nothing Could Fall

The hotel was seven or so floors, surrounded by parking lot, the lot surrounded by trees. As I got out of the car, there wasn't much else to see. I could hear a truck's brakes out on the highway. We went up to our room; Stefan was next door.

James pulled me into a kiss once we were alone.

"Are we going to push the envelope?" I asked.

"Definitely," he murmured, gently tucking my hair behind my ear.

"Don't tire me out too much, though," I said, "because I intend to collect my due of information."

"I will make it worth both our whiles. I promise."

James undressed me and tied ropes around my middle and between my legs so that there was a knot keeping the dildo in place. Then he added various other decorative ropes to me, winding around my forearms and ankles and crisscrossing my chest. He blindfolded me and told me to lie down.

I lay there quietly on the bed while he prepared something else, watching the colors zoom behind my eyelids. Being in ropes had a swaddling effect on me, making me feel peaceful even as I anticipated whatever might come next.

I heard the door open and shut, then silence. Where had he gone? Or had he just opened and shut it to make me think he went out, while he stood there silently, waiting to see if I peeked under the blindfold? I had no urge to peek. I was content, so very content.

Well, except for being extremely horny. After all that penetration without an orgasm, I wanted very much to come. But I could be patient.

The door opened and closed again. "Karina," he said gently. "Move toward me and stand up."

He helped me off the bed.

"Come with me."

He led me by the hand out of the room and into the hallway. I sucked in a breath, thinking about what we had said about pushing the envelope. Did that include potentially surprising hotel guests with the sight of me, blindfolded and in the nude? Or did he have Stefan secretly blocking the way up? For all I knew he had rented the entire floor but wanted me to think we might be discovered. I found that the thought he might be doing it only to make me think I might be seen aroused and thrilled me as much as the thought I might be seen. The next thing I felt under my bare feet was the transition from the rug to a concrete floor. I could smell laundry detergent. I heard another door open.

"Put your hand on the railing, and go up the stairs."

He followed behind me with a hand on my back, telling me when to turn and guiding me to the second set of stairs.

At the top another door opened, and I felt the warm wind from the outside.

We were on the roof. I could hear the sound of an AC unit and the *whoosh* from the highway beyond the trees.

He bound my arms together behind my back, and I felt a few other ropes tugged and added at my hips, my shoulders. He moved me again, and I felt more tugging.

"Bend over."

I bent at the waist and the sound of the AC unit got louder.

I felt his hands at my hips and then his cock nosing between my lips in back. Once he was all the way in, he said, "You're quite secure like this."

"Like what?"

I felt him tugging at the blindfold and then an updraft blew it out of his fingers. I was looking down the side of the building at the parking lot far below. I gasped.

"You won't believe how tight you just squeezed me inside you," he said. "Are you afraid of heights, Karina?"

"I...I don't know. I mean, not usually." I sucked in another breath as he drew his cock slowly back and then drove into me again. "But this isn't usual."

"No. I'm going to come in you, Karina. If you can, you may come, too. I suggest you do it quietly, though, as it wouldn't be very good to get caught up here. And it'll take a little time to untie the ropes that are keeping you secure."

"Yes, James."

He grunted with pleasure. "Every time you say the word 'yes,' it's like an extra caress down my cock."

Then he stopped talking and concentrated on fucking me. Each thrust pushed on the glass dildo, too, and tugged on the rope nearest my clit, not touching it but enough to add to the sensation. In other words, each thrust was a pure surge of pleasure to every possible nerve ending. And maybe, just maybe, the adrenaline from my upper body hanging over the edge of the roof helped accelerate everything.

I was coming within a few minutes, which I let him know by whispering the word "yes" over and over. He whispered it back, exultantly, as he came, his cock pulsing inside me a few moments later.

He didn't savor the moment long, pulling me upright. "Can you stand?"

"Mmm. Just barely." My legs were quivering from the intensity of the orgasm, but they hadn't dissolved into jelly. Yet.

He busied himself with the ropes, undid my arms, and slipped a bathrobe onto my shoulders. I looked around. "Where are we? Looks like the middle of nowhere."

"Pretty much," he said. "Seemed a more isolated place to try rooftop sex than, oh, anywhere in Manhattan."

"Did you know this roof was here? I mean…that it was a good spot for this?"

"I did. Stefan and I stopped here on the way to Ohio." He slipped a bunch of loose ropes into a pillowcase and then belted the robe around my waist, which I hadn't bothered to do yet.

"You know, some people might find it presumptuous that you were planning that when you weren't even sure I was going to forgive you."

"You have made me into an optimist, Karina," he said with a smile. "Nothing could stop me from dreaming about you."

"You know what's different about you, James?"

"What, sweetness?"

"You take your dreams, and you make them reality."

"Does that surprise you?"

I leaned up and kissed him on the cheek. "Not in the slightest."

Back in the room we got cleaned up properly, and then, yes, we ate some granola bars. They were the chocolate-covered kind and I ate mine while sitting cross-legged on the bed, naked, my hair still damp. "So I think you owe me a lot after that one."

"Definitely." He licked melted chocolate from his fingers. He had pulled on an undershirt and a pair of shorts. "What would you like to know?"

"When did you first figure out you were into bondage?"

He sat in the desk chair with casual grace. "Early. I had fantasies when I was a boy. Any movie where there was an interrogation scene became fuel for them." His eyes focused on the ceiling. "I don't know why. Perhaps there is no why. I liked the interrogations where there was torture, and I liked the ones where there wasn't...where there was coercion and capitulation. Both turned me on tremendously. Old movies, current movies, gangsters, spies, cops, superheroes. That's probably where all the role playing during sex came from, too."

"Huh. So there's no sex in the scenes?"

"No, not in the Hollywood movies I saw as a kid, anyway. The sexual part was all in my mind." He shrugged. "It's implicit in some of them, like in scenes in comic books where Catwoman has Batman at her mercy. But it's obvious to me Catwoman was created by a kinkster."

"She is rather dominatrix-like." I tore open another granola bar. *Thanks, Mom.* "Who was the first person you actually did it with, though? I mean took it from fantasy to reality."

"Do you want to hear about how I lost my virginity?"

"Absolutely!"

He picked up the ballpoint pen from beside the phone and twirled it as he spoke. "I was in a school drama club, which led to me and one of the other students having some private rehearsals, shall we say. Improvisational acting is a typical exercise. We agreed to try an interrogation scene and see where it went. It went…all the way."

He looked at me, set the pen aside, and crawled over to me, then on top of me to kiss me. "Fantasies are wonderful. But reality is even better. At least with you."

"Mmm. I feel the same way."

He settled beside me, and we soaked up each other's warmth while the hotel AC droned in the background.

"That was just the warm-up question, you know," I said. "Like how the sex in the car was the warm-up for what we did on the roof."

"Aha, that makes perfect sense. What else would you like to know?"

"You've told me a little about your mother, but almost nothing about your father. You've barely mentioned him."

James nodded. "I note you've barely mentioned yours, either. Though I doubt we've the same reasons. To this day, I'm not sure who my father was."

"Really?"

"Truly. My mother had various lovers during my childhood, mostly high-ranking British officials of one sort or another. When I was born she was living in New York, where she was known for entertaining sundry ex-pats, ambassadors, and the like. I am under the impression now that she had been a kept woman, and although the affair had ended, to keep her quiet, whoever it was continued to pay for the apartment."

"You think that was your father?" I sat up so I could see his face.

"I don't know." The expression on his face had nothing to do with his father and everything to do with the fact that he was looking at me adoringly. "When I was about ten, though, we moved back to England, and she's there still."

"You get very British-sounding whenever you talk about her."

"As well I might. She would spank me if she heard an American accent coming out of my mouth."

"No!"

"Yes." He cracked a mischievous smile. "So I learned to speak British English at home and in front of her high-ranking guests, and American English with everyone else."

"Did you go to public school in New York?"

"Goodness, no. It was private academies all the way." Now his gaze drifted toward the wall, though I don't think he was seeing it at all. "And I went to boarding school in England."

"Who's your best guess for who your father was?"

"Well, the man who tried the hardest to act like one moved in when I was about three. I think merely by dint of the fact that he moved in, he felt that made him the man of the house. He was an actor of some repute. I, being a holy terror at that age, thought that *I* was the man of the house, and refused to submit to his authority. Then again, my mother forbade him to spank me, and now that I think about it, she didn't submit to his authority either." A sly smile spread across his face. "In fact, I'm quite certain, thinking back on it now, that if there was anyone doing any submitting, it was him to her. How does the expression go? The acorn doesn't fall far from the oak?"

I shared his smile. "Do you think she ever went to any of those society parties?"

"If she did, it was only as a guest," he said. "Not as a member. The thought did cross my mind and I had them check. Although there are those rare few who feel comfortable flaunting their sexuality in front of their parents...I'm not one of them."

That provoked a snort of laughter from me. "Don't you kind of flaunt your sexuality in front of everyone, though? I've seen some of your videos."

Now he looked at me, his full attention focusing on me. "That's one of the reasons for the mask," he said quietly.

"Your mother doesn't know...?"

"No. She knows about the glass art, but she doesn't know about my music career." He stood and got a bottle of water, then sat down on the bed to share it with me.

I liked that. Sharing a bottle of water felt perfectly comfortable with him, like the most natural thing in the world.

After I'd had a sip, I said, "No wonder you don't want to take Ferrara to court."

"Yes. My name, and my face, would be everywhere. There would be no way to walk through a shopping mall like a normal person. Much less anything..." Rather than finish his sentence, he trailed his hand up the inside of my leg suggestively.

"I see your point." It was probably easier to keep things a secret from his mother when they had the Atlantic Ocean between them. But Lord Lightning fanatics were everywhere. "Your mother sounds a bit like the woman my mother wished she could have been."

"What do you mean by that?"

"Oh, my mother always wanted to be a kept woman, I think. Or at least she thought she did." I wasn't so sure the experience with Phil Betancourt hadn't changed that. "But she never quite got what she wanted. Not even in her children."

"No?"

"She wanted a daughter just like her and she didn't get one. She got a butch lesbian and me. The only reason I wasn't considered a tomboy was that Jill was more of one. By comparison, I was girly. But I never liked pretty dresses. I never liked fussing with my hair and makeup. And I never liked flirting or dating, which was a constant source of angst for my mother when I was growing up."

"But you do like pretty dresses." He ran his fingers through my damp hair. "I think you didn't like being forced to like them."

"Well, okay, yeah. I didn't like the pressure to be a certain way, act a certain way, and it wasn't until recently I clued in that my discomfort was all about men. Like the only reason to look nice was to attract someone of the male species."

"Male isn't a species," he pointed out. "But I do know what you mean."

"And the thing was, dressing like that does attract male attention, but not usually from anyone I wanted! I mean, why should I be flirty and cute for the guy in the checkout line or at the gas station, you know? I felt like that attracted creeps."

"Do you like the kind of attention you get from me?"

"Yes. And like I said, I discovered I like things from you I didn't particularly like from Damon or any other man. But anyway, that's how my mother operates. For her, it's still all about getting a guy. She's good-looking for a woman in her late fifties, but you know, her relentless need to be with someone is what made her vulnerable to this Betancourt character."

"Karina, may I ask you a question?"

"Of course."

"You've never said much about your father, either."

"That isn't a question and there isn't much to say about him, since he left when I was so young. Jill remembers him better."

He chuckled lightly. "I'm not that interested in knowing what he was really like. I'd rather know what you think, and how you feel about him."

"Oh. Well." I had mostly vague impressions of my father. I remembered photographs of him better than I recalled his actual face now. "My mother never talked about him. He was away a lot when I was a kid. For work."

"What did he do?"

"He was some kind of a project manager for a huge construction firm. He was part of a sales and oversight team that would pitch and sell the project and then also be on-site during the construction."

"Office buildings?"

"And hotels, and I remember him saying they were building a museum, once. It meant that when there was a project going on, he was away for weeks at a time, and when there wasn't a project going on, he was somewhere different every week, drumming up potential clients. We got totally used to him being gone. In fact, as far as we kids were concerned, it was kind of a pain when he was home because all the rules changed. And then one time he just didn't come home. I always wonder how long my mother knew before she told us. I've never asked. He was on a job in Houston that was going to take all winter, and we were talking about the family going there for Christmas, and then the next thing you know, my mother told us not only weren't we going, but he wasn't coming home. I think I didn't really believe it at first. He sent us presents and everything. And it took a while to sink in that she really meant he was never coming back."

"And there was no official divorce?"

"I don't think so. Wouldn't there have been alimony or something? I think they just cooked up their own terms and parted ways."

"You said he left your mother a chunk of money."

"Yeah. She never, ever told us what the deal was. All I know is we carried on pretty much like we had been for about five years. Then she got a job when Troy was in kindergarten. He has no memory of my father at all."

"What do you remember about him?"

"Impressions mostly. He didn't talk to us kids much, and Jill more than me. I have a sense-memory of him carrying me up the stairs to my room, and being scared and comforted at the same time, like he was impossibly tall, but impossibly strong." I closed my eyes. "I don't even know if he's still alive. He was never that big a part of my life. The biggest effect he had was, you know, that feeling at school or when meeting other kids, that I was different because they all had a mom and a dad, and I only had a mom."

"I know that feeling very well."

"I know you do." I rubbed my cheek against him. "I don't know that it actually affected me all that much. I mean, when you're a kid, whatever you have, that's your definition of normal. We seemed like a normal family to me. We were happy."

"Mmm-hmm." We lay there then listening to the AC hum for a while, until James said, "Let's get ready for bed."

We got up and took care of our usual things. After I brushed my teeth, though, I felt a moment of giddy excitement so intense I had to hold the edge of the sink.

"Are you all right?" He hovered beside me, concerned.

"I'm fine. Maybe I'm full of leftover adrenaline. Or maybe that's just how excited sleeping in the same bed with you makes me."

"Mmm-hmm. Excited enough that I question how much actual sleeping we're going to do."

He was right, of course. We slept several hours, but when I woke I had one hand between my own legs and the other on his erection and he was all too happy to pick up where my dream left off.

We slept through a large chunk of Pennsylvania in the car the next day.

As we neared the city, I texted Becky to let her know I would be arriving soon. "Thank goodness I saved up enough of my summer pay to get a little bit ahead with the rent," I said. "If it weren't for Becky, I'm not even sure I'd have an apartment to go back to right now."

James bit his lip.

"What?"

"Karina, I know you haven't asked me to pay your rent and I appreciate that," he said with a tiny smile, "but of course I will."

"Will you? I...I don't know how this relationship is supposed to work. How come I know exactly how *sex* works with you but not any of the *normal* stuff?"

He grinned. "That's what we get for spending all our time working on sex, trust, and love and never getting around to practical things." He held out his hand and I put mine into his. "Here. I'll try to say something practical. Money is no object when it comes to how much I care about you. I want you to be happy."

"And if I want to look for a job in the art world?"

"Then you'll need rent until you find something."

"So you're saying accept the rent like water and granola bars?"

"Perhaps. I'm whisking you off to Las Vegas in a few weeks anyway. It seems only fair I should help you with your housing situation. Do you like your apartment?"

"Well, the place is kind of small. I don't even have a bedroom: I live in the living room."

"I have an idea." He smiled one of those sunny smiles that lit up the car. "Did you like that loft where we ate the éclairs and drank champagne?"

"You mean the one upstairs from the gallery where we performed? It was nice, if a little underfurnished."

"I believe it's still available. What do you think about you and Becky moving there? There's plenty of room for you both, you'd still be close enough to the campus for her, and rent would not be a question at all."

"It wouldn't?"

"I own the building."

I laughed. "Of course you do. I'll suggest it to her and see what she says, all right?"

"All right." He bit his lip again.

"What? What are you not telling me this time, James?"

He squeezed my fingers gently. "I want us to be clear this time. Since you feel a bit sensitive about me trying to control everything in your life. Don't...don't feel as if you have to take the offer to live there. But I will point out one thing. If things with Ferrara blow up, and they very well might, everyone associated with me could find themselves under unwelcome scrutiny. Moving there, you could effectively go off the grid. Get a P.O. box…"

I thought about it. "You know, I was a little freaked out when I heard Professor Renault had showed up at the apartment and ranted drunkenly at Becky." Maybe moving would be a good idea after all. "But, you know, why move me and Becky? It's awesome that you're offering to help her, too, but I'm surprised you didn't offer to put me up by myself."

He paused, choosing his words carefully. "One of the things your mother's abuser did was isolate her from her friends and support. I never want you to think that's what I'm doing, Karina. You know if you wanted a penthouse of your own on Central Park South, I would buy you one."

"Just goes to show I'm not much like your mother," I teased.

"Thank goodness for that," James said, and kissed me.

They left me off at the apartment. I had barely gotten the door open upstairs when Becky seized me in a huge hug.

"Oh, Rina, Rina! I've missed you so much!"

"Hey! I've missed you, too." I felt something soft against my leg. "Hey, even Milo missed me." Her cat looked up at me, then swiped my leg with his tail again.

Becky herself was looking good, her hair loose and fuller than I remembered, but maybe that was the result of spending the summer hanging around with the local Lord's Ladies, some of whom were hairdressers. She was wearing an oversized T-shirt like a dress, belted at the waist, and her feet were bare.

We dragged my stuff in from the hallway, and I immediately proceeded to unpack in the living room so I could dig out the souvenirs and gifts I'd brought her. Some of them were from me, some from Paul and Misha, and it took a while to extricate everything from my luggage.

By the time I was done, it was time for dinner, and we walked to a place in the neighborhood so we could keep catching up. She was working on her thesis, which she had changed to be about feminist themes in the Lord Lightning rock operas. So of course she squealed excitedly when I told her it looked like there was going to be a new production and that I might be in it.

"Oh my God, Karina, I can't believe it! I've been hearing the rumors about a new show but, wow!" She sang a few words from what I guessed was one of his songs, but that was when a waitress came to clear our dinner plates and Becky cut herself off, her cheeks reddening.

When our water glasses had been refilled, she went on in a quieter voice. "Does this have anything to do with what Paul and Misha told me? They said Ferrara Huntington showed up right before you left. The rumors about *Bride of the Blue* started because she leased that Vegas theater. It can't be a coincidence that she turned up in London where you and he were."

Becky put her hands on the table and leaned in, eyes wide and serious. "Karina. You've heard the rumor, haven't you, that they got married?"

"Ferrara told me herself."

"Oh no! Is it true?"

"He says it's not, that it might all be a ploy to get him into court."

"Yuck! That's even worse!"

"He also says she's batshit crazy."

"Oh my God. So is he going to pay her off or something?"

"Well, I guess that's what this whole production is about. You know the Huntingtons divorced, right?"

"Yeah."

"Well, he told me that she actually got the record company in the split. So she's technically the one in charge now. She's the one who is insisting his contract isn't fulfilled, that he needs to record a new song and has to perform in support of the album release. He said he wouldn't tour but he would do this series from Vegas, which will be broadcast all over the world. Hey, would it be helpful for your research to interview people in the production?"

"You know, it might." She bit her lip, looking hopeful. "But I don't want to impose."

"Well, how's this for an idea? Your idol wants to be our new landlord."

"What do you mean?"

I kept her in suspense a moment while the waitress dropped off dessert menus for us to look at. When she was gone, I explained. "He's offered us the apartment above the 624 Gallery. Rent free."

Her eyes got very wide. "That would be . . . *awesome*. Simply awesome."

"It's even got a little bit of furniture in it. There's a couch. And it has big windows overlooking the street."

"And he's okay with cats?"

"I'm sure he's fine with cats."

"Fantastic!" She clapped her hands together, but then looked at me seriously again. "But, Rina, wait. If you and he are back together now . . ."

"Why am I not moving in with him?" I decided I wasn't up to explaining that in my mind James was sort of on probation. This real-world relationship thing was new for us, and so was figuring out our real-world boundaries. Merging our lives was going to be tricky enough. "He's going off to London to record new material any day now. He might be gone for a month. Can you imagine me wandering around some empty penthouse for a month waiting for him to get back? No, thanks."

"I suppose. Well, I'm happy. It was really dull living alone the past few months. I'm so happy you're back. When can we move in?"

"Anytime, I think. I'll ask. I'm starting dance training with him tomorrow."

Becky squeaked and put her hands over her mouth. Her fingers shook as she took them down. "That is so exciting!"

"Yeah." I smiled. "It'll be a lot more fun than the other thing I have to do tomorrow, which is meet with the department."

"Oog. Yeah. I bet." She looked up as the waitress returned. "Oh no. If you're starting dance training, does that mean we can't have dessert?"

"I have a feeling with the number of calories I'll be expending I can have more dessert than usual," I said. "Let's get the molten chocolate cake and split it."

"With vanilla ice cream on the side?"

"Of course."

The waitress approved of this choice with a knowing smile.

Nine

I'll Paint You Mornings of Gold

My meeting with Esther Carmichael, the head of the art history department, went better than I expected. I slept fitfully, nervous about how it was going to go, and arrived at her office feeling muzzy-headed and out of sorts. Her office was in the corner of the art history building, on the second floor, and the sound of traffic came through the open windows. It was an older building, with high ceilings and dark wooden molding around the windows, her walls lined with bookshelves of matching wood.

She had gray hair and wire-rimmed glasses whose perfectly round lenses reminded me of an old bicycle. She offered me some vanilla-flavored iced tea and we chitchatted about the tea shop in the Village where she had bought it. She poured the tea from a thermos that kept it cold and ice clinked into the glass. I barely tasted it, though.

She drained her glass and folded her hands. "I was trying to put you at ease with some conversation, but I can see that isn't working. So I will get to the point."

"Um, thank you." I sipped the tea, trying to stay calm.

"Renault will not be returning. Two other students have come forward in recent weeks to say he made inappropriate advances, and we have received a few anonymous letters as well. Though none have made quite as outrageous a claim as yours..." She paused and took a breath. "Pardon me. I misspoke. Your claim is not the outrageous part. None have yet claimed he acted as outrageously as to offer a passing grade in exchange for, *ahem*, favors, but there are few here now who doubt you."

I breathed a sigh of relief. To know I wasn't alone was huge. To know that I was believed was even bigger.

"In addition, you may wish to know that some of our colleagues who acted inappropriately in reaction to your accusations have been censured, as well."

"Thank you." I assumed she meant the faculty and employees who had done things like e-mail me telling me I was a slut and writing "whore" on my department mailbox.

"Frankly, I'm tired of tolerating all forms of sexist shenanigans and my only regret is it took this long to blow the lid off, which brings me to my next point, regarding your dissertation." She looked at me over the top of the glasses. "I don't know if you've seen the numbers, but we have a terrible success rate with female degree candidates. And by 'we,' I don't just mean the art history department. I mean female students receiving advanced degrees in universities across the nation. Plenty of women start programs. Fewer of them finish than their male colleagues, though, and it can't all be attributed to marriage attrition."

"Surely it can't all be the fault of creeps like Renault, though."

"Oh, certainly not. There must be many factors. And I cannot change the world. However, I am in charge of this department. You are a female degree candidate. I am not going to lose you."

I held my breath hopefully.

"You seem like you would appreciate receiving the degree that you worked so long to get."

"I would."

She stood. "As you may know, I'm not one to compromise academic standards. Not even for the sake of overcoming sexism." She picked up a manila envelope from her desk and thrust it at me. "It's sloppy. In the middle it loses focus. You can do better. Rewrite it."

"I always intended to." I took the envelope and peeked inside. I could see a printout of my dissertation, her hand-written notes filling the margin of the first page. "This was meant to be a first draft."

She sat and gave me a satisfied nod, her lips tight as if she were holding in a smile. "Good. You have until the end of November if you want to graduate in January, or early April if you want to graduate in May. Stay in touch about the paper-work. Call or make an appointment if my notes are unclear."

Her tone made it clear she was dismissing me, and I hopped up, grinning. "Thank you."

She stood also and we shook hands. "My pleasure. The Pre-Raphs are such a fitting subject for a young romantic like yourself. Enjoy them."

I was so happy I nearly ran home, and did skip part of the way. I had to slow down in order to call James. He picked up on the first ring. "Are you in a meeting?"

"No," he replied. "How did yours go?"

"Swimmingly. Renault is gone gone *gone*. What you read in the paper was true. More students came forward to finger him once the word got out. And all I have to do is rewrite my thesis and I'm home free."

"All you have to do?"

"Okay, yes, it's going to be a lot of work, but it's work I wanted to do anyway. And it'll be so much better now that I've seen many of the paintings in person! I took a ton of photos for myself after hours in the gallery." I did a little twirl on the street corner waiting for the light to change. "Next on my agenda. What time are we meeting the trainer?"

"Two o'clock. I would suggest a light lunch. Sabine can be a drill sergeant. I will text you the address. Two other members of the troupe will be joining us."

"Ooh, fun."

"They don't know my real name, though they know my face. You'll hear the dancers refer to me as Jasper. I've known them for years, but the policies stand. Everyone who works for me signs nondisclosure agreements, but you never know when someone could be blackmailed or drunk. It's safer if they simply don't know my real name. Sabine knows it, but she'll never use it in public. You shouldn't either."

"I'll be careful." I'd gotten used to the way Stefan referred to him without any name if he could avoid it. I would have to try to do that, too.

"Now. One more scheduling question I have for you. When would you like the movers to come?"

"Well, I won't have time to start packing until tonight…"

"I have plans for you tonight."

The way he said that made something in my middle clench deliciously. It was like he'd run a hand up my thigh, or slipped that hand into my hair and tilted my head for a kiss. "Do I get a hint what kind of plans?"

"No. But I should point out that the movers will do all the packing, as well."

"Really? I should tell Becky that." As the conversation returned to light and mundane, I noticed the light was green and I crossed the street. "She's probably been excavating her closet all morning."

"They'll bring the boxes, everything. You won't have to lift a finger unless you want to. There are some items you might consider too…fragile…for others to handle."

"Mmm-hmm." I knew he was talking about the set of glass dildoes and sex toys he'd made for me. The issue wasn't so much that they were fragile as that I didn't want a moving man looking into the case. "I'll hand-carry a few things."

"Why don't you bring them with you today?"

"Yes, James. And how many changes of clothes will I need?" I stopped at a corner pizza stand where a single slice was two dollars and gestured for one.

"I don't plan to keep you overnight. You and Becky can have one last night in the apartment and I'll have the movers there tomorrow morning. Say, eleven o'clock? Let me know if that doesn't work for her."

I put two dollar bills onto the counter and took the paper plate. The slice was so large it hung off the plate by several inches. "Will do. I think that should be fine, though."

"Excellent. See you at two."

Since I was supposed to eat a light lunch, I left the two inches of crust where the cheese didn't reach and tossed it into a garbage can as I walked. My phone chimed with the address. There was also a text.

Do not be put off by the others. Remember we will be keeping our involvement a secret so as not to taint the audition. I may seem cold and indifferent to you. I will make it up to you later.

At the thought of "later" I felt that delicious drop in my stomach like I was taking the plunge on a roller coaster of lust.

I felt it again when I walked into the dance studio and caught sight of him in skintight leggings and a wide-necked midriff shirt. He was at the barre, a diminutive woman in a maroon bodysuit as dark as her skin barking at him as he stretched one leg. His hair had been lightened again, and under the spandex he looked like one-hundred-percent pure muscle.

Easy girl, I told myself. Tamp it down. Right now you're supposed to be a prospective employee, not his girlfriend.

Sabine left his side to greet me and show me to a changing room, where I stowed my bags and put on dancing clothes.

I came out carrying my old "jazz" shoes and set them to the side. They were working on a partner stretch, so I began to do my usual warm-ups.

When we were at least partially warmed up, Sabine gestured for me to join them in front of a mirror for some exercises. She led us through various movements that I picked up easily. They were pretty similar to the ones I was used to, leg swings, lunges, and scissors for the legs, then working up to the smaller muscles in back, shoulders, and neck. We sat on the floor to work on neck and shoulder isolations and I could feel I needed a lot of work there. My flexibility was good, but gaining back the fine muscle control and strength was going to take some time.

Then we were back on our feet and she led us through another series of movements from one posture to another, ten times from one to another, then ten times from that one to a third, and so on, forward and back, forward and back. She walked around us as she clapped a steady rhythm, making comments, mostly to James, about his form. "Elbow higher. Straighten your neck."

At one point, though, she was between us and I was facing her. "She's a bit short, don't you think?"

Before I could react with anything more than a startled look, Sabine, who was a good six or seven inches shorter than me, gave me a wink.

James, who was facing the other way, burst out with, "Her height is perfectly adequate!"

"Tsk. You're the boss," Sabine said, giving me another wink and then circling him with a stern expression that belied it. If there was one boss in the room right now, it was Sabine. "No talking. Knee, higher." She poked him in the ribs and he flinched. "Short is good. Makes you look taller and maybe you'll even be able to lift her."

Clap, clap, clap. She paused then to show us the next posture. She had nicknames for each of them. The Teapot. The Hero. The Statue of Liberty.

Eventually we had run through a long set of these and she checked the clock on the wall. "Didn't you say some others were coming?"

James dabbed his face with a towel. "Two others. They are late." He did not sound happy about it.

"Traffic, no doubt," Sabine said drily. "Ah, here comes someone now."

A chime sounded when the front door opened, and

through the frosted glass I could see the shapes of people in the vestibule, but the inner door was locked. Sabine went to open it and then closed it again behind them: two people, a woman and a man.

She clearly knew the pair and waved them toward the changing rooms. Before long they had joined us in front of the mirror, and without any introductions we sat down to do some core strength and more isolation exercises. The man had dark brown hair, gelled back, and looked to be about James's size, while the woman was about mine. Her hair was pulled back in a short ponytail and looked like it had been through a few dye jobs, dark at the top, reddish in the middle, and blond at the ends.

I could see now why James had compared Sabine to a drill sergeant. This was a lot like what I imagined boot camp to be like, except instead of push-ups and sit-ups the moves were artistic.

After almost an hour of that, we had some water, and I finally met the others formally. Roland and Annika had danced with James several times before. I introduced myself as Karina, and James—truthful as always—told them he had seen a performance of mine in London that had inspired him to invite me to audition.

That was also when I first heard the dancers call him Jasper.

Sabine didn't give us a lot of time to chat. For the rest of the time we worked on partner movements, Roland with Annika and James with me at first, and then we traded partners. Sabine switched from clapping to playing a prerecorded African drum, freeing both her hands to demonstrate with and to position us.

We were all sweaty and tired by the time the rehearsal was over. "Enough for today. My regular students will be here soon. I have blocked every day until three for you and your bunch. I like this new one, too."

"Thank you, Sabine." James leaned over and gave her a kiss on the cheek.

In the changing room Annika asked me where I was staying in New York.

"Oh, that's the funny thing," I said, as I pulled on my jeans. "I was only in London for the summer. I live here."

"That is funny," she said with a smile. "Isn't that the way of things? One of the other girls in the troupe, Hayley Williams? You'll meet her. She and I were in a production of *The Nutcracker* when we were thirteen years old. But she went to a different high school from me, I totally lost track of her, and then one day, boom, there she is, right next to me in warm-up exercises. At first I wasn't even sure it was her! We kept looking at each other like, 'don't I know you?' So funny. So you really haven't known Jasper long?"

"No."

"Well, I know he's weird and there are all kinds of non-disclosures you'll have to sign, but he's fair, pays well, and the gig is good. Which is better than I can say for some of the jobs out there. Also, he'll really help your career if you want. And best of all, he'll never hit on you."

I almost laughed at that. I managed to keep a straight face. "He won't?"

"No. I know it's weird. Every dance company I've been in has been totally incestuous, which is perfectly fine, but you know, there are always people in the business who think that it's okay to lech all over the dancers, like because we're in skintight spandex we're there to be hit on. Jasper not only doesn't do it; he doesn't let anyone else do it. Not what I expected from a rock star."

"Huh. Maybe it's because he knows what it's like to be hit on all the time."

"Probably. That's the other thing I should warn you about, though I'm guessing if he brought you here you know it already. Lots and lots of dancers have crushes on him. Heck, I think everyone who works for him has at least a tiny crush. But make a move and you're gone. He's not open to it at all. Honestly, at first I thought maybe he was gay. And yet, the male dancers who have tried got treated the same way. Don't. I know it's hard, especially with some of the sexy dances we do. Just don't get the wrong idea from it. That's my advice. Don't go there."

"I'll keep that in mind," I said, trying to look as wide-eyed and innocent as possible.

A knock came on the door, then Roland's muffled voice. "Annika? Still in there?"

"Coming!" She shouldered her bag. "Want to get something to eat with us?"

"Um, let me check my messages." I picked up my own bag and dug out my phone.

Out in the studio a gaggle of preteen dancers, their hair in buns, was arriving. There was no sign of James. I checked my texts and wasn't surprised to see one from him.

6pm. Hotel where you met RM.

That was it. A time and a place. I wondered where he had gone in such a hurry.

Then I saw who was waiting by the door, talking to Annika and Roland. Ferrara Huntington. She turned and left before I caught up to them.

"You coming? There's a diner around the corner," Annika said.

"Sure. I have some time before I have to be anywhere."

Shortly before six I walked into the lobby of the hotel, wondering if James was expecting me to go up to the room or what. Would he be in the same room as before? It had been 624, hadn't it? Or was I getting it mixed up with the address of the gallery?

It struck me then that if I wasn't getting things mixed up, the number probably meant something to him. Before I could flail too long trying to figure out what to do, Stefan waved to me as he stood up from an upholstered chair and crossed the polished marble floor to greet me, European style, with a kiss on each cheek. "This way."

He led me back out to the street and down a bit, to a two-seater sports car that flashed its lights at us as he pressed a button on the key fob. I opened my own door as he took my bag and put it in the trunk. The bucket seat felt like a giant leather-gloved hand cupping my ass. The fact that I was wearing bike shorts might have had something to do with it.

"Is it supposed to feel like that?"

"Pardon me?" He started the engine.

"Never mind. Is the town car in the shop?"

"No. I'm just giving it a rest. This one has to be driven every so often or it's not good for it. And besides, it's fun." He zipped out of the parking space. "Too bad we're only going a short way."

He turned onto Park Avenue and headed uptown, but we hadn't gone very far before he turned toward Central Park. We went a block south and turned again, spiraling toward our destination the way the one-way streets sometimes forced a car to do.

I was expecting to pull up to a high-rise building, or into a big parking garage, but no, the garage door that faced the curb was built into a brownstone. Maybe five or six stories tall, brick, with a wrought iron doorway, not all that different from a lot of the small apartment buildings in the city.

The door went up and we pulled into a single-car garage. As I got out of the car it dawned on me how rare a private garage was in this city. Almost unheard of.

The entire building was a single mansion. Stefan led me from the garage through a pantry and into a grand foyer. He gestured around. "This is the place. Not really much to see in this room, though."

"Not much to see!" There were two sculptures in the room, one of which was clearly one of James's glass works. The other I thought I recognized as the work of Rodin, a nude woman cast in bronze. "Is this really a Rodin?"

I heard James chuckle. He came down the staircase, barefoot, wearing chocolate-brown pants that looked too luxurious to be called pajamas, slung low on his hips, and nothing else. "It's a bronze cast of one of his originals, yes. The model was a young woman named Camille."

"Wasn't she his apprentice?" It had been some years since I'd studied anything about Rodin.

"And companion," James said, and something about the way he said that, or maybe it was the pantherine way he was padding across the floor toward me, brought that delicious sensation flooding back into my nether regions. Without taking his eyes off me, he said, "Stefan. We won't be needing you for a few hours."

"Yes, boss." Stefan disappeared through the door we'd come through.

James reached me, took the bag from my shoulder, and set it on the floor. "The decision I'm trying to make is whether to take you right here, right now, and then play with you at my leisure once the edge of my hunger is off, or force myself to wait."

I could feel the hardness of him against my stomach as he pulled me close. "If I know you, you'll force us both to wait."

His laugh was rich and low and he bent to kiss me while still chuckling. "Too true," he breathed into my hair. "But you test my self-restraint like no one else ever has. So tell me, which would you choose, if you were given a choice?"

"Didn't you say we should embrace 'and' instead of 'or'?"

"I did. That would mean...taking you right here *and* forcing myself to wait?"

"Take me but let's not come," I whispered, as if Stefan might be listening. Ha. As if he hadn't heard us doing every possible thing in the seat behind him already.

"Since you ask so nicely..." James said, and thumbed the waistband of his pants over his erection. They fell to his ankles in a velvety heap, and I fell upon his cock with my velvety tongue. I couldn't help it. Gorgeous doesn't even begin to describe it. And him standing there in that grand foyer? He was like a third work of art, each muscle over his ribs perfectly sculpted. I ran my fingers down his torso as I sucked him into my mouth, my fingertips skating down the plane of his abs to the creases of his thighs.

He sank his fingers into my hair with a groan, and held me loosely as I bobbed back and forth. Then his grip tightened and he drove deep, hard enough to bruise my lips and deep enough to make me cough once, and then pulled me abruptly free. Keeping his grip, he bent down to kiss my mouth tenderly, the contrast between his gentle lips and the brutal thrust of his cock making me gasp.

"Strip," he whispered, and let go of me.

As I pulled my shirt over my head, he lay back on the parquet wood floor, watching me with his hands folded behind his head.

I wasn't wearing much, so it didn't take long before I was standing naked before him.

He beckoned me with his crooked finger, then gestured, making it clear he wanted me to straddle his face. I put one foot on either side of his head and squatted down, rewarded instantly by the wet suede of his tongue licking up and down my seam. I was already meltingly wet—had been since the moment he'd come down the stairs, really—so this was more about pleasure than preparation.

He disengaged his mouth and slid a long finger inside me, looking up my torso, between my breasts, and into my eyes. "I feel like I want you more and more every time I have you. Like the more deeply I fall for you, the more intense the craving becomes."

"I feel exactly the same way."

"Then get on my cock, now."

I shuffled backward, onto all fours above him, and reached back with one hand to guide the tip of him into me. Being able to have him without a condom had never felt more like decadence, more like luxury, than at that moment. I sank onto him about halfway down his shaft, then had to wriggle my hips to open myself up enough to take him.

Once I was fully seated he let out a long sigh. "I have all

manner of elaborate plans to torture you," he said. "Yet this—this basic, simple thing—is what I want most at this moment."

"Just because the chef is going to prepare an elaborate dessert doesn't mean he can't taste the berry right from the basket," I said.

"True. Perch on your feet. Spread your knees. Display yourself."

I did, looking down at where his cock disappeared into my body. He spread my lips further with his hands, admiring the way our bodies joined, pumping slowly in and out of me.

He bent his knees and sat up, curling his arms under my own and around my rib cage. "Sabine questions whether I have the strength to lift you."

"I don't think this was what she meant," I teased.

"No. And she doesn't know that since she last saw me I've been working with glass nonstop. Glass is incredibly heavy. You're nothing in comparison." He took a deep breath and shifted one foot under us, and the next thing I knew he was lifting me up, still impaled on his cock. "You may have noticed, by the way, that Sabine accepted you as a professional dancer in my employ."

"I guess she did."

"Let's talk about it later. Right now, it's time for this." He pressed me against a wall, pumping in and out of me until I was starting to lose myself in the ripples of pleasure flowing through me from my core.

But then he set me onto my feet and slid free with a wicked grin. "And now, it's time for a tour of the house."

"Like I'm going to see anything but your cock wherever we go!" I said.

"Suit yourself." He took me by the hand, picked up my

shoulder bag, and led me into a kitchen big enough for a staff of ten to cook in. A dining room stood beyond that, and on the floor above it, a more formal dining room. The building had its own small elevator as well as staircases, and we climbed those on foot, leaving our clothes behind on the foyer floor. I never would have guessed he would be so comfortable in the nude, given how he'd seemed to prefer staying dressed as long as possible when we'd first met.

Maybe he felt safer in his own home. And maybe now he felt safe with me. I certainly was pleased to drink in the sight of him, an embarrassment of riches compared to the glimpses of him I was used to.

Parlor, library, master suite, exercise room, on and on we went until we were at the sixth floor, where the upper terrace overlooked the street. "Eight fireplaces, and more bathrooms than there are bedrooms," he said as we went from room to room. "Ten, to be exact." Then he led me back down to a room on the fourth floor he hadn't shown me when we'd passed by it on the way up. This one was at the back of the house, and the door had an electronic lock that took his fingerprint to open, like something from a spy movie.

I was expecting this to be his dungeon, although I suppose "playroom" would be a more appropriate word for a room whose windows opened onto a terrace that looked toward Central Park. Unlike the historical-seeming decor in the rest of the house, this space was sleek and clean—like James himself. Indirect lights came up softly as we entered.

If there was a cache of sex toys here, they were hidden inside Scandinavian design cabinets. There was no St. Andrew's Cross or spanking bench like they had at the club in London. One or two low pieces of furniture were covered with draped cloth. A tall vase contained some minimalist stalks of grass or branches of some kind. The only things that looked out of place were two small paintbrushes on a shelf, as if they had been set there to dry, the brush end hanging over the edge.

"My glasswork studio is upstate, of course," he said. "But this is where I sketch, model with clay, and sometimes paint."

I giggled a little. "When I saw the elaborate lock I thought you were showing me your dungeon."

A catlike smile bent his lips. "I am."

"Your studio is where you have your most private, your most intimate moments at home?"

"That's one way to put it." He closed the door behind us and noted, "It only locks in one direction."

"Fire safety?"

"Yes, but also..." He let go my hand and seemed to falter in his explanation. "I would never want it to seem..."

"Like you were holding me captive?"

"Yes. If you're not here of your own free will, then..." He shook his head, as if he couldn't voice the alternative.

I slid my hand into his again. "Have you brought many women here?"

He shook his head again and pulled me close. "Very few. Very, very few."

"This is your inner sanctum."

"Yes." He caressed my cheek, studying my eyes. "If you were expecting a wall full of whips and chains and implements of torture, I'm sorry to shatter your fantasy."

I smiled. "My fantasy is to be here with you."

"Excellent." He kissed me then, a long kiss that made me forget we were in the middle of talking, made me forget we

were going to do anything other than sink to the floor and
fuck until we couldn't move.

But he hadn't forgotten. "I saw Damon George flog your
clit in London," he murmured.

I didn't answer but my stomach turned to butterflies instantly.

"Flog it until it was swollen and sore and then rub his cock
up and down it." His voice was low with a dark edge that had
to be jealousy. "You don't know how hard it was not to push
him aside and shove my cock into you right there. Forget
manners, forget rules, forget everything but the blinding need
to claim you, Karina."

"But you didn't."

"I didn't, and I'm glad I didn't, because I wouldn't have
forgiven myself for giving in to my anger, nor for invading
you without your consent."

"I bet most people don't have the self-restraint you do.
Now I see why Vanette made me wear that chastity belt."

"Ahh, you know I had forgotten it? I think in my rage I
didn't even notice it." He allowed himself a small laugh. "All
the better that I didn't make a fool of myself then. I've imagined a hundred ways to claim you since, though."

"On a roof?"

"For one."

"What will it be this time?"

"That's what I'm deciding right now." He kissed me on the
forehead. "Remember when I said you don't really like pain,
but you like being challenged?"

"Yes."

"Was I right?"

"Um, I think so." I tried not to visibly squirm. "And sometimes, you know, it's okay if things hurt a little."

"Like when someone flogs your clit with moose hide?"

I couldn't help it. I did clench and bounce once. "For example."

He couldn't hold back his smile. "All right. I'm going to give you a task. If you succeed at the task, afterward I'll give you only pleasure. But if you fail, then a clit-flogging is in your future."

"Hmm, why do I have a feeling that a clit-flogging is in my future regardless?"

"Because you know me well." His grin widened. "At least it might not be *today*."

"What's the task?"

"I'll explain it shortly. First, I do love putting you in bondage."

I followed him to the fireplace, where a coil of blue rope sat on the mantelpiece. An elegantly curved sculpture hung from the ceiling, reminding me of a yoke for a pair of horses.

I soon realized it was a yoke for me. It settled onto my shoulders and he roped my wrists to the ends of it. "And here I thought it was a piece of art."

"It is a piece of art, but a functional one. The winch is for lifting sculptures. It also happens to be useful for lifting people, in certain circumstances. Now bend your knees," he said, encouraging me to squat partway down. I felt like a bodybuilder partway through a lift. He adjusted the chains that the yoke hung from so that they were taut with me in that position, my ass sticking out in back. "Very good."

He walked around me in a circle, admiring the view.

"No blindfold this time?" I asked.

"Not this time," he said. "And no gag, either. I think I want you to have full use of your eyes and mouth for this. There is one more thing I am going to use to restrain you, though."

"What?" I imagined something with leather and buckles.

"I'll show you. It's a very simple thing." He moved beyond where I could see and then came back holding an egg.

"Where is that going to go?" I couldn't imagine he was going to put it inside me, but what else could it be for?

"It goes right between your knees," he said, and leaned over to place it between my two bent legs. He put it just above my knees, where the fleshy part of my thighs began. "So, here is your task. Don't break the egg."

"Don't break it?"

"If it breaks, you get a clit-flogging. If it doesn't break, you get rewarded by pleasure," he reminded me as he moved out of my sight to somewhere behind me.

"Huh. Sounds simple enough…" I couldn't turn my neck enough to see him. "What will you be doing in the meantime?"

"I'll be switching you."

"I thought switching meant we traded places."

He chuckled. "I mean switching as in birching. Although this is willow." He plucked one of the long, slender branches from the tall vase and showed it to me, before retreating behind me again.

"Oh." Birching was something like caning, if my half-remembered knowledge of Victoriana was correct. "So…I guess it's not all pleasure, then?" My voice came out a giddy squeak.

He sounded just as gleeful. "I said that would be after the task. I never said whether the task would be painful or not, did I?"

"You should have been a lawyer."

"I like promises better than contracts," he said, running his hand over my bare bottom. "Negotiation is fun. Contracts are dull."

"If you say so."

"Hush now. Here comes the first one." He stepped back and I heard the sound of something swishing in the air. The sound made me startle, but it was just a test: nothing happened. "Remember, don't drop the egg, or crush it."

"Oh fuck," I said, and I meant it.

The first blow with the switch felt like a slice of fire across my ass, a thin line of burning, a little bit like the riding crop except not as hard. It didn't feel like an impact so much as a sudden blossom of agony across my buttocks. I clenched my fists around the ends of the yoke and realized it was shaped perfectly for that. Kinky handlebars. I wondered if James had made them himself or if you could buy them on the Internet.

My wonderings were interrupted by the next stripe across a fresh part of my skin, and I shook a little, groaning to absorb the pain while fighting not to squeeze my thighs together and crush the egg.

Oh, that egg. It became the center of all my thoughts as he laid stripe after stripe onto me, down the backs of my thighs and across my butt cheeks, never hurrying, savoring my plight. I tried to convince myself that he'd hardboiled it. Surely he wouldn't risk the finish on the fancy parquet wood floor. But could I risk it? I couldn't.

And I couldn't do anything less than my best for him. "Ow ow ow! That's really starting to hurt!" I cried, around what must have been the twentieth one. I had lost track of how many I'd taken a long time ago.

"Back up," he suggested gently.

"Back up?"

"Very carefully, take teensy steps backward toward me," he said. "Carefully. There you go. Stop if you feel like you're going to drop the egg."

I shuffled backward a few inches, then a few inches more, while the winch pulled at the chains attached to the yoke. The result was I was bent forward more, my ass even more prominently thrust toward him, my toes pointed inward as I kept my grip on the floor.

"You can't see it," he said, "but your pussy lips are protruding now."

"Oh fuck," I said, knowing full well that meant that tender area would be his next target for the switch. I had kept up shaving between my legs while we'd been apart, so there was not even hair to protect from the evil implement.

He was merciless now, not pausing between stripes, laying it on five, six, seven, eight times until I was screaming, and then another and another until I lost my footing. I curled instinctively, pulling my feet up, and I swung, hanging from the bar, forward and then back again. He caught me with a hand on my rump before I could go too far, then fondled me, working two fingers inside my wet core.

His voice was warm and sweet in my ear. "You did very well."

"Did I?" My legs trembled a little at the way his fingers were moving inside me.

"So far." With that he gave my G-spot a sudden tweak and I gasped and spasmed...

And crushed the egg. The sound of the shell cracking and then the wet plop on the floor was unmistakable. "Oh fuck fuck fuck."

"Tsk tsk tsk. We're not to the fucking part yet," he said with a gentle laugh. "I guess it's clit-flogging time after all."

He released me from the yoke and led me to one of the covered pieces of furniture, sliding the drape off to reveal a seductively curved…chair? Divan? Imagine if an incredibly high-end furniture maker had designed a luxury gynecologist's table. He folded the sheet and placed it where I would be lying back, and then helped me up onto it. I was reminded of the bucket seat in his car, curved to my body. "Now. Hold your knees with your hands. Keep yourself spread for me."

He leaned down to plant a tender kiss right on my clit, which throbbed wildly in response. I was so aroused.

I watched him saunter across the room to open a cabinet set in the wall. I couldn't see what else was in it, but when he closed the door again I saw he had a flogger with many short tails, only six or seven inches long, in his hand. "I bought this for you, after seeing how you responded to one like it in London."

He came and kissed me on the mouth first, another long melding of our lips and tongues until I was panting, and then he went to stand at my feet. He dragged the tails slowly upward, the friction across my clit making my legs shake.

"That aroused already? My, my, someone really *does* love challenges."

"Someone really does love *you*," I confessed.

"Say that again when you're not high on endorphins." He caressed the insides of my thighs with his fingertips.

"Maybe I'll say it when I come."

"Maybe you will." With that he began to flog my thighs lightly, alternating from one to the other, gradually working his way toward the middle. When at last he reached my pussy with the *whap-whap-whap* of the tails, the blows were still teasingly light, and I gasped and rocked my hips with each blow. Then he returned to beating my thighs, this time with harder strokes, again working his way to the center, where each time the flogger landed on my clit I cried out.

But he could strike even more sharply than that, this time snapping the flogger like a towel, leaving a trail of stinging welts down my already red thighs, closer and closer to my clit. He slowed as he neared it, spending a long time working my swollen lips with blow after blow, with only a stray tail catching my clit from time to time. I began to cry out on every strike then, my pitch rising as I realized how close I was.

And then quite suddenly the flogger was landing right there, at the place where my pleasure centered, at the place where the electricity crackled. I didn't even realize at first that he wasn't hitting me hard there: he didn't have to. I was coming from a butterfly-light stroke now, screaming in ecstasy.

I hadn't quite finished, hadn't quite ridden the orgasm all the way to the end when he was commanding me, "Off the table, bend over, hands on the edge, spread your legs."

I hurried to get into position, and then he was filling me, that part of him I'd craved for so long, bare and perfect inside me. I clenched around him, still spasming from the first orgasm, when he began to flog me again, reaching around me with the whip to beat my clit hard now, fucking me at the same time. When I began to come again, he laid it on even harder and faster, and that only made the orgasm more intense, and my screams louder.

Then I heard the flogger hit the floor, and his hand cupped me from behind, massaging my clit through one more while he pushed himself into me with the speed and intention I recognized meant it was his turn to come.

He came with a bellow and kept going until his thrusts turned soft and slick. Then he pulled free and with the last of the stiffness he could maintain, rubbed it in the crack of my ass, teasing there until he went completely soft.

We sank down onto the wooden floor and he cradled me, leaning himself against the side of the exam table. "You beautiful, fantastic, incredible angel," he said.

I didn't think I could muster words that big yet. "You're not so bad yourself, you know."

That made him laugh and he planted kisses wherever he could reach, my hair, the side of my face, my ear. "And now the drawback of having such a big house. The bedroom is directly below us. Perhaps I should install a trapdoor that would drop us into the bed."

"While you're at it, how about a water slide that slides us into the shower?"

"Also an excellent idea. Unfortunately, right now, we'll have to get up and walk. In a few minutes."

"In a few minutes," I agreed, utterly sated, and gleefully content.

We eventually did get up, of course, and saw two of the ten bathrooms, one that was attached to the studio, and then the one attached to the master bedroom, which reminded me of the bathroom in the Charing Cross Hotel, only ten times bigger. The shower could have easily held five people.

It was just the two of us, though.

And then we got into bed, but only to cuddle, not to spend the night. It wasn't even nine o'clock yet. I was amazed. I was certain he had been flogging and torturing me all night long.

The bed was huge and I couldn't even guess what sheets that soft were made of. Silk? Baby chinchilla down? "All right," I said. "Your turn. What secret will you tell me tonight?"

Ten

Thinking It Must Be Love

What do you want to know?" James had slipped on midnight blue satin pajamas and I nestled in the crook of his arm, both of us looking up at the mural painted on the ceiling. Soft music played in the background from speakers I could not see. Cellos.

"Lucinda. Tell me about her." I draped my arm across his chest. "Stefan seems to think she was no good for you. Chandra, too."

"When did you talk to Chandra about Lucinda?" He sounded curious but not upset.

"I didn't. You talked to her where I could overhear."

"Did I? I must have been careless."

"It was at the doctor's office that time. We did have a... sort of intense time. Maybe that made you less cautious than usual."

"So we did. And it's you, Karina, that makes me want to throw caution to the wind."

"Me? What is it about me?"

"I told you that you're special." He kissed my temple. "Now about Lucinda. I suppose she should have been a cautionary tale, too. We met at a fetish night."

"Fetish night?"

"At a nightclub. A night where everyone wears their leather and rubber and the kinky people can meet one another."

"What were you doing at a place like that?"

"Slumming, of course." He chuckled self-deprecatingly. "By far the best thing about no one knowing what Lord Lightning looks like is that I can move freely in a place like that. Not to mention the grocery store—"

"I can't picture you in the grocery store. You don't buy your own groceries."

"I don't employ a chef except for special occasions. I don't have a butler or a live-in maid. Stefan lives in the so-called 'maid's room' downstairs. I do not send Stefan to the grocery store."

"I still can't picture you shopping for produce."

"I like the farmer's market when it's the season, actually. But are my domestic habits what you want to know about?"

"No! Well, yes, but you were telling me about Lucinda."

"She walked into this place looking like a Swedish super-model, and set every man drooling. I watched man after man strike out. I bided my time, waiting for her to come to me. She eventually did."

"How did you know she would come to you?"

"I didn't. But I knew if I was going to have any chance at all, she would have to come to me and not the other way around. There were only three things that could have kept us from getting together." He held up his hand, counting off on his fingers. "One, she was a lesbian. Two, she met someone before me who interested her more than me. Three, I met someone before her who interested me more than her. Well, no one there interested me more than her, and she wasn't a lesbian. So it was mostly a matter of hoping someone else didn't rival me for her attention."

"And no one did?"

He chuckled. "No."

"Oh, come on. There could have been another man as charismatic and handsome as an internationally known rock star there."

"But there wasn't. She finally approached me to ask what I was drinking. I told her and said if she wanted the honor of getting me a drink, she would have to do it on her knees. She knee-walked to the bar and back."

"Knee-walked?"

"There's a way to do it without looking ridiculous. It's a martial arts technique, from kendo. That got my attention of course. She stayed on her knees at my feet while I sipped the drink she had brought. Then I said I had one simple test that any play partner of mine had to pass. She had to answer one question."

"What was the question?"

"I leaned down and whispered it to her. 'What do you want?' And she leaned upward to speak the answer in my ear. 'To be tested. Just like you're testing me now.' Bam. We stuck together like two magnets from that moment forward."

"I can imagine. So what went wrong?"

"Many things. For one, she had a deep-seated need to be the 'weird' one in the relationship."

"What did she mean by that?"

"She thought I was nothing more than a boring, rich businessman at first. Meanwhile she was the artistic, daring, part-time fashion model who had achieved a modicum of fame, and therefore I was supposed to fawn over her. I did fawn over her, but not because of that. Eventually I revealed who I was, and at first she was delighted. We were very much alike and we made a kind of matched set, tall and aristocratic and kinky. But the secrecy began to chafe her, and although I did much to help her career, I wouldn't do the one thing that she wanted me to, which was to come out publicly at her side. She wanted to star in my videos. She wanted to be in all the tabloids photographed with me. It was very difficult to get her to understand that being in the tabloids would be my idea of hell."

"Wow."

"She accused me of holding her back. Of not understanding what it was like to still be struggling to reach a certain level of fame. Of being jealous of her and sabotaging her success to keep her from eclipsing me." He shook his head. "Nothing could be further from the truth. It was those discussions about fame and celebrity that started me thinking I had to get out of the business. At first my thought was to step out of the spotlight and let her eclipse me. But a person paranoid and neurotic enough to believe that I was sabotaging her was not someone I could get along with in the long term. Our worst fight—the last fight—came when we were arguing almost constantly...except when we were having sex. We were still having fantastic makeup sex, which allowed me to think that deep down we were okay; we just had to work on the relationship a little harder. I truly believed that I couldn't have such fantastic sex with someone I couldn't love."

"But you told me you had tons of sex with groupies."

"Tons of sex. Not particularly fantastic sex."

"Oh. I see."

"So there it was. I was convinced because of how great we were in bed that our differences could be worked out. And there we were in a fight, an epic one, and I confessed that I didn't want to fight, I didn't want to have all this strife, and she burst into tears and told me it was all my fault for not being dominant enough."

"Wait, *you?* Not *dominant* enough?"

"Yes. Because apparently what she wanted was for me to dictate every moment of her life. She felt if only I could control her enough, she wouldn't even feel the urge to argue with me or fight! Therefore the fact that we were having a fight was clearly all my fault!"

"That's...twisted."

"I know. She really believed that if I were more dominant, she wouldn't ever be unhappy, because I'd control her happiness like a faucet I could turn on and off. She confessed she was horribly disappointed by the fact that I didn't require her to walk two paces behind me at all times, and that I didn't spank her if she left the milk out instead of putting it back in the refrigerator."

"Wow."

"I told her that kind of twenty-four/seven role playing would be impossible to keep up."

"Says the man who maintains a secret identity."

"Yes. And you see why I am ready to leave it behind. She told me if I was a real dominant, I wouldn't feel it was role playing. I'd 'really' be like that."

"James, I'm pretty sure you *are* really like that."

"I know. At any rate, we split up. By then I had already

introduced her to the society, and of course she had a crowd of suitors filling her dance card. She ended up in a relationship with the society's regional director and they do, as far as I know, maintain something like a twenty-four/seven relationship. Then again, I only see them at society functions, where of course they are in role. She seems happy. That's what matters."

We listened to the cellos playing for a few minutes while I digested that. "So you have women like Lucinda at one end, and you have women like Juney at the other end."

"Juney? Oh, in London."

"The one you dumped out of your lap."

"Of course I did. Submissives, slaves, servants, whatever you want to call them, should have better manners than reaching into anyone's trousers without permission."

"What do you call them?"

"Lucinda considers herself the director's property. I suppose that makes her a slave, being owned that way. Different people use the words for different things. These owner/owned relationships may have a more equal standing as partners, though, than some who consider themselves servants or service-oriented. In those the inequality of the relationship can be part of what works for them."

"Hmm. So not all slaves are submissive or even servants; not all submissives are servants either."

"And not all service is sexual. Though there's always that undertone, I believe. Juney thinks she wants to be a sex slave, owned more like a pet than a person. And pampered like one, too. Hmm. And I don't mean a pet like the people who play at being puppies or ponies. I mean it metaphorically. She wants her master to play with her and whap her with a rolled-up newspaper when she's bad, but generally just enjoy her. A Persian cat has no duties other than to lie around looking beautiful and to be a source of affection and amusement for her owner. She'll likely find someone whom that suits."

He fell silent again and then I asked what I had been trying to think about for a while. "In other words, labels are complicated. But they have meaning. At least personal meaning."

"Yes."

"So what am I, then, James? I'm not like either of them."

"No, you're not. We don't do what we do because we get off on the roles of master and slave, Karina. We do what we do because we get off on each other."

"You didn't answer my question, though."

"You're mine," he said simply. "You're mine, and I am so lucky that the woman I love fits me like the key to a lock."

I sucked in a breath. "You say that word so easily."

"Which one? Love?"

"Yes."

"You said it first," he pointed out with a smile. He shifted onto his side so he could look at me. "You've worked hard to get me past my fears. You showed me I shouldn't fear to speak the truth. Are you surprised I can say it so easily now?"

I kissed him. "No. Not when you explain it like that."

"Tell me a secret, Karina. What are you afraid of? What do you fear?"

"It's a silly fear." I combed his hair back from his forehead with my fingers. "Because I feel confident it's not true."

"Fears don't have to be rational. What is it?"

"I fear that I'm going to someday discover there's one more

layer of mask, one more layer of you, and when it's peeled back I won't like what's underneath after all."

He touched my chin softly, tracing the outline of my bottom lip. "That's not silly in the slightest, given our history. But, Karina, you have gone all the way to the core."

"I know. I told you I didn't think it was likely." I let out a long sigh. "I'll tell you my worry, instead then, which is a little more rational. I think." I hadn't, until this moment, realized what my worry was. My heart began to beat a little harder.

"What's that?"

"I worry I'm not really going to fit into your life." I sucked in a breath, hoping he wouldn't be hurt by what I was going to say, because my chest and throat suddenly ached as I began to say it. "I worry it's not going to work between us if we don't keep the distance, if we take it beyond you whisking me places in the back of your town car."

He opened his mouth as if to protest, but I didn't let him.

"I worry that no matter how much you love me, you're going to decide you like me best as a plaything, that it worked better when you could simply text me an appointment and snap your fingers to have instant wet pussy on demand."

"Karina," he said darkly, "if you have a problem with me demanding your body—"

"No! I don't have a problem with it! Listen to what I'm saying. I'm saying." I sat up and bunched the duvet in my fists. "Just because I'm the submissive in the relationship, I don't want to be taken for granted."

He moved slowly, sitting up beside me and unclenching one of my hands enough to take it into his. "Listen to me. Karina, if I wanted someone who was merely 'wet pussy on demand' I could have Juney—or a million other women, for that matter. The reason I want you, the reason I want to claim you again and again, is because I need your heart and soul, too. I'm incomplete, otherwise." He kissed the back of my hand and I felt a thrill whip through my core like a gust of fresh air. His voice was quiet, but his words pinned me. "If I decide I'm going to fuck you on the foyer floor every time you walk into the house, it's not because you're a slut who does what I say. It's because I need, beyond all reason, to have you. And I need, that badly, to know you need me, too. I need you beyond all reason, because I love you. Love is the only possible reason for me to be this out of my mind."

I kissed him then, and found myself pressed back into the bed by his body, the thin layer of satin between us. When his lips moved from claiming my mouth to my neck, I said, "Love is the only possible reason why I never resist you. Why I never get enough of you. Even if I'm mad at you. No matter what you want to do, I leap in and try it."

He held himself above me and looked into my eyes. I could feel his cock hardening against my leg. "The day will come when you'll refuse me. But as long as you aren't refusing me because you've ceased to love me, we'll survive."

"Today is definitely not that day," I whispered, rocking my hips against him. I sucked in a breath and trembled a little as he slipped his pajama pants down and slid the searing hotness of his cock along my thigh.

"Are you sure?" he whispered back.

"I'm just...sore."

"I'll be gentle."

Those were the last words we spoke for a while, as he pressed against me slowly until he was between my legs.

The slippery head of his cock nudged between my lips and he moved his hips in a small circle, not teasing so much as doing exactly what he promised. Soon the first inch of him was in me, pumping back and forth, and then another inch, and another, each time penetrating slowly before he resumed the undulation of his hips.

I don't think sex had ever felt so good, not even with James previously. Where our bodies met was a fusion of liquid pleasure, nerve ending against nerve ending feeling nothing but a frictionless glide. The sensation of penetration had always sent sparks through me, but this was like the sparks had turned to a white-hot glow, edgeless and growing the longer it went on.

We didn't kiss. He didn't play with my breasts or change my position or anything, nothing to distract me from the pure pleasure of his penetration.

I began to quiver once he had worked himself all the way in. It was as if the ceaseless, gentle rubbing had erased the soreness of earlier, had taken away the stinging marks of the whip and the places where I was abraded and bruised from being fucked so hard. And on and on and on it went, too, until I realized I was having an orgasm that had blossomed so gradually I hadn't felt the usual blast of fireworks at the beginning of it. Instead it was like the middle of one, stretching on and on. I let out a long "aaaaahhhh" as the pool of pleasure spread from my center all the way to my fingers and toes.

I opened my eyes as it ended, as the pleasure of him moving inside me had not lessened but my peak had passed. He kissed me then, and pulled free, and finished himself with a few very quick tugs, spattering hot droplets on my stomach.

He kissed his way down my breastbone, then a few extra-gentle licks to my clit.

Our next kiss was salty with my sweat. "I love you," I said.

"I love you back," he answered, his forehead pressed to mine. He held my gaze for another long moment.

And then a gentle chime sounded from nearby.

"You had best get back to Becky," he said. "You're going to work with Sabine six days a week now, remember."

"I remember. Wait. Are you not going to be there?"

He shook his head. "You proved today you fit in just fine with the others."

"Does that mean no audition?"

"We'll still have an audition, to pick who the principal dancer will be from among the women in the troupe."

"I still don't think I'm that good…"

"Which is why we planned an audition in the first place, right? It'll still fulfill that purpose. You'll see how you measure up. But there's more. I need your help to keep her in check, Karina. I need you to do this."

I gritted my teeth. "And I do love a challenge."

"Yes, you do."

"Okay. But what's this about you won't be coming to practice at Sabine's anymore?"

He looked down into my eyes as if he were reluctant to move or to let me go. "I have to leave in the morning for London."

"Already? I thought you weren't going until next week."

"So did I. Right before you arrived, I discovered I can't wait. We need to grab the studio time now."

"How long will you be gone?"

"At least a week, maybe two."

"Well, it's going to take me a week to recover from tonight anyway," I teased.

"I am going to be desperate to have you by the time I get back."

"Maybe it'll have to be one of those fuck first, talk later kind of greetings, then," I said in as sultry a voice as I could muster.

He growled and rocked his hips against me. "You're lucky I'm completely spent, or I'd take you again right now for inflaming me with talk like that...!" An evil glint came into his eye. "Leave the case here."

"The case? Oh." Of the glass toys.

He pressed me back into the bed with a flurry of kisses across my neck and under my chin. "You can share my deprivation. Nothing into you until you have my cock again, hmm?"

"Evil! But fair. Am I allowed to come?"

"Yes. In fact, be sure to send me video of yourself masturbating. That is, unless you can catch me live."

"And if I do catch you?"

"Then I'll join you."

It was nearly midnight when Stefan dropped me off, by which time I was starved again. Becky and I got our last Chinese takeout meal in the apartment. We prepacked a little but mostly we talked. She told me her parents had started pressuring her to get married, and that the only reason her mother didn't go wholeheartedly into arranging a marriage for her was because she and Becky's father (who had been an arranged match) were fighting a lot. Meanwhile, back in Ohio, my own mother was doing well. Tera convinced her to buy all new curtains and bed linens, she said, and there had been no sign of Phil.

The movers came the next day. Stefan himself met us at the gallery with the keys and supervised the men a little, but they were unfailingly efficient. It was going to take us ten times as long to unpack everything as it had for them to pack it up. They had even labeled all the boxes, and they piled the ones full of books by the floor-to-ceiling shelves that lined one side of the living room, put the ones from Becky's bedroom into the room she picked, and the ones with my name on them into the front bedroom with the windows overlooking the street. They set my futon up as a bed instead of a couch, and the room had a somewhat worn-looking but huge antique dresser, so for the first time in years I had somewhere to put my clothes besides in shelves made of milk crates.

I quickly slipped into a routine of sleeping late, having a quick breakfast of a little granola and yogurt, and then taking the subway up to Sabine's dance studio. By the end of the first week, the group had grown to eight or nine dancers. The first hour was almost always the same: warm-ups, isolation exercises, moves that built strength or flexibility or both. In the second hour Sabine would change what we did, though, sometimes making us learn short routines, pushing us. One exercise we did every few days involved crossing the floor. She wouldn't tell us what to do here: it was up to each dancer to improvise what moves to do as we crossed from one side of the empty floor to the other. Ballet-style jetés, spins, jazz sidesteps, you had to make it up as you went along. We usually went three or four at a time, one group, then the next, and then waiting on the other side until everyone had crossed and then going back. It was one way to build stamina and also keep your brain sharp, and it was a chance to be creative after a solid hour of doing nothing but following instructions and imitating moves.

One day she introduced a new twist, which was that we had to make the floor pass in pairs instead of solo. Sabine called that "pass de deux," a bilingual pun. Sabine was from Martinique and could pun—and curse—in several languages. The goal was to make it look like we were coordinated with our partners, which was a fun challenge, even if we weren't all that coordinated.

Ferrara came by about once a week to check on our progress. She didn't appear to recognize me at all, which didn't surprise me given that she'd seen me only once. That night she hadn't given me a second glance after Vanette told her I was a society trainee, as if I weren't even there. The dancers as a whole spent a fair amount of time hanging out together but Ferrara didn't join us, which suited me fine.

The only complication of hanging around with the dancers was that—as Annika had told me—they were an incestuous bunch. Everyone had slept with someone there, and it seemed like the possibility of hooking up with one another was always alive. I brushed off a few advances and then stopped spending a lot of time with them beyond grabbing a bite to eat after Sabine would throw us out each day to make room for her students. Not that some of them weren't nice—not to mention attractive—but I was very, very off the market, thanks to the one person I couldn't tell them about.

James and I talked or texted every day. I gathered that things at the recording studio were going slowly, sometimes badly, but he did not want to talk about it. I imagined he was something of a perfectionist in the recording studio and I knew beyond any doubt he was a control freak. So it didn't really surprise me that three weeks later they still weren't done.

A little over a week before the audition for the role of principal, he told me that each dancer needed to prepare a solo dance of no longer than two minutes. He advised me to adapt what I had done at the ArtiWorks. "Adapt" was putting it mildly since everything about that performance had involved interacting with a massive installation of glass sculpture that would not be present in Vegas. But it did give me an idea, which was to build the dance around an absent partner. At first it didn't go very well, but then I hit upon the idea to use an empty stool as a focus and that went much better. Fortunately, the living room was mostly empty in the new apartment and there was still the large space where a dining room table should go, so I had room to practice. The date of the trip grew nearer.

"You'll have to fly to Las Vegas without me," he told me a few days before we were set to leave, as I lay in bed under the windows. It was a voice-only call while he was taking a quick break from recording, and I had my earbuds in to hear him in stereo. "I'll need to be here until the last possible moment and I'll meet you there. I'm having you and Chandra and a few others take the same flight."

"What about Stefan?"

"He's here with me now."

"Ah, of course." I rolled over onto my stomach. "So I've been meaning to ask you something for Becky."

"Ask away. Has she been liking the new apartment?"

"She loves it. It's so much bigger than our old place. Plus the sink here isn't cracked, and we don't have to jiggle the toilet handle to get it to flush. Even her cat likes it better." I looked at the blank wall across from my bed and wondered if I should get some art to hang there. "Anyway. She's writing her thesis on representations of feminist utopias in your rock operas."

"Excellent!" He sounded giddy about it.

"Is it? Does that mean she's right?"

He cleared his throat and tried to sound more serious, but I could still hear the glee. "Whether she's right or not doesn't matter. Being taken seriously as an artist is the rarest reward."

I decided this wasn't a good moment to remind him that Becky's fan nickname was Baroness Babelicious. "Well, anyway, I said I'd ask if she could interview your choreographer."

"She might be better off interviewing me, if she is trying to ferret out the source material. Though isn't that cheating? Going to the source? I thought postmodern critique discounted the influence of the creator."

"She's not a postmodernist. She's a feminist. I mean, she uses a feminist school of critique, which I think actually takes into account the intention of the artist more than most of the others."

"Ah. Is she in the women's studies department?"

"I don't think we have 'women's studies.' She's in the department of cultural and social analysis, with a fellowship from the Institute for Gender Studies."

"That's quite a mouthful."

"You should see it when guys try to hit on her. Their eyes glaze over before she can get halfway through an explanation of it. Half the time she just says 'Culture Studies' and changes the subject. Anyway, it's her dissertation, and I promised I'd ask."

"I'd be more than happy to speak with her and introduce

her to whoever she wishes. Hang on." I heard the phone rustle as he turned to speak to someone else in the background. "Sorry about that."

"Do you have to go?"

"Soon. They're still setting up a piece of equipment we need. Almost done. I'm yours until then."

I teased him. "I thought you were mine forever."

"That, too," he said drily. "How has rehearsal been going?"

"Well, we're not really rehearsing anything with Sabine, you know. It's exercises and exercises and exercises, but it's not like we're learning any routines."

"Of course. That's what I meant. You won't start learning the actual steps until the whole troupe is together."

"How many dancers are you hiring?"

"The full troupe is twenty. Several of them are already in Vegas. A few got gigs there after the last production. Everyone else has been hired and vetted."

I imagined the ability to keep a secret was what they were vetted for. "Some of them have been talking about trying out for the part of principal. I really do think some of them are better dancers than me."

"Karina, please don't worry about it. I know one of my goals is to make it harder for Ferrara to meddle in the production, but I didn't hire you for nepotism and I'm not hiring you because of the hard-on I have for you, either. Speaking of which…"

The delay in his return meant I had masturbated every day, often with his supervision and input, but as planned, there had been no insertion. Not even my finger. "Don't you have to go soon?"

His voice was low and silky. "I do, but touch yourself until I do. Describe to me what you're doing."

"I'm running my fingers along the edges of my lips where I'm shaved. Slowly. Lightly." I pushed my panties down to my ankles. It was good to have the privacy of my own bedroom, again! "Now I'm letting my middle finger graze the tip of my clit where it sticks out. *Ngh.*"

"How long do you think it will take you to come? Can you do it in under two minutes?"

"I don't know, James. It's like you rewired me! I feel empty. It's hard to come sometimes from my clit alone."

"You don't know how much I wish I was there to fill that emptiness." He sucked in a breath and I wondered if he was rubbing his cock through his clothes or what. "I am somewhat tempted to bend the rule."

"To let me slip a finger in?"

"You know, you can always use your ass."

"It's not the same!"

"Have you tried?"

"Well, not yet, but—"

"I suggest you try, if you're having trouble coming. But no, I was thinking of something small that would make the long flight to Vegas more interesting for you…"

I rubbed myself harder and faster as he talked.

"Perhaps if you were flying alone," he concluded. "No, you'll just have to wait, and so will I. And now I must go, sweetness." He made a kissing sound into the phone and hung up.

The flight to Vegas was uneventful. The most interesting part was getting to know Chandra a little while we were sitting around at the gate waiting to board. She was older than I realized. She looked to me like she was in her twenties, her dark brown skin flawlessly wrinkle free and her figure fashion-model tall and thin, but she had just turned forty. She had been a dancer and backing singer when she and James met, but she had a knack for organizing and that led to him hiring her as a personal assistant for a tour a few years back. She'd quickly moved from tour assistant to full-time assistant to full-time manager.

The hotel was quiet and luxurious, exclusive rather than touristy. Once we arrived, Chandra checked in for us as a group and provided our keys. As we rode the elevator upward, the others in our party got off on lower floors until it was just her and me.

I wasn't surprised to see we went all the way up to the top floor, the "club" level. We came to my door first. "Your room has a connecting door to a suite," she said. "I suggest keeping it closed for appearance's sake."

She didn't have to tell me who would be staying in the suite.

"I'll be directly across the hall," she added. "And you have my cell phone number. The van to rehearsal leaves right from the driveway outside the lobby at ten-thirty a.m. Don't be late."

"I won't."

"Order room service if you want it." She looked me up and down like she had something more to say, but she didn't say anything other than, "See you in the morning."

Eleven

Leading Us On and On

We would have two days of rehearsal on the main stage in the theater before the actual audition. I was soon very grateful for the rehearsal time. I knew I was going to want to get used to performing in the space, but it hadn't occurred to me that the stage would be raked. It had a tilt down toward the audience so that people in the orchestra seats could still see the whole stage. It took some getting used to.

The other thing that took some getting used to was the fact that there were two dancers who looked like James, at least at a glance. The only reason I didn't think he'd arrived early himself was that when I caught sight of them they were talking to each other, so I knew at least one of them couldn't be the real thing...and on closer inspection it was obvious neither of them was. I wondered if he used stunt doubles at various times in the show. That seemed likely.

Chandra introduced us first thing to the choreographer, an Asian-looking woman named Alicia Bogovich. I was expecting a Russian with a name like that, but Annika told me later it was her ex-husband's last name, and she kept using it professionally after they split up. She was American, from California, and she ran us through some warm-ups before giving us the schedule for the rest of the day. She was in tights and a sports bra with a chic-looking knee-length knit cardigan over it, a clipboard tucked in one arm as she paced the edge of the stage, looking over the rest of us sitting scattered across the stage.

"Nice to see you all again." She was answered with a smattering of claps and "you too" from the dancers. "You all know Barnaby, the house manager." She pointed to a guy walking through the auditorium. His T-shirt was untucked, his hair grown over his eyes, and his pot belly protruding over the edge of his jeans. He waved without looking back. "And of course Ramon, my assistant." A young-looking guy with a thin mustache waved from the sound board, which was placed among the curved tiers of tables. The whole main floor was made up of tables, while the upper level was regular theater seats, and there were opera-style balcony boxes on the sides.

"Now. Jasper's not here yet, but he'll be conducting a review for a partner role the day after tomorrow. *Female* partner, I should specify." She walked along the footlights as she talked. "You ladies who are working on solo pieces for that, I've blocked the four hours at the end of the day today for you to have a half hour each on the stage. Tomorrow, same thing. I've got you in alphabetical order today, the reverse tomorrow. Right now, I want us to get started on an ensemble piece. Any questions?"

One of the male dancers from Las Vegas I hadn't met yet raised his hand. "Are we doing *Bride of the Blue*? I've heard we were, but I've also heard we weren't."

Alicia nodded at him. "There's a reason for that confusion." She looked at the clipboard and touched it with her finger, making me realize it was actually a tablet computer, not a clipboard after all. "Let me play you something. This is the brand-new overture to a show that incorporates a few elements of *Bride of the Blue*, but which also pulls in songs from several other Lightning albums. The title is still to be determined." Music came from the sound system then, the sound of synthesizers and violins soft at first, but then growing louder. Then the drums came in. It reminded me of the music from a Cirque du Soleil show, only not so French-sounding. I liked it.

A voice from the wings made everyone look up. Ferrara pushed a curtain aside and strode onto the stage. She was dressed in skintight jeans with lace-up boots. Her heels were loud on the hollow stage. "What the bloody hell is this?"

Alicia faded the music out. "Ferrara, I was wondering when you were going to grace us with y—"

"I asked you a question, Bogovich."

Alicia pursed her lips. "As I was just telling the group, it's an entirely new overture."

"I didn't approve this."

"I wasn't under the impression that your approval was necessary."

Ferrara laughed and gave Alicia a feral smile. "I'm the executive producer. I'm financing *Bride of the Blue*."

"Jasper told me he calls the shots."

"Jasper likes to feel like he's in control. You know that." She glanced around as if she were expecting that line to get a laugh. No one moved. "And this whole principal dancer shite? Totally unnecessary."

Alicia looked like she was trying hard not to roll her eyes. I liked her already. Her attitude made me feel less afraid of Ferrara, too. "Jasper intends for the principal to do a lot more in this show than the bride did in *Bride of the Blue*."

Ferrara waved her hand like she was dispelling cigarette smoke. "Oh, does he? Well. Jasper knows best." She snorted dismissively.

"Could I ask you to clear the stage?" Alicia cleared her throat. "We've got a lot to learn in a little amount of time."

"You're wasting your time. We're doing *Bride of the Blue* and that's final. Anyone who participates in this audition non-sense can put their names on my shit list right now." Ferrara stalked toward Alicia, but turned before reaching her, going down the hidden steps at the front of the stage and up the side aisle to the back of the theater. The sound of the door opening and shutting echoed loudly in the empty auditorium.

The moment she was gone people began talking. "Is she serious?" Annika said to Roland.

"Yeah, is she going to arm wrestle Jasper for control of the troupe or what?" he said back, before Alicia demanded everyone quiet down and get to work.

We worked on learning the first part of the overture, and before I knew it, it was time to break. Alicia called us all in close.

"Okay, people," she said, looking around to see if Ferrara was about to pop out of the curtains again. "I guess I need to know who's still planning to audition for Jasper."

I raised my hand.

"Okay, Karina, that's one. Are you the only one?"

I looked around. They were all looking at me. "Annika, weren't you planning to try out, too?" I asked.

"What if she blacklists me?" Annika answered. "Jasper's getting out of the business."

"Yeah, that's what he said last time," someone I couldn't see in the back of the group said, causing laughter.

"No, seriously, you guys, it's not worth it. Karina, don't make an enemy."

What Annika didn't know, of course, was that Ferrara was already my enemy. "I'm still going to do it. Jasper's my boss. It's going to be up to him."

A girl with a black bun and part of a tattoo visible along her collarbone raised her hand then. "I'll try out. Ferrara doesn't scare me."

Alicia nodded. "All right. Change of plans, then, people. Let's break for lunch, except Karina and Natalie. You do your rehearsal runs with Ramon. Everyone else take thirty. When we come back, we'll continue blocking this piece and let Jasper and Ferrara duke it out later."

Ramon climbed onto the stage and came toward me while the others drifted away. "Are you Karina? You're the one I haven't met yet."

"Yes, nice to meet you." We shook hands. I introduced myself to Natalie, too, and she exchanged fist bumps with Ramon.

"What are you guys planning to use for music?"

Natalie shrugged. "I haven't prepped anything. This was a spur-of-the-minute decision. What have you got in your iPod?"

"Here." He dug a music player out of his pocket and handed it to her. I got the feeling they had a bit of a history together. "Go in the back where it'll be quiet and come back when you've picked something."

"Thanks." She slipped easily off the edge of the stage and disappeared.

"I have my song in my phone." I dug it out of my bag and pulled up the track. "Here it is. And I need a stool for a prop. I saw one in back?"

"Okay, cool. I saw it, too. Hang out here while I go get it." He came back with a chrome-legged stool with a round black seat and set it down. He spun the seat with his hand, which gave me an idea. "Now, let me go set the music up." He held out his hand for the phone and I gave it to him with a little pang of worry. He loped up the aisle to the sound control board, though, never leaving my sight, and a moment later the sound of the drums echoed through the huge sound system.

Fortunately for me, Ramon didn't care how many times I needed him to start it again at the beginning, because I had to have him try it many times. But the rake of the stage didn't bother me too much, and the moves I had been working on in the living room of the apartment seemed like they trans-lated well enough to the big stage. At first I had put the stool at center stage, but then decided it worked better downstage and off to one side.

Then my time was up, and I grabbed a sandwich from the green room where everyone else was getting ready to con-tinue. I didn't have much time, but I checked my phone for messages: none. I texted James:

Ms. Trouble is here, scaring off everyone else from audition-ing. She insists we're doing Bride of the Blue *and she doesn't like the new music you sent. Is that why things are taking so long in London?*

I was surprised a reply came back right away. *No, that's not why. You have inspired me. Must go. Love you.*

He said nothing about Ferrara, but I figured I'd ask him later. *Love you, too! Get here soon!*

I failed to reach James for the next two days, other than to receive text messages from him so brief they were almost cryptic. I gathered that he was working until the last possible moment and then he would hop on a plane, arriving only shortly before the audition was to be held.

He wasn't there yet when Chandra and I got in the van with some others to head to the theater. One of them was a black man with some of the most impressive biceps I had ever seen. He took off his suit jacket to keep it from getting wrinkled as he got into the van. Under it, his chest and arm muscles stretched a plain black T-shirt to its limit. Chandra introduced him as Ty, head of entourage security. He gave me a professional smile and a nod as he shook my hand. I got the impression he was ex-military.

Once in the green room, I changed into dancing clothes, black tights and bodysuit with a wisp of a light blue gossamer skirt around my hips.

When I got to the stage I found Ferrara terrorizing Alicia, or trying to.

"You've got to be kidding me. You hate my guts, Bogovich." Ferrara was wearing a black leather jacket over a catsuit studded with rhinestones. "You think I'll accept you as an impartial judge?"

"Ferrara, contrary to your self-centered fantasies, I don't give a fuck about you," Alicia shot back. "All I care about is how the show looks. If Jasper wants my opinion, he's going to get it, no matter what you think."

"I want all of your opinions," came a voice from the balcony box immediately to the right of the stage. James stood at the railing, looking down at us all. "Chandra. Give everyone a score sheet."

Ferrara looked like she was shooting laser beams out her eyes at him. "This is not a democracy!"

"No, it isn't. Because *my* decision will be the final one." His voice, and the authority in it, carried easily through the auditorium. He turned on his heel, then disappeared through the archway. A moment later he reappeared at the foot of the stage in the orchestra. "Now, let's get this under way."

But for Ferrara, the argument wasn't over. She loomed over him from the edge of the stage. "I'm the producer. You need my input."

He looked up with a mild expression on his face. "No, I don't. A producer might have some say if she threatened to pull her financial backing, perhaps, but I don't need your money, Ferrara."

"You're being ridiculous."

"I'm not the one who insisted on a ridiculously strict interpretation of our recording contract." He lifted himself onto the stage with his arms and swung his legs like a gymnast onto a vault horse, then stood close enough to kiss her. She refused to back away. "Why don't you try reading the production and performance agreements I signed? Auteur clause. I get complete creative control of all sight and sound in the production. Every detail."

"You—"

"Right down to the length of the false eyelashes on your face." He knew exactly how to push her buttons.

She snapped. "You're a monster! You put the freak in control freak!"

"Of course I do," he said mildly. "Now, come on, people. Everyone into the seats." He looked up into the catwalks overhead. "Hey, Barnaby."

"Yeah?" came a voice from above.

"You know anything about dancing?"

"A little."

"Can you even tell my dancers apart?"

"Not really."

"Excellent. Get down here and serve as an impartial judge."

"A'right."

Everyone but me, Natalie, and Ferrara took seats in the VIP section of the orchestra, the posh tables closest to the stage, James included. Ramon went back to the sound board. Ferrara looked at me, then, examining me. I think until that moment she couldn't have picked me out of the group of dancers. Now she was looking at me with an expression of hate and disgust, like she couldn't believe she was even bothering to scrape me off the bottom of her shoe.

I tried to keep my chin up. But the sheer force of her disdain for me brought all my worries to the surface. What if I really was about to make a fool of myself in front of everyone? What if I was kidding myself and James was just besotted with me, he was no judge of whether I could do this, and everyone was going to see how pathetic a dancer I was?

Then I remembered that was the point of this audition. To find out. To prove to myself that I could hold my own, or to find out that I had no business there. That was why James wanted everyone to see it. Because if I really, truly sucked, he would know from the reactions of the others.

He cleared his throat. "Karina, why don't you go first? Natalie, take a seat."

"I'm happy to go first," I said.

"Fine. Ramon?" James called as Ferrara went into the wings.

"Almost ready, boss. Karina, don't forget your stool."

"Ah! Right!" I ran into the wings where it was stored.

Of course, when I found the stool, Ferrara was sitting on it. I decided to try the polite approach. "Excuse me, but I need that."

She had a compact in one hand and was putting on a fresh coat of lipstick, focusing on herself in the tiny mirror. She looked up at me slowly, her gaze taking a leisurely path up my body, her nostril flare increasing the longer she looked. "Who. Are. You? I don't recognize you."

"I really need the stool now."

"*What* are you? Are you his latest fuck toy? Is that it? Am I being tossed aside for a new piece of trash?"

I'm sure I blushed.

"Ahh, I'm right, aren't I?" She brightened suddenly. "He is a master of manipulation, isn't he? So that's why he insisted on this charade. I know what he's doing now. This is all some kinky humiliation game, isn't it? He's going to make you go out there and make a spectacle of yourself, and then what, spank you for doing a terrible job? Or just fuck you raw in the restroom? Fuck you until you're so sore you come out bowlegged and everyone knows what you've been doing?"

The longer she talked the more desperate I got, my face redder and my breath shorter. "Please," I begged. "I need the stool."

She uncrossed her legs and stood with deliberate slowness. "You're not the first little chickadee he's ravaged," she said. "I know you think you like it. I know you think you love the attention. Maybe you even like pain. But just you wait until the day you say no to him."

She stepped aside and I grabbed the stool.

"It'll happen. He'll keep pushing you until you say no, and then he'll get what he really wants. Then he gets to rape you."

I clamped my mouth shut tight and wished I could do the same with my ears.

"He'll rape you and then leave you by the side of the road, and his money will shut you up..."

I hurried back onto the stage, banging my shin on the leg of the stool as I did. I put it down where I wanted it, panting and trying to keep from crying. She was full of it. She had to be. She was saying any outrageous thing she could to mess me up.

I remembered Stefan telling me once that he'd seen James do that, fuck a woman and then leave her.

But that had been a lame attempt to scare me off. And you know what? Ferrara was trying to do the same thing. Had to be. *Had to be.*

I heard Ramon's voice through the PA. "Whenever you're ready. Take your mark."

Right. The performance. I took a deep breath. I had to put everything out of my mind. Remember what the dance in London had been like. The whole audience had been rapt. And the audience of one I'd intended it for had reacted just as I'd hoped, cracking his shell and giving in to his lust for me.

I could do this.

I went to the back corner of the stage, opposite the stool, and nodded to Ramon. The music began, and I crossed the stage almost in a ballet-like pass, coming to the stool, dancing in front of it and around it as if James were sitting there.

As the drums kicked in, my moves became more sensual, as if I were teasing the man sitting there. I flowed across the stool with two kicks in the air as if I had taken a quick pass on his lap, and then straddled it with my back to the audience for a circular hip grind that Sabine would have called "stirring the cake batter." I'd made an edit of the music so that it was exactly two minutes long, and the ending slipped into another minor mode, almost a mournful one. Here's where I had to sell the idea that the stool wasn't only empty; it was permanently so. Maybe I relied on too much mime, but I hugged myself and wiped a tear, then danced away from the stool, and back, away, and back, until finally running off the stage entirely as if too grief-stricken to even look at the stool anymore.

They clapped. Hard. A few of them even whistled! I tiptoed back onto the stage and they got louder. I took a small bow, then ran down into the audience to sit next to Annika, who hugged me.

"It was great!" she whispered. "You're really good!"

Then it was Natalie's turn. Her music began before she was even on the stage, and she came bursting forth from the wings into a leap and a split in the air that defied gravity. She came down and went directly into a slide along the stage, effortless and mind-blowing, as she flowed right into the next upright spin and then another leap. I heard dancers around me gasp. It was a serious "wow" opening, and it kept up like that for the full two minutes, ending with her all the way at the front of the stage, as she slid into one final dramatic pose.

There were claps and a couple of male voices in particular shouted "yeah!" as she hit that last pose. But I think the clapping had been louder for me. It was hard to tell.

I brought her a towel and we hugged. "You're really an acrobat!"

Natalie grinned. "I figured I may as well go all out. You were really good, too. Good luck."

"Good luck," I said. I knew if James was picking on his own, he was picking me, but I really wasn't sure how this was going to go.

Chandra collected the score sheets. James did not look up at me. He appeared to be checking something on his phone.

Chandra handed him the score sheets and whispered something in his ear. He began to look through them. Now that I was closer, I could see the dark circles under his eyes. He had been traveling for what, fourteen hours?

Ferrara walked to the edge of the stage. "You can't seriously be trying to choose between them based on that alone."

James looked up from the scores. "Why shouldn't I? Is there something in particular you wish to see?"

"Well. If one of them is going to be a principal, we need to see what kind of compatibility she has with you."

James sighed.

"Don't you agree? If you're going to do this mad idea of a production, you don't need a soloist. You need a partner. You remember Sabine's exercise she calls 'pass de deux'? The one with the cross-stage improv?"

"Ben, Pascual," James said, calling for his two look-alikes.

Ferrara clucked her tongue. "You should do the passes yourself. You're the one the girl needs to be compatible with."

James glanced at me, but I couldn't read his expression. He addressed the group then. "I've come directly from the airport. I had to be on the shuttle to Heathrow at five in the morning, London time, and it's, oh, almost midnight there now. But, she's right. I should do it. Who's got a dance belt to lend me?"

There were laughs, but then someone threw one that landed on his head, and that set the entire troupe laughing, James included. He took it and held it up to examine it, and nodded as if he approved of it. "Thanks for your support," he quipped, and that prompted more howls of laughter. "Be right back."

He went to change clothes, and the dancers and crew fell to chattering among themselves. Ferrara stalked off, probably to harangue him. I wanted to text him a quick warning, but my phone was still plugged into the sound board. By the time I reached it, she'd have found him anyway. Well, I might as well get it, I thought. I went up to the board and found it.

The phone was blinking to get my attention: a video call coming in. I clicked it.

On the screen I saw the green room. James had set the phone down and was changing his clothes. At another time I would have thought it was him winding me up by showing me his body, but this time I got the feeling he wanted a witness for the conversation he was having.

"James," Ferrara said. "I really think it's time to abandon this insane course."

"I know you do," he said. He wasn't visible in the frame now. I could hear rustling sounds.

Her voice was smooth and reasonable. "There simply isn't time for the company to learn an entirely new show."

"Ferrara, I'm tired, I'm at the end of my rope, and I didn't come back here so you could harass me about it one more time."

"And I told you you're being ridiculous, dear. In fact, it

seems you're being even more ridiculous than we first discussed. What is this new music you sent to Bogovich without my knowledge? We don't have time to learn a whole new production. The whole point of returning here, returning the same cast, and doing the same show, is that it's doable in two months' time."

"You underestimate how talented this group is." Something flew past the camera. His shirt, perhaps.

"And you forget who is in charge of your career."

"Would you excuse me, please?" He cleared his throat.

She clucked her tongue and then purred, "I own you, James. I have every right to look at what's mine."

He was silent, and so was I, my hand over my mouth. Although she'd probably seen him make costume changes plenty of times, this was open ogling, open harassment. My cheeks burned scarlet again as I imagined how mortified James might be. When he was relaxed and open with me, like at his house on the Upper East Side, he wandered unselfconsciously naked. But I had almost never seen him like that. He was always covered, always discreet.

Maybe this was why. Had she been getting an eyeful of him since he was eighteen years old and too young and powerless to say no? Was this why he was so controlled, so closed, so wary? It might be why he was so touchy about certain things.

He picked up the phone and the video cut off. A few moments later the two of them came onto the stage.

"Karina," he said, gesturing for me. "You first again."

He was in plain white spandex tights that only came to below his knee, his chest bare. Under the tights I could clearly make out both the outline of the borrowed dance belt and the sizable package it held in place. As I made my way to the stage, he called out to Ramon for some appropriate music. "Five passes. Make each one faster than the previous."

"No problem," Ramon said, hurrying back to the board from where he had been sitting.

The first piece of music was some kind of soundtrack, the music swelling and sweeping but without much rhythm. I followed James's lead and we floated across the stage, circling each other like two leaves on the eddies of a lazy river. Next came a classical waltz, and we zigzagged back to the other side like two marionettes being made to dance in time. The third pass was some kind of funk, and though neither of us was really a hip-hop dancer, we clapped and strutted and popped our way. James was easy to dance with. It was like the music suggested the same ideas to us both, and then it was a matter of staying in synch, reading each other's cues. On the second to last pass the music was worldbeat, with bursts of horns and washes of marimbas, and James lifted me on a horn hit, then spiraled me around him as the marimbas took over again. And the last pass was to a rousing section of the 1812 Overture by Tchaikovsky, the part with the cannons going off. James swept me off my feet and let go of me at the top of the lift, my arms flying wide like a swan, and then he caught me, and swung me around, almost like ice skaters do. We were both grinning as we ended, and took bows to the enthusiastic clapping of the company.

Then it was Natalie's turn. I sat down with a sinking feeling. What if they could do so much more? She was such a daring, athletic dancer, and they had danced together before. Would it be obvious to everyone that James was choosing me only because of how into me he was?

On the very first pass, though, I could see they weren't in synch. She tried too hard to keep control of what they were doing, to show off her athleticism, and they had some moments of disconnect. As the music got faster, she pushed harder and that only made it worse. On the final pass she took a leap and he tried to catch her, but the catch wasn't completely clean and they both went down.

Thank goodness as the music cut off they were laughing. James was flat on his back he was so exhausted, and Natalie was cracking up. "Oh, that wasn't how that was supposed to go!" she said, poking him. "Karina, you win! You can have him." She kicked him playfully and climbed to her feet.

James got up more slowly, looking exhausted but still smiling. "Very well. I would say we have a definitive winner."

And it's not Ferrara, I thought, as I stood and took a bow, to the applause of the rest of the company.

Ferrara, who had been standing at the edge of the stage, shook her head and left.

James spoke to the group, still seated in the tables. "Thank you, all, for being here. I know I said good-bye last time, and I truly meant it. But circumstances are such that here I am, here you are, and the opportunity to put on a damn good show is in our laps."

He hopped down and went to the sound board, then continued. "We're not doing *Bride of the Blue,*" he said. "We're going to do a new rock opera that incorporates my greatest hits, with a few new songs and a new storyline. Ferrara was afraid we wouldn't have time to learn it, but the band is already cranking on the new material, and we have two months, people! That's more than enough time to work up the numbers where the whole ensemble is needed. There will also be opportunities for each of you to feature if that's something you want. Alicia and I will both be working with you..."

A huge yawn cracked his face then, and he had to wipe sudden tears from his eyes. "...Tomorrow. I'll be working with you tomorrow. Right now...it's been almost forty hours since I slept. I was in the recording studio all night, on the plane first thing this morning..." He sat down on the stool at the board. "I'm sorry. Alicia."

Alicia clapped her hands for attention. "Listen up, everyone. Take the rest of the day off. It'll be your last one for a while, so enjoy it."

Chandra was already moving to help James to his feet and push him toward the van back to the hotel. I grabbed my bag and joined them, as did a few others. As the van crept through the backstreets toward the hotel, James slept with his head on Chandra's shoulder and I couldn't help but feel envious. But now wasn't the time to reveal our relationship to everyone. I knew that.

I consoled myself with the thought that when he woke, no matter when it was, Chandra wouldn't be the one he turned to. I considered whether I should sneak into his room, and into his bed, entirely naked, to wait for him to wake up. It seemed a good bet.

I took a shower. As I closed my eyes under the flow of the water, moments from our dance improvisation played in my mind. We really were great together, so in synch, so perfect. I remembered dancing with him in that Cinderella dress at the society mansion, how perfect that had been, too. What would the first dance at our wedding be like? I wondered.

I could almost hear my conscience in Becky's voice: *First*

dance at your wedding? Really? Karina, aren't you getting ahead of yourself?

Maybe I was, but at that moment it seemed really possible. We could be partners in synch forever. He'd called me the love of his life, as if anyone else there had been before paled in comparison. He had used the word *forever.* He was moving slowly because he was trying his best to preserve the relationship, not ruin it by rushing. But once the concert series was over, we had our whole lives ahead of us. Together. The mere thought made my heart pound and I felt like singing in the shower. Heck, even though I was a much worse singer than I was a dancer, I let loose with a few bars of the 1812 Overture. That was how excited and amazed and ready to explode from happiness I was.

I got out of the shower, put on the luxuriously thick hotel bathrobe, and was combing out my wet hair when a knock came at the door. I could hear a muffled female voice saying, "Karina? Karina, I know you're in there."

I looked through the peephole.

Standing there was Ferrara Huntington.

Twelve

Made of Lipstick

I opened the door.

"May I come in?" she asked, her face quite sober and serious.

"Ferrara, what's this about?"

"Please, Karina. I...I promise I won't bother you about this again. I have some things to tell you, and show you, so you don't have to take my word for it. Just give me fifteen minutes of your time, and then I will never speak of this again."

"Speak of what?"

"There are things you don't know about James."

I prickled to hear her use his name and suppressed the urge to look around the hallway to make sure no one had overheard. "Fine. Come in. Fifteen minutes."

She glided in, head high like a swan, and I closed the door behind her. She went to the small table by the window, sat down, and then pulled a laptop computer out of her voluminous shoulder bag. It was some fancy designer brand, but once she had the computer on the table, she tossed the bag aside like it was worthless.

I sat in the other chair, my hands folded on my knees, telling myself to count the minutes until she'd leave. Then I'd get in bed with James and that would be the end of it.

"Pardon my presumption, but you have to realize how obvious it is that he's sleeping with you. One new dancer comes along and all of a sudden he wants her to be the star of the show? Oh, perhaps I shouldn't be such a cynic. Maybe he hasn't started sleeping with you yet. Either way, you need to know what it is I'm about to tell you," she said.

I said nothing, waiting for her to go on.

"If you're already sleeping with him, then you know all about the whips and chains. He talks a great game about consent, doesn't he? About boundaries and all that? He makes you feel completely safe, even when he's menacing your cunt with a straight razor."

I swallowed, my thighs clenching involuntarily, as I remembered the first time he shaved me. I hadn't been scared at all. No, wait, I had been kind of nervous, but then he made it obvious he'd been making me nervous on purpose, and then he made it all better, *so* much better...

"I know I was harsh with you before. I was upset. You can imagine how I felt, can't you? I arrive in Vegas thinking I know what's going on and then, wham, Alicia Bogovich drops a bomb and tells me, oh by the way, we're not even doing the show you commissioned? But that's the kind of coward James is. He wouldn't tell me directly."

I still said nothing. I'd had no idea if James hadn't spoken to her, but I could easily believe he'd told her and she'd dismissed it, the way she had dismissed his request for her to leave him alone so he could get undressed earlier.

"Anyway, I apologize for being so bitchy today, but unfortunately, what I said was true. You probably know that he gets off on hurting you. Nothing makes his cock harder than seeing you in pain or seeing you helpless. Am I right?"

I couldn't keep my mouth shut any longer. "You know, I haven't tested the hardness to see how it compares to him seeing me in pleasure or in ecstasy."

She smiled and I realized I'd given her an advantage by confirming I was having sex with him. But then her look softened, turning sympathetic. "Oh, dearie, I know. He can play normal when he wants to. And you know what? You're probably a great lay. And James, well, his dick gets hard if the wind blows. That's just how he is. But back to what I was saying. The thing that will excite him to the next level is when you start to resist. And the thing that he's waiting for, the thing he can't fucking wait for, is the day when you actually say no."

"He and I have discussed it," I said.

"You think you have," she shot back. "You'll see. You'll say no, and he'll keep right on going. He won't stop until it's full-out rape."

"No," I said, before I could stop myself.

"Yes. He's pumped you so full of talk about consent and boundaries and stuff, but you know what? You'll probably blame yourself at first. You'll blame yourself for miscommunication. Or worse, for disappointing him. But that'll just build up a nice wall of resentment. Eventually you'll resist because you have to find out if you're really a prisoner to that cock of his, or if you have the free will he claims you have. He claims he'll let you go so that you'll come back to him, and prove that you love him. But it'll happen. You'll say no. He'll fuck you anyway. You'll fight and scratch and claw to prove to him you're serious, and that'll just excite him even more. And if it looks like you might actually win the fight or hurt him, well, he'll just put you in bondage, and then you'll truly be fucked."

I tried to argue with her. "But... but I offered to him that he could take me anytime, anywhere. I wanted to give him that. I did that myself, without him prompting me."

Her eyes were misty with sympathy. "Oh, darling, I know you did. And it's a great romantic notion. That's so Romeo and Juliet, that level of devotion. And I know you truly believe it. But when push comes to shove, there'll be a day. Maybe you'll feel ill or you had a death in the family or maybe you just want to test the boundaries, and you'll refuse. And he'll say *so what*."

"Ferrara—"

"I told you you wouldn't have to take my word for it. I brought proof." She woke up the laptop and pulled up a video player that filled the screen. The thumbnail image, I could see, was of someone's bare ass. She hit play.

James's bare ass. He was walking past the camera toward a bed, where a woman lay sleeping atop the covers in a sheer nightgown. He looked younger here, slimmer, but he moved the way I expected. He eased himself slowly onto the bed at the woman's feet, and then gradually separated her knees. He pulled the nightgown up to her stomach, showing that she was shaved down below. He slid the back of one knuckle up and down her seam while he stroked his cock with the other hand.

I felt myself growing slick and tried not to squirm in the chair.

"You're so wet," he murmured to the woman, and any thought I had that maybe this was one of his body doubles vanished. That was his voice. I was certain. "You must want me, eh? Even in your sleep, you want me."

He plunged into her suddenly and she screamed, making my hair stand on end. She fought him and he laughed and kept on fucking her. At one point she managed to maneuver so that he wasn't inside her, and he got a hand around her throat. "Lie still and let me fuck you," he growled. "If I choke you unconscious, then nothing will stop me."

She lay still then, whimpering, while he humped her, keeping one hand on her neck. He slapped her breasts with his other hand and the whimpering sounds increased.

Then his grip slipped or he got careless, and she escaped off the bed. He tackled her from behind and they landed with her face right up close to the camera.

He got one of her arms twisted behind her, though, and she was trapped again.

"Harder to get at your cunt this way," he said. "Guess you want it in the rear."

"No, oh no, no, please no," she said. He put a ball gag in her mouth then, and using his one free hand, strapped it behind her head.

"There. Now I won't have to listen to your lies," he said. "When I know you want it."

At that point, she started to cry.

And so did I.

Ferrara closed the laptop and sat for a moment in silence, then dabbed at her own eyes with the edge of her sleeve.

"That's enough, I think," she said. "I know that was difficult to watch. Believe me, I know."

I tried to catch my breath. "Who was she?"

"Some groupie, one of dozens, maybe hundreds. He was doing this night after night! I was his tour manager, you understand. It was my responsibility to do something about it. Imagine the position I was in. He was legally an adult, and when these women went to his room, at first they were consenting. Of course they were! He was a rock star! They'd have epic, wall-shaking sex! And then he'd wait until they were asleep or helpless and…this would happen. What could I do? I couldn't go to the police. This was my golden goose, after all, and none of the women I could find—and that was if I could even find them at all—would speak out against him! Or if they did, they wanted money. Money to keep silent about it. At any rate, I had to confront him with irrefutable evidence that I knew what he was doing. So I started leaving a hidden camera in his room. And that's how I made these tapes."

"There are more of them?"

She nodded gravely. "Many more."

I put my head in my hands, trying to think, but I was in turmoil. The sound of the woman screaming echoed in my ears. But this was Ferrara. She wanted me and James to break up. She wanted James for herself! Wait. Did I know that? That was what James had told me, but was it true?

I looked up. "Has he raped you?" I asked.

She froze, and then her face crumbled and her eyes closed. "Yes," she whispered, with a choked sob. She put her hand to her throat. "Many times."

And although my heart was doing flip-flops of sympathy, something in the back of my head said it didn't add up.

"Why do you still work with him, then?" I wanted to ask why she was claiming to be married to him, but I didn't want to give away that I knew that. "Why stay?"

"I help protect the young ones, the new ones, like you. Except I hope I'm not too late in your case."

That didn't add up, either. Annika told me James never, ever got involved with the dancers, and if a dancer made a move on him, they were gone. Was she wrong? Was it that he only liked them when they were illicitly taken, and once they revealed an interest he got rid of them?

I almost, *almost* could make Ferrara's story believable. Then I remembered what James himself had sent through video to me earlier that day. Ferrara being the one who got off on crossing boundaries. Ferrara who liked to watch him…

There was only one person who could fill in the missing gaps in the story here, and that was James himself. But I sure as hell didn't want to talk to him with Ferrara there.

I needed to get rid of her as quickly as possible.

I covered my eyes as if I were crying. "I think…I think I'd like to be alone now. It's a lot to take in."

"I know it is, dearie. I know it is. Here is my card. Call me anytime you want to talk further." She passed me her card and patted me on the hand. I looked at her card instead of at her. I wasn't sure I could really pull off the act of being distraught. I mean, I was genuinely upset by what she had shown me, but I worried if she got a good look at me she'd be able to tell I wasn't convinced she was telling the truth.

She stood then and swept the laptop into the bag.

"I'll just see myself out," she said, while I pretended to still be so stricken that I couldn't even raise my head.

The door slammed behind her. I stood up and wished I

had something to smash or throw. I didn't believe she was telling the truth about James. Yet, what was the real story behind that video? That was definitely something James hadn't told me. And I was getting tired of discovering there were still dark secrets to uncover.

After I washed my face and calmed down a little, I went to the connecting door, which was disguised to look like a paneled section of wall, except for the round lock in it. I unlocked it and discovered that either James or Chandra had thoughtfully unlocked it from the other side already.

The suite was huge, the bed huge to match, and there was James, lying in the middle of it, the sheets wrapped around his middle but his torso exposed. The curtains had only been partly drawn, which meant the late-afternoon sun was streaming in, making his hair look as blond as it had been when we first met and his skin golden. The dark circles of his nipples stood out against his chest and the muscle of his stomach was lean and flat. A gorgeous picture and all for me.

I felt even calmer just looking at him. This was James, my James, a man I knew better than he knew himself sometimes. Or at least I had fewer illusions about him. Didn't I? Didn't he say himself that he was afraid he might push me too far one day? Was that a setup, a warning? Was I clinging to an illusion about what our relationship was, about what his desires and needs were?

Or about my own? I hadn't seen him in a month. It had been so hard to sit there in that auditorium and pretend to be just another dancer when I had wanted desperately to run up to him, kiss him, run my hands through his hair—and then the dancing, partnering with him, I could practically taste the sweat on his skin and I imagined what it would have been like for him to lift me up, carry me backstage, and have his way with me.

I dropped my robe into the pile with the duvet and the pillows he had knocked off the bed. I slipped under one edge of the sheet and settled, naked, next to him. Ferrara was wrong. She had to be. I'd prove it.

I'll do it when he wakes up, I thought. He'll want sex and I'll say no and see what happens.

But when he realized I was there, I think he was still asleep. He rolled over and wrapped an arm around me. Then his hand stroked between my thighs and until he found the wetness. A finger worked its way into the wet cleft, rubbing up and down my clit and my hips shifted wantonly, lust spiking in my belly.

"Karina," he murmured. "I've been dreaming about you."

"Oh? What kind of dreams?"

"This kind." He reared up suddenly, quite awake, and pushing my leg aside. I struggled purely instinctively against how rough and brusque he was, not even thinking about anything Ferrara had said, and then quite suddenly he had the head of his cock fitted snugly between my slick lips.

I wanted to remind him that it had been a month since I'd had anything there. I wanted to remind him that once he had caused me so much pain with penetration that it had taken him a week to train me up to taking his size. But all I could do in that moment was make a helpless whimpering sound. All thought of testing his resolve, or my own, was erased. *This is James. He knows. He knows.*

Wasn't I the one who had teased him, saying that maybe our reunion would have to be a "fuck first, talk later" one?

He paused only a moment, looking into my eyes, before he began to push into me, and I began to wail. A firm, solid, never-stopping push, more and more of him entering me with each passing second, and my scream rising in pitch. Not because I was in pain, no. Because the moment he breached me like that, I had started to come, and the deeper he went, the more explosive the orgasm got. I'd never come from penetration alone like that before. I beat on his back with my fists and my heels and my screams broke into desperate gasps as he began to fuck me hard and the pleasure kept going off inside me like fireworks, *pow pow pow.*

I lost it completely, cursing, screaming, sobbing, and then crying my eyes out as he switched from the punishing, rough thrusts to the gentle, tender rolling of his hips that melted my insides and my heart.

"I've missed you," he said, "and I've missed fucking you. And it would seem you've missed me, too."

I couldn't even answer, I was crying too hard. I managed a nod, and then he pulled out suddenly, causing me to cry "No!" even though what he was doing was sliding down my body to put his head between my legs and pleasure me with his tongue.

I came once more, shuddering against his mouth but feeling empty and bereft of what I needed most. He crawled up my body again and ran the length of his shaft up and down my clit, sending vibrations through me that made me incoherent with need.

"Tell me what you want."

I writhed against him, trying to answer. "Your cock."

"It's right here." He moved it slickly.

"Your cock inside me."

"Hmm, in your mouth?"

"No, no!" I struggled against, him, lust-crazed, trying to impale myself on him, but he held me in place.

"Or is your ass ready?" He slid it lower.

"No!"

"I will claim your rear, too, Karina."

"No, no!" I thrashed helplessly. "Fuck me! James, just fuck me! Fuck me until you come or I don't know what I'll do! Please!"

"Ah, there's the magic word."

"You mean *please*?"

"No. *Fuck*." He drove into me as he said it. "Ahhhh, yes."

Oh God, yes. No more teasing. From there he fucked me steadily as he went up the ramp of his own arousal until he couldn't keep it steady anymore and I knew he was close. Then five or six hard jerks against me and a long growl that ended in a sigh, and he was done.

He collapsed atop me, and I think was drifting to sleep again when I made him roll to the side. "Hey, no sleeping, Jet Lag Boy. I have questions for you."

"Hmm? Oh, yes, of course, Karina. I wouldn't dream of skimping on your answers." He rubbed his eyes. "If you want me to stay awake long enough to answer anything, though, I had better get into the shower."

We made our sticky, sweaty way across the room to the immense bathroom and he turned on the water, but then sat on the edge of the separate Jacuzzi tub while waiting for it to get hot.

Now that the ecstasy of sex was ebbing away somewhat, I tried to wrap my head around the questions Ferrara's video had raised. I sat on the edge of the tub next to him.

"You look like you're about to ask a big question," James said.

"Yeah, I think I am." I waved at the shower. "Let's get clean first while I get my head together."

"All right."

He was somber, or perhaps merely subdued from being exhausted, as we washed. He helped me rinse my hair, his long fingers sluicing away the water and lifting it in the spray, and he gently soaped between my legs, kissing my belly reverently when he was done. I scrubbed his back and lathered his balls, remembering my earlier conclusions, that James was fundamentally afraid of the act of intercourse. He certainly hadn't felt afraid in bed just now, and he hadn't looked afraid in that video, but...

We got out and toweled dry. He ordered a pot of coffee from room service, put on an undershirt and yoga pants, and then belted a bathrobe over that. I put my robe back on and we settled on the couch together.

"You seem troubled, Karina. You've never taken this long to come up with a question."

"I know. This one might be a doozy, though, so I'm psyching myself up for it."

"Take all the time you need. May I make a guess, though?"

"Sure." I turned sideways on the couch so I could look at his face.

He pulled one of my feet into his lap and began massaging my foot. "My guess is that this has something to do with Ferrara."

"Good guess. What makes you think that?"

"It's a fact: Ferrara will want to drive a wedge between us any way she can." His hands were warm and strong. "She's not blind. I'm sure she saw the rapport between us at the audition. So tell me. What did she say to you?"

I sighed. "It started backstage at the audition. She said all kinds of stupid things to bait me. I managed to block it out. But"—I looked at him, the picture of ease, a demeanor I had almost never seen on him before, except after sex the last few times. He no longer looked like a man who was holding everything in. "She showed me a video."

"A video?" He frowned. "Of my early work?"

I took deep breaths, trying to stay calm and rational. "You're much younger in the video. You're...It's..." How could I say it? "In what she showed me, you're—I mean, it's definitely you, not a fake—"

"Karina, what does the video show?"

"Um. It looks like you're raping a girl in it."

A glimmer of suspicion came into his eye. "A video, you say?"

I nodded, took another breath, and let it all spill. "She said you used to do it all the time, to groupies. You'd wait until they didn't want it, and then force yourself on them, and...and...and..."

"Breathe, Karina."

I gulped. "And she said she taped it so she could confront you about your behavior instead of going to the police."

He had stopped massaging my foot, but kept his hands still and warm on my ankles. "Was that the whole story?"

"Pretty much. She only showed me one video, but she made it sound like there are more of them."

He nodded. "Let me ask you one question. Does me forcing myself on girls seem likely?"

"Well, no. And I told myself she's a nonstop liar. Still, it was pretty upsetting to see. I told myself there's surely an explanation. But if there is, that means there's something more you haven't told me."

He nodded. "Remember when I told you my past with Ferrara was sordid?"

"Yes, but you said you never slept with her."

"I didn't." He stretched tiredly. "May I tell you the other thing I've been holding back before I tell you the untold secrets about Ferrara?"

"Of course."

He shifted until he was cross-legged, facing me on the couch, my feet still in his lap. "I haven't told you yet the thing I fear."

I swallowed and said nothing, not wanting to derail him.

"You told me two things, you said, a silly fear and a serious one. I can't tell if mine is silly or serious. I think whether it is or not depends on you." He ran a hand through his hair. It was growing out longer again now, and his fingers made damp furrows. "I fear you're in love with Dom James, not Real James."

"Ah." I sat up and pulled his hands toward me. "I can see why that might be tricky. However, I have a strong feeling that Dom James is a big part of Real James. That's just part of who you are. It's part of how your sex drive works and it's part of how you love."

He gave a small nod.

"Remember, I've also met Performance Artist James—and Neurotic Artist James, too, come to think of it. Not to mention Boss Whose Staff Loves Him James, and Dancer James. In fact, Dom James is the James who's the most prone to fits of pique, petulance, and emotional turmoil." I crawled forward and kissed him on the cheek. "And yet, I love him anyway. I love all the Jameses I've met so far."

"You haven't met Rock Star James yet," he pointed out.

"I don't think Rock Star James exists. Maybe he used to, or maybe he only exists on the stage. I think that's why you're leaving him behind. There's no place for him in your life." I sat back while he let that sink in.

"I think you're right about that," he said. "Rock Star James is a creation of Ferrara's. He's who she wants. He'll fuck anything that moves, for one thing, and he's moldable, trainable; he'll do whatever she says."

I nodded. "So where does the video come into it?"

"I'm getting there. The reason I ask about how much you care about my dom persona is…well, some women—some *people*—can get that bubble burst very easily."

"You told me that. Women who had a perfect fantasy dom, or master, or king in their minds, who couldn't handle it when you were a real person. You know I'm not like that."

"I know. It's one of the reasons I've fallen so hard for you, Karina." He kissed my hand. "But there is still a thing, sometimes, where submissives especially lose all respect for a dom if they find out he ever bottomed or subbed."

"Did you forget you and I switched in Ohio?"

"I didn't forget. I'm saying it's still my instinct to be careful when telling you about my past. Because there are who those who can't handle the idea of their top bottoming."

"Hey, but I thought it was kind of normal for tops to get trained by starting at the bottom, isn't it?"

"It is, in some circles, not others. You know, people still get ideas in their heads, and when a relationship is based on ideas, on fantasies, well—"

"James. I'll say it as many times as I need to. It's the real you, not the fantasy, that I want."

"Thank you." He closed his eyes and took a deep breath, letting it out slowly. "Turn back the clock to the days when I was—as the saying goes—young, dumb, and full of come. Trying to get noticed as an artist and as a performer. I was more of a songwriter than a singer, really, but I had to sing them or no one would ever hear them. And besides, singing in clubs was an excellent way to meet sex partners, something I had a keen interest in at the time. Ferrara and her husband courted me. At the time I made no distinction between them wanting me for the record label and wanting me for anything else. Maybe they didn't make a distinction either. Anyway. She's the one who introduced me to the society."

"Yeah, you told me that."

"What I didn't tell you was that she insisted I go through six months as a trainee."

"Really?" The thought of James prancing about half-naked while rich men and women paddled his bum when they felt like it was a shocking thought. "Did you like it?"

"Not particularly. I liked that I had found this haven of sexuality that was unlike anything I knew of in the rest of the world, and I was at the age when I was game to try anything to do with sex. However, there's no getting around the fact that I am essentially dominant by nature. I didn't get much out of submitting to others or in serving them, except as a kind of acting exercise.

"The one person I was concerned with pleasing, though, was Ferrara, and not merely because she and Huntington were the avenue for a record deal. Her idea of being a loyal wife was that she never had intercourse with anyone except her husband. But that one rule left a lot of leeway. She would blindfold him, put earplugs in his ears and headphones on top of that, and mummify him so the only parts of him that were accessible were his face and his cock. She'd have slave girls fluff him with their mouths. And then to arouse herself enough to ride him, she liked to see me dominate other women." He didn't meet my eyes. Rather than blushing he looked bloodless, as if telling me this was draining him. Or maybe he was that tired. "Tell me about the video you saw."

"Well, there's a girl lying on top of the covers of a bed, wearing a kind of see-through nightgown."

"Looking rather ready to be ravished?"

"Yeah, now that you mention it. And you, um…" I closed my eyes, trying to sort out the images, which had turned into a jumble in my head. "First you kind of teased her like you were trying not to wake her up, and then you sort of leaped on her."

"Was there a struggle?"

"Yes. She fought you, and you choked her and told her to lie still, and then she almost got away, but you pounced on her back and put a gag in her mouth since she was protesting so much. That was all I saw."

He took my hands in his. "Your hands are shaking."

"The way she screamed was pretty convincing."

"If it's who I think it was, she's a very good actress. Didn't you recognize Vanette?"

I blinked and sat up straight. "What?"

"Have you ever seen her without makeup and her hair down?"

"No! Are you sure that was her?"

"If it's the scene I remember, yes, it's her. And it took place in one of the bedrooms at the society's club in London."

I thought back to what it had looked like. "You know, I was so focused on you and her, I didn't even look at the room. Or really look at her face." What I remembered, though, certainly didn't contradict the idea.

"I'm certain Vanette would confirm the story if you asked her about it," he said. "We were both trainees then. She was developing a specialty in ravishment."

"Ravishment?"

"For those members who wanted to playact that they were forcing her. Some of them had elaborate scenarios, with bodices to rip from the lady of the house and that sort of thing, while others were just playing at intruder in the night." He shrugged. "It was one of her favorite things. She was brilliant. Could cry on cue. I certainly couldn't have played her part."

I shifted until I was lying against his chest. "All right. Is that the whole story, then? No more secrets left in the closet?"

"Pretty much. I mean, there are more scenes I could describe, but I think you get the gist. Now, where is that coffee I ordered?" He tightened his arms around me.

"And that was what you were worried about? That I would flip out if I found out how it really was?"

"Well, there is one more thing you should know. The whole reason my recording career has been kept a secret from my mother is because I met Ferrara and did these things for her before she gave me the recording contract."

"So it really was the 'casting couch' but with the genders reversed?"

"Not really, but you can see how someone could interpret it that way. My mother, I feared, would interpret it as extortion, that these people from the entertainment world had corrupted her son and extorted sexual favors from me in exchange for the contract. I feared she'd try to put a stop to it. I most certainly didn't want that. When you're young and have stars in your eyes…" He shrugged. "Understand, I didn't feel taken advantage of. I didn't feel preyed upon. It merely seemed a part of the world I was entering. I thought, when I bothered to think at all, that it was cool that this kinky, wild woman was into me. In the beginning, of course, she kept me hooked with a continual thread of teasing that one day she might let me fuck her. She might as well have put a ring through my nose and led me around by a chain; that's how hooked I was."

"I can imagine." He had certainly learned how to apply delayed gratification and withholding to his own advantage. Not that I minded. "Are you ever going to tell your mother?"

"I plan to tell her about Lord Lightning someday. But not today." He nuzzled me. "I imagine I'll tell her about *you* long before that."

"Have you not told her yet?"

"Sweetness, the moment I tell her, she will demand to meet you. Let's get past the show and put that all behind us, and then we can fly to London to meet her. Or perhaps she'll be ready for a trip to New York. She does love the city."

There was a knock at the door. Most likely the coffee. I excused myself to the restroom while James answered the door. I heard the room service cart being wheeled in.

When I came out, the waiter was getting James's signature. He was an older man and his white tuxedo jacket looked a little too small for him. He was holding a hardcover book and James was signing the check using the book as a surface.

"Thank you, sir," the waiter said, and I suddenly recognized his voice.

"Phil Betancourt?" The man who had stolen my mother's engagement ring and who knew what else was standing there, right in front of me.

"Um. My name's José," he said, and then broke for the door.

Thirteen

People on the Edge of the Night

Betancourt took off like a sprinter. James lunged for him but missed, and then went tearing off down the hallway after him. I wanted to follow right after, but I was worried that we'd get locked out of the room. I went back through my own room and grabbed my key, then hurried down the hall in the direction they'd gone.

I met James coming out of the door behind the elevator lobby that led to the service elevators and laundry. He was shaking his head. "Lost him. You're certain that was Betancourt?"

"Sure of it. What did he want, though?" We walked back to the room together and went through my room into his again. "Spying on me? Or you?"

"I'll call Stefan and hotel security. Meanwhile, you should call your mother to be sure there's been no more trouble for her at home."

"All right." I went into my room and got dressed while waiting for my mother to pick up the phone. She eventually did.

"Karina! How are you, dearest?"

"Fine, Mom. Are you in the bathroom?" I could hear the echo of the tile.

"I have you on speaker. I'm curling my hair. It's grown out so much and Velvet showed me a great way to do it."

"Awesome. Hey, has there been any more trouble from your ex?"

"I have not heard a peep, dear. No sign of him. I think you were right. He must have been no more than a common criminal and is certainly not worth my expending any more thought about. Did I tell you I met a nice man at the gym?"

"Um, no."

"He's a research librarian at a university in Chicago, but he's here on sabbatical while he takes care of his aging mother after she had a fall."

I wondered if the aging mother was real or if this was another one of her ways to work herself into a conversation. "That's sweet."

"He is. So smart. We're going to a book club together tomorrow night, and the Rosemonts are coming over for dinner Friday. His mother's in bed asleep by seven every night. Can you believe that? So he's free every night of the week."

"That sounds great, Mom. Just take it slow, okay?"

"Oh, I'm taking it very slow. Don't worry. I've only let him kiss me so far."

"Mom!" I really did not want to hear about her sex life.

"Honestly, Karina, you'd think your generation had invented dating."

"I'm just saying if you're seeing him every night of the week, that doesn't sound like going slow to me."

She was silent a moment, and I heard the clack of the curling iron being put down. She picked up the phone then. "Karina, I know you want the best for me, but let's get one thing straight. You've made it completely clear to me I don't get to pick your boyfriends. Well, you don't get to pick mine."

"Okay! Okay, Mom, yes, I totally agree with that. I wasn't trying to criticize your choice. He sounds great. It's just, you know, after what happened, I get worried."

"Well, now you know how I felt after you and your sister moved to New York City," she said smugly. "Stop worrying. I admit I may have done some unwise, maybe even nonsensical, things in the past. God forbid you should be alone when you're older, Karina. I don't wish this lesson on anyone, even if I do wish you'd understand me better."

"Okay. I'm sorry, Mom. I guess I just didn't think. You know, I always think of you as so self-sufficient. You did such a great job raising us as a single mom. We certainly never felt you needed a man around."

"There's a big difference between needing a man and wanting a man," my mother said.

"Yeah. Well, keep me and Jill posted about how it goes."

"I will, darling. Speaking of Jill, she told me you're in Las Vegas? I thought you were going to rewrite your thesis."

"I am, but I have a couple of months to do it and this chance to be in a dance production came up."

"You didn't tell me you had started dancing again! Karina, that's wonderful!"

"Well, I just found out today that I got the part."

"Even more wonderful! Should I start making plans to come see this show?"

"Oh, maybe! I'll get the dates and details and send them to you."

"And what about your own man situation? You haven't even mentioned him yet. Does that mean you're quits now, and off to Vegas like a showgirl?"

"Goodness, no, Mom. We're getting along pretty well now. I mean, it's not all smooth sailing, and right now he's got this crazy ex trying to make our lives difficult, but I think it's going to work out eventually. He's here, too..." I heard a knock and went to look through the peephole, but I didn't see anyone in the hallway.

"So glad to hear it. Was there anything else you needed, Karina? My hair's done and I have to go soon."

"No, that was it. Bye, Mom. Have fun."

"Give your fella a kiss on the cheek from me, then, dear. Bye."

I hung up the phone. My mother had gotten really direct after that blow to the head. I think I liked her this way, but it was going to take some getting used to.

The knock came again and I realized it was coming from the connecting door. I opened it and Stefan came in with two men from hotel security. "We're checking for spy devices," he said. His expression was as serious as I'd ever seen it. All trace of his usual baby-faced look was gone.

"Spy devices?"

"Bugs, cameras, that sort of thing. Just in case." He was trying to sound light, but he failed.

James spoke to him from the doorway. "Have you heard from your contact with the local police?"

"Oh, yes." Now Stefan cracked a small smile. "They'd be all ears, if we were to involve them."

One of the two suited men with Stefan spoke up. "We'd prefer to handle it internally, of course."

"As would we," James said. "But I like to know where we stand. Good work, Stefan."

I followed James back into the suite. He shed the robe and slipped back into bed.

I crawled across the bedspread to kiss him on the cheek. "There. That's from my mother. She says everything's fine."

"Excellent," he said with another yawn. "Stefan told me that in Ohio he suspected you were being tailed."

"He told me it wasn't unusual for your car to be followed."

"No, no. I mean he suspected you were the one being tailed. And it's too much of a coincidence for Betancourt to show up here right after Ferrara spoke to you. He and Ferrara must be working together."

"Ohhh. And you think that's how they met? He was following me while she was following you?"

"Something like that. Perhaps he had your mother's house staked out. Anyway. If he fled here to report to her, Ferrara probably knows by now that her bid to get you to leave me didn't work." He yawned again and closed his eyes.

"Tsk. Here we are in one of the most exciting cities in the world, and you're falling asleep," I teased.

"You try getting by on four hours of sleep in the last forty-eight," he said. "No one's heard from Ferrara or seen her since her visit to you. And her things are gone from her room downstairs. I wonder if she has withdrawn from the field of battle." He yawned again. "I'll have to worry about her later. How about you? Want a nap?"

"I suppose a little rest couldn't hurt."

"Excellent. Get undressed and come under the covers."

I looked behind me at the door connecting to my room. The men were still in there, poking around. I slid under the covers and undressed while under them, flinging my clothes off the bed one item at a time.

James was in satin pajama bottoms and nothing else. He groaned as I pressed myself against him.

"You'd think I'd be completely sated," he complained.

I slid my hand up his leg to find him hard and needy again. "Here." I slipped my hand under his waistband and stroked him gently. "Bet I can make you come in under two minutes. And then you can nap in peace."

"You bet? What do you wager if you fail?"

"That'll be up to you, but I won't fail."

"All right, sweetness. Go to it."

I licked the palm of my hand and began to stroke him. Two minutes might be ambitious, but I figured whatever penalty he decided to exact if I failed would be as much fun as any reward for success. BDSM was win-win that way.

I'm sure it was longer than two minutes. More like four, before he was straining and groaning in my hand, his own long fingers interlacing with mine in the final seconds before he erupted. He curled away from me, pulling me to spoon with him as he quaked through the aftershocks, and then was asleep before either of us could let go.

The men were gone from next door. Once I was sure James was deeply asleep, I slipped out of the bed to clean up. There wasn't much, since he hadn't had time to replenish his supply. Then I got back in and snoozed contentedly with him.

*   *   *

When I woke, he was sitting up in bed with his phone, apparently texting back and forth with someone. He saw I was awake and reached down to stroke my hair.

"Anything going on?" I asked.

"Nothing exciting," he answered. "Get this. Ferrara told Alicia she was checking into a different hotel because she developed a sudden gluten allergy and the pasta bar in the restaurant here was setting it off."

"That sounds less than plausible."

"If she is caught out she will no doubt say she made up the story to protect our sensibilities from a more awful truth." He shook his head. "Am I terribly cold to her? I'm afraid I've grown very hardened to her nonstop attempts to rouse my sympathies, whether fake or genuine."

"I'm probably not a good judge of that," I admitted.

"It's a large reason why I want to get out of the business," he said. "To get free of her. Her advances after she divorced her husband became relentless. I don't think I've convinced her that the way I felt when I was a starry-eyed, horny twenty-year-old isn't how I feel about her now. I thought I had at least convinced her to give it up, but as we know, what I thought was a done deal didn't stick."

"What's she going to do when she finds out her ploy to get me to leave you didn't work?"

"No idea. I will worry about it once we know." He turned to me, setting the phone aside and propping his head up on one folded arm. "Let's go out."

"Out?"

"Yes. I have an idea." He slipped from the bed fully naked and retrieved one of his suitcases, which looked like they hadn't been opened since he'd arrived earlier. He lifted it onto the bed. When he unzipped it, at first all I could see was folded clothes. Then he dug through and took some items out. He tossed something toward me that looked at first glance like a small dog caught in a net.

A wig. I took it out of the net and held it up. Sandy-colored, shoulder length. "Is this for you or for me?"

He took out another one, orange-red and spiky, and twirled it on his finger. "Which one would I look least like myself in?"

"I've never seen your hair orange before…"

"All right. Wait, I have another red one for you." He dug into another pocket and brought out a long wig, gently wavy, in a red auburn color.

I tried to pull it over my head, but he wagged his finger at me. "There's a way to do it. I'll show you."

Next thing I knew, we were in the bathroom, and he was using bobby pins to secure my hair atop my head so that no stray bits hung down. He showed the inside of the wig where tiny combs clipped to my hair.

"Shake your head."

I shook it gently at first, as if saying "no" to him, then more vigorously, like a go-go dancer. The wig stayed secure. "That's amazing."

"Let me make up your face, too."

"You know how to do makeup?"

He looked at me impatiently. "Do you doubt me?"

"Well, yeah. Most guys—"

"Have I ever struck you as anything like most guys?"

"No…"

"Bend over. Ten for that."

I grinned as I felt a sudden thrill like the start of a roller-coaster ride. "Yes, James." Why had I even bothered to pull a bathrobe on? I let it drop, leaned over, and braced my hands on the side of the tub.

I expected him to start light and ramp up, but no, the smacks were fierce and quick and over in a flash, leaving me gasping and suddenly very wet.

"Stay still," he said, and in the bathroom mirror I could see his erection coming to full hardness. He stepped close, running his hand up and down my reddened ass, and then using one finger to test how wet I was. He made a pleased, satisfied noise when he felt the ample slickness.

"You have my body trained," I gasped as he slid one finger into me.

"No," he corrected. "I have *you* trained."

"Yes, James." I blushed at how proud he sounded as he'd said it.

"Let's see if we can train you a bit more. Come suck on the head of my cock. Only the head."

I started to kneel, but he said, "No, no, stay bent over. Put your hands behind your back. And walk over here." He hefted his balls, making the head and shaft of him bounce up and down.

I put my hands behind my back and walked toward him like some kind of awkward, hungry flamingo, my mouth open and reaching for the prize that awaited me.

But as I was about to close my lips over him, he stepped backward, out of reach. I took another step forward, and again he teased me by backing up, stepping out of the bathroom this time. He led me that way, like a horse and a carrot, until he was up against one of the beds and sat on the edge. My mouth closed over the tip of him.

"Now. Suck gently, gently, good. Now swirl your tongue in a circle. Fantastic." He stood and I stayed with him, never letting his cock free. "Try to stay still now," he said, as he pushed himself more deeply into my mouth, and then deeper, and deeper until I gagged. He withdrew slowly, seemingly not bothered by my coughing with him still in my mouth. "Good girl. Try to take another inch this time."

He thrust in and again I gagged, this time gasping to try to catch my breath, which had only been cut off for a second, but that was enough to kick in my instinct.

"Do you know why I love putting my cock in your mouth?" he asked.

I shook my head, not wanting to let go of it unless told to.

"First and foremost, because I can. That it feels good is also a plus. That you do it so obediently is another. That it brings tears to your eyes and tests your control"—he grabbed me by the wig and thrust three, four, five times into my throat, making me gag and snort, then changed to holding me by the chin with one hand, slapping my tongue with the head of his cock with the other—"that is wonderful. Hands on top of your head."

I laced my fingers and put them on top of my head, atop the wig.

"Keep your tongue out."

He kept slapping my tongue with his cock, then switched to slapping my face with it, wetting my cheeks while I kept my tongue extended.

Then he put his cock back into my mouth and thrust deep,

though not deep enough to choke me. "Suck," he said, and as I did, he slapped me lightly on the cheek. It barely hurt the slap was so light, but it startled me.

After that one I was prepared for him to do it again, and as he thrust in and out of my mouth, he slapped me on one cheek and then the other, several slaps to each side.

Then he thrust again hard enough to cause tears to spring into my eyes, only this time as he switched to gentle thrusts, my sobs and spasms didn't subside. I was crying for real.

He pulled free as soon as he realized I was crying and cupped my cheek tenderly, searching my face for the source of my distress. I only cried harder and as I sank to my knees he kissed me lovingly. "Good girl," he whispered.

I felt a sudden pang of relief and my breath went out of me in the rush. Just like that, the storm cloud that had rained tears dissipated and the sun came out. He kissed me again, slipping to the floor next to me. Dear James. I turned the kiss more passionate, and by the time he paused to take a breath, I had almost put the sudden bout of tears out of my mind.

But he hadn't. "You all right?"

"Fine." I took a deep breath.

He caressed my cheek, wiping away some of the dampness with his thumb. "What was going through your mind, sweetness?"

I thought back to the moment. "Not a really coherent thought, just a feeling that...I don't know. You never hit me in the face before."

He kissed me on one cheek, then the other, looking into my eyes with concern. "They say we react instinctually to being struck in the face differently from anywhere else on the body."

"Huh. Yeah. I guess I felt a little shocked. And then I wondered if I had done something to make you angry or disappointed you somehow."

"Not at all, sweetness. There was nothing more in it than it was exciting to slap you while taking your mouth. Nothing more than how enticing and beautiful and thoroughly mine you looked." He planted another kiss on my lips.

"You know what makes me feel thoroughly yours?" I whispered as he pulled away. "How protective you're being of me now."

"I don't take your tears lightly," he said. "How are you feeling now?"

"Much better." I grinned. "So I'm beautiful while I'm blowing you. Good to know."

He smiled back at me. "I'm glad I waited to do your makeup until now, though."

"Ha! I thought the runny mascara look was in nowadays."

He stood and offered a hand to help me up. Once I was standing, he pulled something else from the suitcase, a slim, peach-colored dress, almost more like a long T-shirt, but a bit flared at the hem. I pulled it carefully over the wig and shimmied to settle it over my hips. The hem fell at mid-thigh.

"Should I go back to my room to get underwear?" I asked.

"No," he said casually, beckoning me into the bathroom. He put down the lid of the toilet and washed my face gently with a washcloth, then retrieved a zippered makeup case. I sat quietly while he worked on my eyes, my cheeks. His hands felt deft and sure on my face.

"Now, have a look." He swept his hand toward the big mirror.

I stood and looked. My eyes were huge, my cheekbones

high, and my chin an elfin point. With the wig it barely
looked like me, and I said so.

"That's the point," he said with a smile. He stood behind
me and kissed me on top of the wig. "If only I had some
appropriate rope, I'd tie you a thong to wear between your
legs. Lift up your dress and show me your pussy."

His eyes were on my reflection, and I pinched the fabric of
the dress in my fingers and lifted slowly, baring myself.

"Perhaps we'll do that another time. I'd tie a thong shape
over your hips and through the middle of your legs. If I
wanted to be cruel, I'd leave a knot right over your clit, which
you'd feel with every step you took. Then we'd go walking
up and down the Strip."

"Until I was so wet I was leaving footprints?"

"Or maybe until your clit was so engorged you were beg-
ging me for some other torment. Anything else. I wonder
what I'd make you do to earn some relief. Expose yourself to
a stranger? Service me secretly with your hand? Take another
Ben Wa ball?"

"We haven't played with those in a while."

"Was that a request?"

"Maybe. Although it might not be the best idea if I have
no underwear on."

"It might not be the best idea if I want to fuck you on a
whim." He rubbed his erect cock against my back. "Now,
let's go, before I am tempted to succumb to my whims right
here."

He got dressed, in blue jeans and a tank top, a loose,
short-sleeved shirt over it. The jeans were somewhat baggy,
meaning his erection wasn't completely obvious. He put the
orange spiky wig on and it looked surprisingly natural on

him. His pale skin made the red hair seem fitting and gave him an almost Irish look.

In the mirror we looked like a pair of tourists, which I guess was the point.

Out we went, and caught a cab, and James directed the driver to take us to the Strip. We drove past several casinos, the Luxor looking like a pyramid from outer space, New York New York with its funny, crunched version of the big city skyline, the Eiffel Tower of "Paris." We got out in front of Paris, in fact, and then walked a bit, James holding my hand. The sun had set and crowds of people were making their way up and down the wide sidewalks. James steered us around hawkers handing out flyers and coupons. I was very aware of my lack of panties. I knew no one could see, but I could feel my slick lips rubbing together as we crossed the avenue on a pedestrian bridge.

"Have you seen the fountains?" he asked.

"I haven't seen anything but the inside of the hotel, the inside of the van, and the inside of the theater."

"I meant on TV or in movies, but it doesn't matter. Here they are."

We descended from the bridge and joined a group of people all looking expectantly toward the palatial front of the Bellagio and the dark lake of water in front of it. Behind us, crowds continued to go up and down the avenue, but in the tightly packed group of spectators by the railing, everyone faced the same direction. James stood behind me, his arms around me.

Music began to play and sprays of water waved back and forth, lit from below by lights. I recognized the tune, "All That Jazz." As the music reached a crescendo, all the jets shot upward at once, and I sucked in a breath at the powerful display. A sound like thunder mixed with the music as the water fell back into the pool. James rubbed himself against my back and I felt how rigid he was.

When the song ended, most people turned to wander on, but many lingered.

"The next song will start in about ten minutes," James said. "Let's stay for one more." He led me to the edge of the ornate, concrete railing, under a tree. He leaned against the corner of the railing and I settled back against him so we could people-watch while we waited for the fountains to begin again.

A constant parade of people made their way up and down the Strip while others lingered like we were, waiting for the next show. Compared to many of the glitzy, lit-up places on the Strip, the spot we were in was relatively dim. There were many trees planted along the edge of the water, I supposed to make an oasis of darkness so that the bright lights in the fountain would look more dramatic. Crowds were still stopping to take photos at the railing, catching the lit-up Bellagio in the background on one side, or Paris on the other side of the street.

One couple had clearly come directly from a wedding chapel. They were in typical tourist wear, flip-flops and shorts, but she had a short veil in her hair and a small bouquet clutched in her hand, and he was wearing a bow tie around his neck like a collar. They were beaming with giddy, fat-cheeked smiles, and trailed by a happy, drunken entourage of well-wishers. After they took some smoochy photos with the Bellagio as a backdrop, she climbed precariously onto the concrete rail and flung the bouquet into the air. It came apart as it flew and flowers rained down on the laughing group.

"See! You're all next! YOU'RE ALL GETTING MARRIED NEXT!" she squealed, while her beau held her steady and kept her from falling into the fountain. He helped her down as the next song began to play.

James chuckled. I wasn't sure what was funny at first, until I recognized his voice. It was a Lord Lightning song.

A huge spray of water and light shot up into the air and people *ooh*ed like they did at fireworks.

James murmured in my ear, "Everyone is looking at the show." Meaning, *No one is looking at us.* He slid his hand up my thigh.

I swallowed and sucked in a breath as his other hand lifted my dress. I felt air on the damp part of my thighs. Was he lifting it high enough that if the bride and groom in front of us turned around, they'd see all of me? One of his fingers snaked lazily between my lips and circled my clit. I held in a moan as my arousal leaped.

Then he slid his hands down my legs again, smoothing my dress. "How far will you let me go, Karina?" he said into my ear, as the fountains danced.

Everything between my legs was throbbing in time with the music. There were a thousand sensible reasons why we shouldn't tempt fate here. But lust overrode sense. I turned my head to say "All the way" as I reached back and tugged on his hips.

"Are you sure?" He slid his palms over my nipples, which were hard as glass. "I would love to lift you onto my cock right now. You're plenty wet. Your dress would hide it. But nothing would hide the look of ecstasy on your face."

I wiggled back against him, trying to be as much of a tease to him as he was to me.

But the song came to an end and he stood up straight, turning me to face him and kissing me as the final chords played, then faded.

"Can we stay through one more song?" I asked, my arms around his neck.

"I'm not sure either of us has the patience for that," he said.

"James." I ground my hips against him.

"Patience," he repeated. "I know. You want to push the envelope. You want to go further, do more than we've ever done before. The more deeply in love with you I fall, the more I do, too." He spun us in a slow circle, like we were in the center of the world's grandest ballroom.

I remembered what he'd said, about discipline and self-discipline being equally important. About control. Ferrara was the one who was going too far and getting too carried away. "You have a point."

"I want nothing more than for all of this to be over with. Ferrara, the rehearsals, the contract, I want all of it behind me so I can concentrate on you. Hmm. Maybe I will build a playroom or a dungeon after all, once I'm done having you in every other room in every twisted way my mind can imagine."

"You tease."

"Always. Or at least until we get back to the room." He smirked. "Come on."

As we walked away, hand in hand, a young man in a military uniform at the railing dropped to one knee next to us and held a velvet box up toward the shocked woman beside him. Camera flashes lit up their faces as she grabbed him and kissed him. I guess that meant yes.

Fourteen

Your Soothing Hand

Rehearsal started for real the next day. Before we left the room in the morning, as we were finishing our room service breakfast, James said to me, "I want to ask you something. About how you relate to the other dancers. Because you have the role of principal, that already sets you apart from them somewhat."

"Is that a problem?"

"I'm getting to the question. I don't think we should pretend anymore."

"Pretend what?"

"That you're just another dancer."

My heart jumped suddenly into double-time. "You mean, tell them about us?" I hadn't thought James would be so ready to acknowledge me.

He nodded. "Even if you could keep up the facade, I don't think I can. I'll be too tempted to put my arm around you, look lovingly at you, and kiss you when the opportunity arises." James was trying hard to maintain his usual cool exterior, but he couldn't keep himself from a smoldering smile. Which was his point. "I'll try, if you think it'll make things too difficult for you with the others, but I don't think I'll succeed."

"What if they turn catty like Ferrara and hiss at me?"

"On the contrary, I think they'll be highly amused to see me letting my hair down. I expect we might both have to accept some good-natured ribbing, though, Karina."

"Why, because I'm the new dancer? Or because these people are your extended family?"

"There is that word 'or' again. Can you think of a reason it wouldn't be both those things?"

"Ha-ha, no. But I'm right, aren't I? These folks are your real family."

"You may be right about that." His eyelashes looked long as he dropped his gaze to the empty plate in front of him.

"I know I am. I've never seen you more comfortable around people. They clearly have a lot of history with you, and a lot of affection for you."

"Performing together builds a certain kind of bond," he said, as if it needed explaining.

"So does sharing a secret," I pointed out. He nodded as if he agreed with that, too.

When we got to the theater I realized my analogy of the troupe and crew being his extended family was even more apt when I met his "brothers," the musicians in his band. In contrast to James's groomed appearance, they were a disreputable-looking lot, sitting at a front table and talking cheerfully like they owned the place.

James would be splitting his time between rehearsing with us and rehearsing with them. They were still writing some of the music, though from the signs of jet lag on their faces, it would be another day or two before they were up to the task. For the next several days, as Alicia taught us the steps, it was mostly to her counting out the beats, anyway. I worked a lot with Ben and Pascual, who each learned all of James's parts as well as an ensemble role. When I was up close with them, of course, I could tell they weren't James, but they were really excellent mimics. During one lunch break, Pascual entertained the group by imitating Roland, only to be one-upped by Ben, who did an impression of Annika. I literally laughed so hard I rolled on the floor. (It helped that I was already sitting on the stage at the time.)

We settled into a comfortable routine of rehearsal. There was no sign of Ferrara or Phil for more than a week, and I was beginning to think maybe we weren't going to hear from them again. James often had dinner delivered to his suite in the evenings, and invited various people to join him on different nights. That night it was Alicia and Ramon, and the four of us shared a bottle of wine and talked.

At one point James excused himself to take a phone call, so I asked Alicia, "How long have you been working with James?"

She glanced around instinctively, then relaxed as she realized all three of us were in that exclusive club that could call him by name.

"Almost ten years." She counted backward on her fingers. "Yeah. Ten years. Time flies when you're having fun!"

"Did he always do such elaborate stage shows?"

"Oh, not always thematic operas like this one, but he usually had a dance component to his live performances. He was much more raw in the beginning."

I had no idea what he had been like ten years before, though Becky kept telling me to watch the old videos. "Raw?"

"Well, you know how he is. He's physically expressive when he wants to be, but he was more or less untrained as a dancer. Self-taught. But Sabine whipped him into shape quickly."

"Did she?"

"Oh yes. Polished off all the rough edges, the asymmetries. I'd say it took two years of fairly diligent work to really give him the chops he has now, though." Alicia took a sip of her wine. "You look fascinated."

"I am fascinated! Not every rock star has legit moves."

"Not every rock star works as hard as he does."

Ramon lifted his wineglass. "Amen to that. Now, seriously, how does a workaholic like that retire?" He looked at me for an answer.

I shrugged. "I think he'll find other things to do. He said the music industry is too depressing. Too many crooks and liars."

"He's right about that," Alicia said with a sigh. "I keep hoping he'll go more seriously into conceptual dance."

Ramon snorted into his wineglass. "He keeps hoping *you'll* go more seriously into conceptual dance. You could be the next Moses Pendleton, Alicia. You know he'll bankroll it if you say the word."

"Yeah, yeah. If he's retiring for real this time, maybe it is time for me to think about that. It's a risk, though."

"Art always is," Ramon said.

James returned to the room, a dire scowl on his face and Chandra in tow. Before any of us could ask what was wrong, he put his phone down in the middle of the table. It was in speakerphone mode. "Go on, Ferrara. Why don't you say to everyone here what you said to me just now? Issue your ultimatum."

"Oh, do you have your guard dogs there?" Ferrara's voice was thin but recognizable. "It doesn't matter anyway. They can't keep you out of court. James Byron LeStrange, you married me in secret and now you're trying to deny it."

This time it was my heart that jumped into my throat at the sound of his name.

"You're deluded. Utterly deluded," he said.

"Name-calling will get you nowhere. I have proof. So here are your choices. One, we carry on as husband and wife—"

"Never."

"Or, two, we go through divorce court, where I drag your name through the mud and take you for everything you're worth, you heartless bastard."

She made a snuffling noise and I wondered if we were supposed to think she was crying, or if she had allergies.

"Ferrara, don't be ridiculous. Listen to me. You can't force me to have feelings for you that I don't have. There has to be something we can work out."

"Something like what, James? You mean something like a payout? Why would I settle for any less than a good divorce lawyer would get me? In fact, since we're looking at the breakup of not only our marriage but the loss of my company's most vital intellectual property, hmm." She paused as if doing math. "How much would you earn for the record company if you kept your career going? I'd say that would be at least a gross income of twenty-five million dollars."

"That—"

"*Per year.*"

"What!"

"For ten years. Plus half your current assets. Half of every-thing you're worth is what I'd get in a divorce. Including half the inheritance you'll be getting from your mother."

James clenched his jaw, struggling to stay cool. "My mother is in perfect health and if you are thinking to threaten her you are making a grave mistake."

"James, James, James. I'm merely pointing out the folly of trying to pay me to go away."

"You are insane."

"How about this? Why don't we go on a honeymoon together? Our wedding night would truly be one to remem-ber, don't you think? And we can have some quality time away from work and stress. I know that work has really come between us. Three weeks on the Riviera, or Paris? Perhaps after that if you are truly not convinced we belong together we could discuss an amicable separation agree—"

"Insane, I tell you!"

"Think it over. I'll talk to you tomorrow." There was a beep as she hung up.

Alicia's mouth was hanging open with shock. "What an unbelievable witch! My God. I knew she was terrible, but I didn't think she was this terrible."

Ramon was just shaking his head.

James was gritting his teeth so hard it was a wonder they didn't crack.

"Is she really going to take you to court?" I asked. "Hasn't she threatened that before?"

James closed his eyes. "This is the first time she has laid out her terms so plainly..."

Alicia frowned. "I don't quite understand the outlandish marriage claims. Even mistresses have had some wins in court."

James shook his head. "She was never my mistress."

"Oho." Ramon perked up suddenly. "So you mean she's trying to get you in bed for the first time?"

"Essentially." James let out a long breath. "It's rather complicated."

Alicia nodded. "I hate to say it, but maybe what she needs is to get laid. Maybe she'll calm down, then."

James clenched his teeth again. "She'll have to look elsewhere. I am not available. And even if I was...No. I won't be made into a whore."

"Do you know what kind of proof she has?" I asked. "She said she'd prove you were married."

"She has claimed to have proof before, but she has never shown it."

I looked at Chandra. "She claims they got married. We're here in Vegas. If it supposedly happened, it would have been here, wouldn't it?"

"That's what I suspect, anyway," he said. "Chandra, is it possible to do a search on the marriage licenses issued to see if there is one with my name on it?"

Chandra crossed her arms. "It's possible. I'm not sure how easy it is to search."

"Narrow the dates from the run of *Bride of the Blue*," I suggested. "Knowing what kind of proof she's got, or lacks, might give you some leverage."

"Definitely. I agree with you there." Chandra looked at James. "She hasn't sent you anything?"

"Nothing. As much as I would've liked to have deleted every message she ever sent me, I've been checking them all. Nothing we can use yet."

"Tell me immediately if any of you hear from her again," Chandra said. "I'll bring Stefan up to date." She swept out of the room with purpose.

Alicia and Ramon didn't linger after that, and we pushed the room service cart into the hallway.

James sat on the edge of the bed and stared at his phone like it had betrayed him somehow.

I stood to one side, wondering if his anger meant I was going to be in a lot of pain tonight.

I sat down next to him, so my hip touched his. "Hey."

It took him a moment to focus on me. "Hey."

"I have a question for you."

"Oh? A *question*-question?"

"Not sure, which is why I figure I should ask it first. You'll understand when you hear what the question is."

He tossed his hair out of his eyes. "Now I am intrigued."

"Good." I set his phone on the nightstand and held his fingers in my hands. "Would sex distract you from...everything that's bothering you? Or would it be an even bigger reminder?"

One of his eyebrows rose with his puzzlement. "Are you offering yourself as a distraction?"

"That might depend on whether you think it'll work or not." I examined his face. "If there's one thing I've learned, it's that there are a million ways to do this. BDSM, I mean. I don't want you to think I'm starting this conversation to try to seduce you if you're not in the mood. Do you see what I'm saying? But I want to know if I should...How did you put it? Offer myself?"

James lifted one of my hands to his mouth and kissed the backs of my fingers. His voice deepened. "Your hands are trembling a little."

"Are they?" Yes, I was a little nervous.

"They are. As for offering yourself"—he kissed my other hand—"your offer is always appreciated. Your willingness is one of the things I love about you most, Karina. Don't think that just because I have you all the time, I take your surrender for granted." He nuzzled my neck then and bit me just hard enough to make me suck in a breath, anticipating more pain, but the nip turned to a kiss and I melted against him.

He went on. "But I think maybe I'm still not clear on what you're asking. What about you could possibly serve as a 'bigger reminder' of Ferrara Huntington? Other than being female, you have nothing in common with her."

I swallowed. "Well, you're angry at her and you probably want to do terrible things to her, and I thought that might mean you might do them to me instead?" I shrank back a little as his ire flared.

It wasn't for the reason I feared. "Karina. Back up a moment. First of all, yes, I'm angry at her. But let's get one thing clear: I don't picture spanking her as punishment her for 'being bad,' or anything else. I don't imagine assaulting her. Spanking is only for those I love, not those I loathe."

"Okay, but wouldn't it be natural for you to work out your aggressions on me?"

"Like you're a punching bag at the gym? I had a bad day at the office and so I'm going to blow off steam by taking it out on you?" He winced. "That doesn't sound healthy, not unless we negotiated it in advance."

Ah. The picture began to clear in my mind. "When you put

it that way, I feel almost like I should offer myself for that, then. Sex is a great way to relieve tension."

He kissed the tips of my fingers separately, his eyes closed. "Yes, it is. But you're not talking about mere sex. Trust me, Karina. If you want to negotiate a scene where you role-play as Ferrara and I somehow give you her comeuppance...I have no interest in that. I want her to have no part at all in our bedroom. If you're thinking that me delivering a good, hard spanking might clear my mind and restore my bruised ego, well, yes, it might."

When he put it that way, I found myself suddenly eager for that spanking. My clit throbbed between my legs and I discovered I was gripping his fingers crushingly tight. He didn't seem to mind. He watched me very closely. I cleared my throat. "I, um, I would be honored if you would use me that way."

His voice was low. "And you're not afraid I'll let my anger get the best of me? That I might hit you too hard or demand too much because of how pissed off I am at her right now?"

I realized he had led me in a circle. We were back where I had started the conversation, but now I understood what I was asking, and what might happen. "Of course I'm afraid of that," I said. "But I think you are, too. Which is why, if it happens, I know you'll take care of me."

He pulled me close and whispered into my hair. "You're a gem. Strip and bend over, hands on the top of the dresser, legs apart."

I practically flung my clothes off in my hurry to get into position. James took his time, though, pacing back and forth behind me, brushing past my legs and trailing a finger over my bare ass as he slowly removed his clothes. I swallowed, my anticipation winding up tighter and tighter each time he passed.

"Were you spanked as a child?" he asked, his voice casual as he let his hand stray over one of the globes of my ass cheeks and then between my legs. "As a punishment."

"Not that I can recall," I said.

"Good. Remember that this isn't a punishment, Karina. I'm spanking you because you give me your body to use as I need." He trailed his erection along my thigh. He felt rock hard and all he'd done was undress. It wasn't only me he wound up by forcing himself to go slowly.

I felt him back away before his voice came from behind me. "Over my lap. Head on this side."

He was sitting on the edge of the bed. I folded myself over his knees and his warm palm came down to make circles on my butt cheeks. "Remember, if it becomes too much, you can tell me to stop."

"What word should I use?"

He chuckled that low, evil, dominant chuckle. "I would say that any of the following would work: *no, stop, don't, James I can't take it anymore.* If you think of other variations, I would like to think we communicate well enough that I won't mistake them for something else."

I grinned. "So our safe word is *no*?"

"It's a perfectly good word, isn't it?"

"Yes, James. Perfectly good." I wiggled my butt and he gave me a quick swat.

"Someone apparently really wants this spanking!" He ran his hand down my thighs.

"Well, now we've been talking about it for fifteen minutes. Of course I—!" I didn't get to finish my sentence because the first real spank landed then and made me suck in a breath. Then he matched it on the other cheek and I yelped.

The blows at first were fast, *smack-smack-smack,* but as they grew heavier and harder the pace slowed, as if he let each one sink in. My skin got redder and hotter and my ass got more sensitive as it went on, but at the same time it was like I could take more and more. Endorphins kicked in and the longer it went on, the more aroused I became, too. I wasn't quite in the right position to grind against his leg, though, but every smack felt like it went right to my clit.

Then he began to speed up again, still hitting me hard but faster now, piling each swat on top of the last, as he loosened the rigid control he had on his own passion. He struck me harder and harder, until I was screaming and crying and squirming a little, not enough to be trying to get away from the blows, but enough to make him clamp down on my back with his other arm.

And then he pulled me with him as he flung himself back on the bed, pulling me down to his chest, my legs straddling him as he went after my ass with his other hand. Now every smack really did drive my clit against him, rubbing in the gloriously rough patch of his pubic hair. He didn't tell me not to, so I drove my hips against him. He switched to both hands, smacking me on both sides at the same time, while I drove my clit against him, trying hard now to come.

Smack-smack-smack, I was getting closer and closer for a while; then I leveled off and my cries turned to whimpers.

"Get on my cock," he growled. "Now."

I lifted up on my knees, and before I could do much more, he had thrust upward into me. I had barely settled against him before the spanking began again. This time he would deliver one hard double-smack, then grip my ass and pull me toward him three or four times, grinding my clit and thrusting into me at the same time, then deliver another hard smack with both hands. I cried out equally loud on the spanks as on the thrusts, his rhythm never breaking until suddenly he pulled me down in a rib-crushing hug, driving into me and groaning almost as if he were in pain himself as he released inside of me.

I hadn't gotten there yet, but that was okay. Feeling him lose control was completely worth it.

He hadn't let go, and he was still somewhat hard inside me, when he whispered in my ear, exhausted but firm: "Make yourself come. Use your fingers if you must. Come on, Karina."

I ground against him and felt him starting to slip free of me. I didn't need my fingers, though. I was so close, I could come from rubbing on him now, just like that. Like that. *Like that!* I screamed as I spasmed, the throb spreading from my clit through my whole body.

And then he was kissing me, pulling me up so that my mouth met his, his passion completely unbridled now.

"I love you," he said, when he finally let my mouth go and caught his breath.

"I love you, too," I said. "Now, I have a question for you."

"Already?"

"Not that kind of question. That can wait until we at least clean up a little. A simpler question. My room is on that side of the suite. Who's on the other? Whoever it is had better enjoy the sound of screams."

James grinned. "I left it empty. Stefan would normally have

it, but he might need to actually sleep sometime, and something tells me sleeping through that would have been beyond even him. Now, what's your real question?"

I blinked. "I have to think of one."

He clucked his tongue and chided me jokingly. "You mean you weren't thinking of one that whole time?"

"I couldn't think of anything during that!"

"Funny. Me either. Mission accomplished, my dear." He let out a long, satisfied sigh.

"Let me check my list."

"List?"

"I made a list of questions I wanted to ask you. Back when we were separated and I was in London. Let me get it and you can pick one." I climbed carefully off him, then made a detour to the bathroom before I got my laptop.

James made a trip to the bathroom as well. "Let's get in your bed now. No wet spot."

"True."

He slid under the covers and patted the space next to him. I sat cross-legged on top of the covers and looked up the file. "Here it is." I got under the blanket next to him and showed him the list.

Why did you abandon me at the party?
Why didn't you tell me not only your name, but who you were, sooner?
When had you planned to tell me, if not then?
Is there some reason you're so hung up on secrecy?
What's the story with Lucinda?
What was art school like?
How did you meet Paulina and Michel?

Were you rivals with Damon Georgiades?

Why don't you ever talk about your father? Did you know him?

When can I meet your mother?

How did you become Lord Lightning?

Why did you keep your artist identity a secret, too?

What drew you to glass art?

How did you get into the society?

How did you know you were into BDSM in the first place?

Why do you love sex in public places so much?

Are you proud of me for turning in Renault?

Why didn't you shut off my phone?

Have you had your heart broken (before)?

"Karina," he said. "I've answered nearly all of these now. The only one we haven't touched on is…well…what drew me to glass art."

I scanned the list. "Well, nearly all is not the same as all."

He gave me a quick kiss. "Yes, I'm proud of you for turning in Renault. I didn't shut off your phone because I couldn't actually bring myself to cut you off when I knew I'd made a huge mistake."

"And the heartbreak question?"

"Oh, there was puppy love and disappointment but…I never let myself love someone enough to get my heart broken, Karina." He kissed me again. "Until now, that is."

"Let's talk about glass later," I said. "I'd rather make out than get a question answered."

His answer was another kiss that went straight to my soul.

Fifteen

Nothing Seems to Make a Dent

Ferrara waited twenty-four hours before she made her next move. By then Chandra had located the marriage license and it looked, unfortunately, legit, right down to James's signature.

We were gathered around the table in the suite, James, me, Stefan, Chandra, and Ty, who I had been seeing around but hadn't really gotten to talk to, looking at the copy of the license.

Chandra gave James a stern look. "You're absolutely sure she didn't slip you a roofie and take you off to get married at one of those drive-through places?"

"If I had any blackouts I think I'd at least remember that," James snapped. "More likely this is a forgery. My signature isn't that difficult to fake, and she has it on my recording contract. She could have copied it from there."

"Or got you to sign this when you didn't know what it was?" I asked.

"What, like signing my room service bill? I have a different signature for that."

Of course you do, I thought.

"What about the witnesses on the certificate?" Stefan asked. "Who are these other two?"

"Probably employees of the wedding chapel," Ty pointed out.

James shook his head. "And of course they don't know what I look like. So they had no way to know she was marrying an impostor. Presumably someone she taught to forge my signature. For fuck's sake."

Chandra shook her head, too. "I knew there had to be a drawback to total secrecy."

My phone chimed with a text then at the same time James's rang. He picked his up as I checked my message.

It was from Becky: *OMG Karina have you seen the video? What is going on please call me ASAP!!!!!*

James was saying into the phone, "What video?"

I called Becky immediately. "Becks, what's up?"

"Karina! Oh my God, I don't know what to do. You know how I'm the webmaster of the NYC Lord's Ladies website?"

"No, but go on."

"Well, I am. Geri couldn't do it anymore. But anyway, the reason I'm calling. Someone just sent us an anonymous video, and it's freaky and scary."

"Let me guess. It's of what looks like a woman being raped and whoever sent it is claiming it's Lord Lightning."

"Yes! Have you seen it, too?"

"Maybe. Can you send it to me?" I could hear her keyboard tapping in the background.

"Done. So it's fake, right?"

"Becks, I haven't seen it yet."

"Then how did you know?"

"One thing at a time, okay? Let me look at it. I'll call you back."

"Okay."

I hung up on her and then brought the video up on my phone.

James was just hanging up the phone himself. "That was Paulina. Someone, presumably Ferrara, has sent her a video that sounds like the one you saw, Karina."

I put my phone down in the middle of the table. "Becky got it, too. Here it is." I hit play.

What played was a highly edited version of the ravishment scene with James and Vanette. It wasn't until a minute or two in that a clear shot of his face appeared, and then it was pixelated over. Still, you could hear his voice quite clearly.

"It's fake, right?" Ty asked.

"For at least some definitions of fake, yes," James said. "That's me, and the whole scene is consensual, but no one who sees this is going to believe that."

"Which is exactly why Ferrara is using it as blackmail," Chandra said. "Did Paulina say if anyone else received it?"

"It hasn't appeared on any of the fan websites yet," James said. "But Ferrara only just sent the thing out. Once they get over their shock, I'm sure some of them will post it."

"This was a warning shot, though," I said. "She made it so that your face doesn't clearly appear, but the implication is she could release the unedited version anytime. She's trying to get you to cave."

He closed his eyes as he thought. "I can't. I can't do what she asks."

"There must be some way to stall her," Ty said. "Until we can come up with a better plan."

"Let me talk to her," I said.

"No. I don't want you anywhere near that poisonous snake," James replied automatically. "Besides, what would you say to her?"

"I don't know. I'll think of something."

James shook his head again. "No. Chandra, let's get ready for spin control. The video is out there and we need—" He looked up suddenly, looking right at me. "I have an idea."

"Let's hear it," Chandra said.

"It's something I'd rather discuss with Karina first, alone," James said, standing up.

"You're sure it's that you just can't wait to get into Karina's pants again?" Chandra chided as she stood, too. "You've really got it bad if you can't make it through a whole meeting."

Stefan and Ty were clearly trying to hide their smiles and were failing. They hurried out while Chandra sauntered, giving James a raised-eyebrow look.

I stayed seated. Once the door closed behind them I copied the raised eyebrow. "Something to ask me in private?"

He leaned on his knuckles on the table. "Yes. Though now that we're alone, I'm tempted to tell you to get on my cock before we discuss any more."

"Yes, James," I said, standing up and undoing the button on my jeans.

"Now, now, I said I was *tempted* to. That's different from telling you to."

I gave him a disappointed look. "All right. What's the idea?"

He narrowed his eyes. "You're being very impatient tonight."

"Hey, I wasn't the one who couldn't make it through a whole meeting."

He grinned. "And impertinent. So mouthy. I think you had best come here and put that mouth to some better use."

I grinned back. So that was how it was going to be tonight. "Yes, James."

He settled himself in his chair again, a few feet back from the table. I stripped off my shirt and jeans but kept my undies on for now as I crawled over to him. I made a show of putting my hands behind my back and went to work on freeing James's cock using only my mouth. His scent was intense and I drank it in like the heady perfume of an exotic flower.

He was large enough that my jaw grew tired of sucking him quickly, but he didn't let me go on too long. He lifted my chin with his fingers until I was looking in his eyes.

"The idea is we pretend the video is part of a publicity campaign for the new show." His grin was little more than the suggestion of a smirk, but the glint in his eye was predatory. "By tomorrow, everyone on the entire Internet will have seen that video and be talking about it. Then we make it seem as if we released it intentionally to get everyone buzzing. We could even follow it up with a video of our own."

"Aha. That's a brilliant idea…and I take it the video of our own would include me?" I licked my lips. From where I knelt between his legs, I could see the spot under the point of his chin where he had trouble shaving as closely as the rest of his face.

"Yes. Which was why I wanted to ask you about it in private, so you wouldn't feel put on the spot by the others." He hefted his cock with one hand, keeping his grip on my chin with the other. "Though this is a nice side benefit."

"Chandra knew the second they left we were going to do something."

"Chandra is very observant." James licked his own lips. "Reach into your panties and touch yourself."

I did as he asked while he still held my face tilted upward. He kissed me, my arousal deepening.

"I'm not sure exactly what we'll put in the video," he said. "But you have an inkling, I imagine?"

I spread my fingers apart and flicked my own clit. "Will it be more extreme than what we did at the 624 Gallery?"

"Perhaps not, though having the audience of a piece of performance art see your bare ass is one thing. It's a bit different to have it all over the Internet. So you should think it over before you agree."

"Hey, who says it's *my* ass that'll be bare in the video? You're the sex symbol."

"True." He stood, pulling me up until I was standing, too, my hand still working in my panties. "Hands behind your head."

He circled behind me and then reached around so that his hand replaced mine, and then continued talking to me as his fingers ran in slick circles over my clit. "What I haven't told anyone yet is that this actually plays perfectly into my plans for the theme of the show."

I could only make a general sound of agreement as I tried to relax into his expert touch. But then he seemed to stop talking. "And that theme is?"

"Well, I was thinking I'd explain it to the whole company in the morning at rehearsal." He lightened his touch as I tightened, nearing my peak.

"Does that mean you're not going to tell me now?"

"How about I give you a choice? Which would you rather

have delayed, your orgasm, or finding out about the show? You can have one now and one tomorrow."

"Oh, you're evil. Ah, fuck." I was too close now and didn't have the willpower to stop. "Make me come, please, James? Please, oh, God."

"Gladly, sweetness, gladly." He brought me off with one hand over my mouth, stifling my screams, while the other hand milked every last shiver of pleasure from my pussy he could wring, four or five orgasms in a row, until I was limp against him and gasping.

"One more choice for you," he murmured, as he shifted us to the edge of the bed. "Shall I come in your mouth tonight or your cunt?"

"My...cunt." I blushed intensely, trying to remember if I'd ever said the word out loud. When would I have had the chance? But it was easy to blurt out when I was this soaked in sex already. James wasted no time getting inside me, but once there, he slowly inserted himself with long, soothing strokes, in no hurry at all.

The next morning he made good on his promise to explain what the show was about, although he and Alicia ran us through the number we'd been working on for an hour first. Then he gathered all the dancers in the VIP tables around the runway of the stage while he sat on the edge, his feet hanging down. He was in his dancing clothes, but wearing an Oxford shirt over them, unbuttoned like a jacket.

"Thank you for being so patient with the artistic process," he began. "The idea for this show struck me quite suddenly and putting all the pieces together has been an interesting challenge. Since the record company wants to release a greatest hits collection, I was looking for some way to incorporate several songs from the past into a single storyline, and add one or two new songs. As it turns out, what I've come up with could only be performed here in Las Vegas."

"Does it have a burlesque theme?" Annika asked brightly.

"No, but good thought. It has a sort of futuristic bondage theme, hence the title, which is being revealed in the marketing campaign later this week: *Bonded to the Black*. The plot is simple enough. Dystopian future ruled by a master computer, which has divided people into the haves and have-nots. Nobles and serfs, or masters and slaves, if you will. Our two principals find each other. If the rigging can be done the way I want, it may end with the two of us literally flying off together. When they get together, she is elevated from mindless drudgery while he is liberated from his role as a cog in the machine."

"Kind of like *The Matrix*?" asked Pascual.

James thought a moment. "Perhaps? I was actually inspired by a Kurt Vonnegut story. The production will have a bit of a *Matrix*-y appearance though, since we'll be using a modern fetishwear look to key the metaphor of bondage. The underlying message is about consent and mutual respect being empowering."

Alicia raised her hand. "You mean 'no means no'?"

"And 'yes means yes,'" James said. "Come to think of it, that might end up in the chorus of the finale. And on T-shirts. And on that note, if you'll excuse me, now that the band is awake, I had better go and work with them."

He slipped away, while Alicia made an announcement about costume fittings and hairdresser appointments for that afternoon. After lunch we had to clear the stage for a while as some work that couldn't be done at night had to happen on the sets, and the guitar player from the band came by with a tape for Alicia of all seventeen songs that would be in the production. Only six would have the full complement of dancers, including the opening overture and the finale, and two others would have a small ensemble of me, Annika, Ben, Pascual—and James.

I had my costume fitting early in the afternoon and then was sitting around listening to the tape with some of the others when I got another text from Becky.

Another video. This one's worse. Or better. Depending on how you look at it.

I excused myself from the group. From a stall in the women's room I texted James to let him know, and then I put my headphones in and texted Becky back. A few minutes later I was watching a video.

She was right. This one wasn't as "bad" in that there was no fake rape. No. It was a shaky, grainy cell phone video taken at what was clearly a Las Vegas wedding chapel. Ferrara holding the phone and pointing it at herself as she primped her miniature veil and mugged for the camera, then pointing it quickly at her tall, blond groom.

At a glance it sure looked like James. But the camera never focused on his face except as it tried to capture the actual kiss after the vows, and then it was Ferrara's face we could make out, not his.

The entire ceremony couldn't have been more than five minutes long, and this was an edit of it.

A text came from James. *Have you seen it?*

I texted back. *Yes. It's of Ferrara and someone who looks a lot like you getting married in a Vegas wedding chapel.*

James's sarcasm came through, even in a text: *Gee, I wonder where she would find someone who looked just like me for her charade? Tell Ben and Pascual I need to meet with you all. I'll be there shortly.*

Of course. I should have thought of Ben and Pascual myself!

I went back into the green room and found Annika first. For half a second I couldn't remember which name I was supposed to use for James. Not Jules...What was his dancer nickname? Jasper. Right. "Jasper wants a meeting with the small ensemble. Are Pascual and Ben here?"

She looked around. "I just saw Ben go into the men's room. Pascual might be outside the door?"

"I'll get Ben if you look for Pascual."

"Okay."

I caught Ben coming out of the restroom and led him back to the green room. Annika had Pascual in tow. We sat down together. My plan of having it look like it was about discussing the small ensemble pieces worked perfectly. Annika had no idea there was anything wrong, so she chatted away, keeping the other two fully engaged so they had no chance to notice I was a little distracted.

When James came sweeping in, the first thing he did was kiss me on the cheek. Then he looked around at our little group. "I'll talk to the boys first," he said, "but come with me in the car. Multitasking is my life."

If the two of them found this in any way odd, they didn't let on. I peeked out the side door as they got into the car. Stefan was driving one of the larger limos today.

Well, that would be an interesting ride, I was sure. If one of them was guilty, he certainly couldn't run away easily. And the car was probably a lot harder to bug or eavesdrop on than a room like this one.

When James hadn't returned by the time we wrapped for the evening, I went back to the hotel in the van with the rest of the crew. Upstairs, Ty made a nightly check of our rooms to be sure no new surveillance devices had appeared. After he left, I checked my e-mail and then saw I had a video chat request from Becky.

I joined the video chat to find Becky, Paulina, and Michel already in mid-chat.

"Karina!" Becky exclaimed. "Oh my goodness, this is so exciting!"

"Which thing is so exciting, Becks? Fill me in."

"Okay, so I'm all set to come out there and interview people for my thesis, right? And then Paul and Misha told me they were talking with him about spreading these videos around, and so I'm going to do these promo videos, too, while I'm there. I'm flying in tomorrow."

It took me a moment to realize that she wasn't talking about the ravishment—or whatever it would be—video that James and I were planning to make. "Fantastic! I've really missed you, Becks. And there's so much going on here." *So much that I haven't been able to tell you over the phone or e-mail, that is.*

"And we're going to come too, Karina, for the press conference and party," Paulina said.

"Is Las Vegas as odd as it is portrayed in movies?" Michel wanted to know.

"Odder," I said. "This place is hard to believe. I can't wait to see you all. It'll be great to have some friends here!"

I got the details about the press conference from James

later. He didn't come in until nearly ten o'clock and he was ravenous. So was I and he chided me for not getting something for myself earlier. But I had gotten sucked into rereading my thesis and marking it up with revision notes anyway. It had been forever since I'd read it, and parts of it now were very obviously weak and in need of shoring up. But having spent the entire summer looking at and talking about the paintings hanging in the special exhibit at the Tate, I found myself easily tossing out whole sections and making notes for what to fill them in with.

Now wasn't the time for art analysis, though. Now I wanted to find out what happened with Ben and Pascual. "Well? What did you learn on your car ride?"

"I will have to tell you later," he said, making a gesture like he was still worried the room had ears. I knew Ty had checked it only a short time ago but I also knew this was one thing we really didn't want Ferrara to get wind of. "I can tell you that I've made some plans for our counteroffensive, though."

Our video, I assumed. "I talked to Becky, Paul, and Misha earlier. Becks will be here tomorrow, she said."

"Yes, I talked to her myself earlier today. She's quite sharp, your roommate! I'm impressed. I put all kinds of references and things into the songs and the music but I never expect anyone to actually *get* it."

I laughed in amusement. I don't think he quite understood that there were millions of fans out there analyzing his every word, every breath, on hundreds of websites, forums, and chat rooms all across the world. But Becky was quite sharp, too. "Just don't get her started on Foucault or you'll be talking all night."

"You don't like Foucault?"

"I like him just fine. You can't study art in the postmodern era without him. That's why Becky and I talked about him all night one night."

Of course, that meant that James and I stayed up late talking about art. Not too many men could keep up with me on the subject, but James had no trouble, and we ended the night with some artistic fun of our own.

Things got very very busy after that, as the night of the debut was only a few short weeks away, and there was still so much to learn, sets to be built, costumes to be made, et cetera. Rehearsal hours doubled, and for James they tripled since he was also rehearsing the songs with the band at some music studio a mile away. He and the band did most of their work in the evenings—as he put it, rock musicians were not morning people—leaving me some time to see the Vegas sights with Becky and to work on my thesis.

And yet, in spite of all that, he still found the energy to play games with me, tying me, spanking me, sometimes fucking me to the edge of orgasm for both of us in the morning and then making us both wait until night to finish.

We had special fittings for a Peter-Pan-style flying rig that would allow both of us to fly together, as if joined in a somewhat suggestive pose. We tested it extensively as well as practicing how to get into it quickly. Leading up to the moment in the show when we would take off over the audience, Ben and Annika would briefly replace us on the stage. Because of lights and smoke no one would likely be the wiser that for those thirty seconds or so we were actually inside the set, getting the flying rig on, and then *whoosh*, out we would come as part of another switcheroo. I'd be on the bottom, with him on top. When we practiced it, the pose put his dance-belted cock right in the crack of my ass.

Becky was fairly busy, too, interviewing Alicia, Chandra, and the dancers about their interpretations of various works. Chandra got a bright idea then, as well, following on James's that we might have to release some videos of our own. She got Becky to interview various women, me included, about our thoughts on the bondage theme, and about James's statement that consensuality and mutual respect were empowering. I didn't feel like much of an expert on the subject, and I didn't want to talk much about our private life, but I could definitely see how it would be helpful to spread these videos around later, to undo any damage that the "rape tape" (as the ravishment video was being called) might have spread.

And Becky and I finally got to go shoe shopping, this time with no budget restrictions. I thought she was going to die of ecstasy. Amusingly enough, after trying on twenty pairs of shoes at three different insanely expensive designer stores, what she ended up buying was a Gucci scarf. She wore it everywhere, so I guess she really liked it.

In the midst of this, Ferrara released two more videos. One was another ravishment tape, only this time it had herself as the victim, and again the face of the man was obscured, this time by an elaborate carnival-style mask over his eyes. Snippets of James's voice were interposed at various points where his mouth was not shown, but it was overall smoothly done. Ferrara's face, of course, was huge, right in the camera. Her crying on camera was nowhere near as convincing as Vanette's had been, though. James brushed it off. It continued to play into his plans to create a publicity frenzy.

The next video she put out a few days after that, though,

incensed him. It was a music video, using the music from *Bride of the Blue*, that began with some snippets of the Vanette ravishment video, then had some of the more recent one with Ferrara, this one making it look more like it was as if the couple in the wedding video had made a sex tape that had gone wrong, with more footage of him tearing her clothes and her trying to push him away, and then toward the end, some footage that made my hair stand on end, too.

It was us, James and me, in bed. And it looked bad. It looked like I was struggling and shouting "no, no." He threatened to fuck me in the ass and I continued to shout "no."

We were watching it on my laptop in the suite. James stood abruptly and went to stand at the edge of the bed, staring at the spot where it had been filmed. "When did they get that? When was that?"

"I'm trying to think. When was the last time you teased me about fucking me in the ass?" I backed up the video and watched it again. "Damn it. I'm actually struggling to get your cock *into* me here, but in the context of the other footage, it sure doesn't look that way."

He turned and stared at the media center shelf. "The camera vantage is from here."

"And a good thing, too, so your face doesn't show." I moved to stand next to him and it dawned on me. "Phil. The night he snuck in here dressed as a waiter. He must have taken the camera when he came in."

James pointed to the books. "Yes. You're right. Remember when I signed the room service check? He had me lean on a book, which I thought was odd since the folder was adequate enough for that. But that's it. He ran off with the book. It wasn't a book. It was a camera." He cursed loudly.

"Well," I teased, "we were planning to put out a film clip featuring me of some kind, weren't we?"

He sat on the edge of the bed. "True. But I do hate having choices taken away from us. From you especially."

"It's all right, James." I sat next to him. "Don't let it bother you. That's what she wants. Does this mean we don't need to do a tape of our own?"

"We might not," he admitted. "The press gala is coming up, though. Did I tell you Mandinka is going to come in to do hair and makeup for it?"

"For you?"

"And you. And more important, Ben and Pascual, so that the two of them and me will be perfect matches. But we were speaking about me doing something wicked to you."

"On video?"

"At the press gala. I was thinking of making you into a kind of centerpiece of bondage art. What do you think about that?"

"I think that would be a great way to avoid having to make awkward cocktail party talk."

The next day, Ferrara got even more impatient and desperate. She e-mailed me herself, though from an anonymous account, of course.

A different edit of the video of me and James having very rough sex was attached to the e-mail. The message read:

> The first thing that will happen if you don't help us is that this video will be sent to your mother.
>
> You will threaten to drop out of the show if he doesn't meet our demands.

*If he refuses, then you will drop out of the show. If you
do not, the second thing that will happen is we will send you
back a tape of this happening to your mother. Do you understand? We know where she lives.*

I don't know what Ferrara was thinking. Did she really,
seriously think she could blackmail me into betraying James?
She'd already tried to play on my worst fear, and failed. I
showed him the e-mail immediately.

He sighed. "Call your mother. Invite her here. Free vacation
on me. I'm having my own mother come here, too. It's long
past time when I should have told my mother about what I
do. I'll feel better when they're in our security's hands."

I had to agree with him there. "So you're going to come
out to your mother."

He smiled. "Yes. 'Mom, I have something to tell you. I've
been hiding it from you all these years.' 'What, son? Are you
gay?' 'No, Mom, I'm a rock star.'" He sighed. "Honestly, I can't
imagine she's going to have a problem with it now. When I
first started keeping the secret from her, she was having terrible empty-nest syndrome, clinging to me fiercely and the only
thing I could think of was I had to get away. I didn't want to
seem like I was anything less than a dutiful son, though. So
I rebelled...but I didn't tell her. It seems rather stupid now."

"I wonder if my mother will be cool with it, too, or if
she'll flip back to being the judgmental person who drove
me crazy ever since I got old enough to date." I held out
hope that she'd be accepting, but I figured if not, our rapport
was nice while it lasted. I hadn't ever really expected her to
approve of my life choices, so if we went back to that, well,
I'd live with it.

Sixteen

As Long as There's Fire

My conversation with my mother went something like this.
"Mom, you know that show in Las Vegas I was telling you
about? James and I would like you to come to here to be with
us while we work on it."

"Oh?"

"Yes. We've got a whole floor of a hotel to ourselves, and
we'd love if you could join us."

"You didn't tell me James was involved in the dance show,
too. Is he a financial backer?"

"Yes. James is inviting his mother, too."

"Oh! Oh, well, I should definitely come, then!"

"Great! I actually already booked your plane tickets. A
driver will meet you at the airport here."

"Fantastic! Karina, it will be so great to see you! And I'll
finally get to meet your mystery man!"

She sounded so happy and so unquestioning of the situation that I didn't say anything more. I figured all explanations
would be better done in person.

I didn't hear how James convinced his mother to come. Rehearsals became even more intense for me, Annika, Ben, and Pascual. Everyone was working like crazy, but we had more to learn than most. We were so busy that my mother had already been in Las Vegas for several hours before I saw her. It looked to me like she had already been to the spa and the salon when I met her for dinner. I wasn't looking anywhere near so fresh, after rehearsing all day and then throwing some clothes on before hurrying down to the hotel restaurant.

The first thing she said was, "Karina, this is quite a nice hotel."

"Is it?" I fussed with my napkin, deciding to wait to put it in my lap when something to eat arrived.

"Oh, yes. The last time I came to Las Vegas all I remember is seedy, tacky places. But, well, I suppose your James counts as a high roller."

"I think he wanted somewhere quiet, away from the tourists," I said. "And with good security."

"His staff have certainly been taking good care of me," she said with a happy sigh.

We ordered then, me without looking at the menu since I had long since memorized it. "So, Mom, there are some things I have to tell you. They might sound kind of weird."

"What kind of weird, dear?"

"Well, there's something we've been keeping from you because we were afraid you wouldn't give James a chance."

"Don't be silly. Why wouldn't I like James?"

"Well, you know, sometimes people get funny ideas."

"They certainly do."

Come on, Karina, I thought, *get to the point.* "So, the thing is, he's an internationally famous rock star and performer."

"Oh, is that all?" She made a motion like she was throwing an imaginary napkin into a basket. "Karina, why would I care about that?"

For half a second I couldn't remember why we'd kept it a secret from her. "Well..."

"I mean, seriously. I was a teenager when Janis Joplin and the Beatles were doing LSD."

Right. "Okay, cool, but the thing is that we didn't just keep it a secret from you. It's a secret from everyone."

"Ohhh. I get it. You mean he's like Bruce Wayne and Batman. All right. Well, that's nice, dear. Doesn't that rather complicate things?"

My mother, queen of the understatement. "Yes, it does. But the whole point of the concerts we're doing here is that he's retiring. These are his good-bye concerts."

"And then what? Ride off into the sunset?"

"Oh, well, he has other pursuits. It's just the rock star thing will be over."

"I see." She nodded much more knowingly than I expected. "And will I be allowed to see these concerts?"

"Of course!"

And on the conversation went. She seemed perfectly happy with me and with the situation. Only when we finished dinner and I was eager to get upstairs and find out if James had returned from music rehearsal did I finally bring up the last difficult topic. "Mom, there's one more thing you should know."

She folded her napkin carefully as she placed it on the table. "And what's that, dear?"

"The show. It's a little...risqué."

"Are you topless in it?"

"What? No!"

She made the dismissive motion again. "Karina. It's Las Vegas. If you're not showing your boobs, you're fine. You shouldn't worry about it. Dancing is perfectly respectable."

"I'm not worried for myself! I just didn't want *you* to be shocked!"

"Honestly, Karina, you're acting like it's a stripper bar you're taking me to. James sounds like a very tasteful individual. Very artistic. I'm sure you're in good hands. Now, seriously, when can I meet him?"

"I'll have to ask about that. Rehearsals are crazy right now. But I know he's been looking forward—"

Damn that James, though, for having impeccable timing. He swept up to the table, took my mother's hand in his before she was aware of what has happening, and kissed it.

"Mrs. Casper. I am so sorry I could not greet you before this moment," he said, dropping to one knee so he didn't loom over us at the table. "I do hope my staff took excellent care of you during my absence. I'm James."

My mother blushed like it was Cary Grant or Richard Gere looking her right in the eye. "Oh, well, yes, very good care. Nice to meet you, James. You can call me Charlotte."

"A beautiful name for the beautiful mother of a beautiful daughter." He kissed me on the cheek and pulled up a chair. Almost instantly a waiter appeared, then disappeared with the mandate to bring us coffee and dessert. "Is it your first time in Las Vegas, Charlotte?"

"My first in a very long time. I was just telling Karina that either the place has cleaned up a lot or this must be a better class of establishment than I stayed in before."

"The town has upscaled quite a bit," James said. "I do hope you'll have a chance to see some of it while Karina and I are ensconced in rehearsals. My own mother is flying in this week as well, all the way from London. Dare I suggest the two of you might take in some sights together?"

"I'd like that. London, you say? I was there before Karina was born! On my honeymoon."

And off they went, talking about London. She was completely and utterly charmed by him, I could tell. He asked her questions about me and Jill, and listened to her answers and laughed in the right places, while encouraging her to tell more. She deftly avoided actually talking about my father, which she had years of practice doing, and she told some stories about me that had previously mortified me when she'd brought them up to boyfriends.

Maybe once you've had your ass beaten in front of someone, that story about the time you fell in the lake didn't seem all that exposing anymore.

No, that wasn't it exactly. It was because with James I wasn't pretending to be someone else. He insisted on me being myself and he already knew me far better than I thought my mother did. There was no silly story she could tell that would make him think any differently of me.

I said very little, enjoying my coffee and dessert. I didn't have to. My mother loves to talk, and she loves to have an audience. James kept me saying just enough that I stayed a part of the conversation without having to carry it.

It was an odd opportunity to watch James at work. I'd had

a glimpse that night at the gallery, but this was different. I watched him charm my mother and convince her he was the greatest thing since sliced bread without really telling her anything about himself. I suppose that was the point. The important thing about him was that he was the man in my life. The rest was just details. And I should have known that next to Dancer James and Artist James and Rock Star James, "Someday I Could Be Your Son-in-Law" James would be a piece of cake for him to pull off. My mother loved being treated like a queen, and that was one thing James was very good at.

The day the publicity gala arrived, I wondered if my mother would remember that she had called him artistic and tasteful when I mentioned the content of the show might be somewhat risqué. The crew had taken over an entire restaurant inside one of the casino hotels, catered it to the nines, and invited all manner of celebrities, as I guess one does. Becky and Michel were wielding their cell phones as cameras, live-streaming some to the Lord Lightning Internet channel, as well as recording interviews and asking people what they thought the new show would be like. James had kept the information to the public about the actual show very minimal, but nearly everyone there had either seen the "publicity" videos or seen the news about them. I definitely heard the opinion multiple times that the videos must be fake and the difference was whether the people felt fake videos that were made to seem real for the sake of going sensationally viral was a terrible or wonderful publicity tactic.

I got to hear a lot of opinions at the party, because I was in bondage for it, suspended above the crowd. James had rigged me himself, of course, starting my preparations with a remote-controlled bullet vibe, then a spandex bodysuit, and then the flying harness. The vibrator inside me buzzed while he added ropes and a blindfold.

The preparations took place in a room high above the main floor of the restaurant where I was hooked to a motorized track and then flown slowly over the crowd. I was comfortable, with all my limbs supported by ropes, but I guess from the reactions of the people I passed over that I made a striking image.

James wasn't out there, though. He stayed in the prep room, and each time I came through, he would check on me, kiss me, fondle me a little, and make the vibrator go on and off.

"Don't you have to go out there?" I asked, on one of my trips through the room.

"Don't be silly," he said. "My public appearances are rare and fleeting."

"Ah, right. Of course."

"Ben and Pascual will each appear at moments, along with some of the band. Chandra, Alicia, and some of the others are there to actually speak about the production. But this is mostly about unveiling the cover of the album."

I had a sudden thought. "Am I on the cover?"

He chuckled. "You might be." Then there was no more time to talk as I reached the trapdoor that swung open and let the sound of the crowd wash over me. As I glided away from him, I felt the vibrator click on.

I wondered if he meant for me to come while flying over all these people. It had been nearly an hour of the vibe going on and off and I was edging closer.

As I passed over the crowd, though, I thought I heard a familiar voice. An unwelcome voice. A slightly nasal twang and an oily manner, that sure sounded like Phil Betancourt. I tried to see, but no matter how I moved my head there was no seeing past the blindfold, and my wiggling intensified the sensation of the vibe inside me. Then I heard people making comments about my movements so I stopped. The vibe stopped when James must have seen me squirming. Long agonizing minutes passed before I reached him again.

"Are you here?"

"Yes, I'm here," he said, running a hand down my side. "Are you all right? Do you need to come down?"

"No no, it's not that. It's just…I thought I heard Betancourt's voice, schmoozing someone. I mean, maybe it's how smarmy people sound, but can you look? Can you see?"

"I will look once you're out the trapdoor. From up here I can see almost everyone in the room. As you go over, listen again and see if you can figure out where he is."

He didn't turn the vibrator on this time, I guess so I could concentrate on listening. Most of the voices weren't familiar at all, and I couldn't make out much other than the general buzz. The room seemed to have gotten more crowded, as if anticipating something. Perhaps they were waiting for the cover reveal.

I heard the doors swing open as I sailed slowly into the prep room again. "James?"

The doors swung shut behind me and I could hear the whirring of the motor that kept the track moving. I sensed as he stepped close to me.

The whirring suddenly slowed and stopped. "James?"

Someone's hand ran along my side, but no one answered me.

I shivered. Was he doing it to freak me out? The vibe came on suddenly and I relaxed, thinking that meant he was giving me the silent treatment but it was all another game he was playing.

A rough hand massaged between my legs, where I was getting quite wet under the spandex. Gushing it around like that was surely creating an obvious wet stain. I moaned into the touch.

The next thing I felt, though, was the cool fabric being pulled away from my skin, the pocket of air forming, and then I heard the unmistakable sound of scissors, *snip-snip-snip.*

My pussy was now bare to the air. A finger traced the edges of my lips and I jumped. That wasn't James. That was someone with long fingernails. "Who is that? Who's there?"

"Just me," came Ferrara's voice. The vibrator clicked off and I heard her put the controller on the ledge.

"Ferrara, what the fuck? Where is James?"

"I'm here to tell you the bad news, Karina. It's all been a setup. I tried to warn you, didn't I?"

"What the hell are you talking about?"

"James is about to come back in and fuck you like the little fuck toy you are. And you have a choice. You can either shut up and take it like a good girl, or you can scream and cry and protest. Either way works for me. When the video hits the Internet, you won't be able to deny it. Everyone at this party saw you in bondage flying overhead. They'll all know it's real."

"Ferrara, don't be stupid. You're going to film this? This is rape. You'll go to jail."

"Will I? Karina, don't be naive. Judges and juries blame women for their own rapes simply for wearing a skirt. You've been displayed to everyone as a sex object. Are you going to convince the judge that you were coerced into this? Hmm, let me see. You've been on the payroll for months. That harness was specially fitted for you. You were even in one of the earlier rape tapes that came out. Oh, weren't those faked? Well, obviously this is faked, too."

"You're crazy!"

"I'm driven. There's a difference. Here's what's going to happen. James is going to come in and fuck you now, and the entire thing is going to be on the Internet."

"That doesn't make any sense!"

"Doesn't it? Think about it." She flicked her nail across my clit and I tried to squeeze my legs together to no avail. "It doesn't matter if you fight, because afterward we're going to fly you over the audience with your ravaged cunt hanging out, just at the moment we unveil the album cover, which happens to be a painting James did of you in rope bondage. If you fight though, you'll see I was so right about him, that that's what he really wants. That'll work better with the theme of the publicity videos we've been releasing. Haven't they been brilliant? The whole campaign is brilliant. The whole Internet is on fire about it."

She was lying. She had to be. That old fear fluttered in my stomach, that maybe there was one more layer to James, one more layer of deception.

"If you don't fight, well, it'll still be a good show. I love a good, hard assfucking. Especially of an anal virgin. But that's why I think you'll fight."

Was that why he kept winding me up about anal sex? Because it was all a setup for this?

"Now, stay where you are. *Don't move.*" As if I could. She

laughed at her own joke as she went to open the door to let someone in from the hallway.

I heard the shuffling of feet. It sounded like more than one person came in. One of them squeaked in distress. Becky?

I swung in the suspension, unable to move my arms or free myself. I couldn't even kick my legs. I felt large hands massaging my buttocks.

"Get the camera closer," Ferrara hissed. "Film his thing."

I could hear the wet, rhythmic sound of a penis being stroked. Then hands on my thighs as someone positioned themselves between my legs.

"You don't want to do this," I said.

A hard erection rubbed my thigh.

"I'm telling you right now to stop. I didn't consent to this." That couldn't be James. It couldn't.

Ferrara egged him on, though. "Go on, James. Her ass is ripe for the taking. Why are you going so slowly?"

His hands pulled my buttocks apart, massaging my flesh. For a moment I felt a flicker of fear, but his touch felt unfamiliar. "You're not my James!" I cried out. "I don't know who you are, but this is rape!"

I heard Becky sob.

"Becks! Tell me who that is! That's not him, is it?"

"No, Karina, it's not! I don't know who that is!"

I heard a scuffle then, and Ferrara's voice. "Of course it is! You don't know what he looks like!"

"I do! I've met him! The real him!" Becky cried. It sounded like they were wrestling. "That's not him."

"Ben? Pascual? Which one of you is it?"

I heard Pascual's voice then. "Ferrara, this isn't the way you said the scene was going to go."

"Pascual, let me go! She lied to you! Where's James? Where's Jasper! Get me down!"

My heart surged with relief as I felt him working at the ropes. He couldn't quite figure out how to get them off me, but he did figure out how to release my legs from the suspension and my feet touched the floor. He took the blindfold off next and then unhooked me from the track, which freed my arms. I still had gauntlets made of rope running up my forearms and shins, but they didn't hinder me from moving now.

I turned around to find Becky had Ferrara in a headlock. I guess those self-defense classes her parents made her take were good. I slipped the Gucci scarf from Becky's shoulders and got it around Ferrara's wrists.

"You bitch!" she shouted. "Now who's committing assault?"

"Enough. I've had it with you and the videos and the threats to my family." I stepped back so I could see her face and I put my back against the door. "Now we're going to talk."

I noticed Pascual had put his clothes back together, at least. He was in a typical James-style suit, no tie, his jacket slung over one shoulder. He stood to one side, looking calmer than I would have expected.

"Becky, put the camera on."

Becky did as I asked, but she gestured at me, as if asking if I wanted to cover up or something. I looked down. There wasn't much to see now, with the flying rig hanging down and my legs together. Plus I didn't care. Nudity didn't make me weak unless I made it out to, so I ignored it.

"Pascual, do you mind telling me what's going on here?"

"Honestly, Karina? I'm hoping to find out. I mean, when

you take a Lord Lightning gig, you know that a whole lot of secrets come as part of the territory. I've been a stand-in for Jasper for years now. Hell, that first six months he was so cagey I thought he was some kind of stand-in, too." He took a step toward Ferrara.

"Uh-uh. Stay put. I'll tell you what's happening. Ferrara has been trying to blackmail him for months, claiming he married her and now she's entitled to half his net worth."

Pascual looked at her curiously. "Using that video we shot?"

"Yes. She's claiming that's Jasper. Or as she calls him, James."

"Well, he couldn't go do it himself, so I stood in." Pascual shrugged.

Ferrara sobbed.

"All right, Ferrara, spill it," I said.

She shook her head. "I'm not telling you anything. You have no proof. All you have is a lot of lies. It's a house of cards. Just let me go and I'll never bother you again."

"I believe that about as much as I believe your lies." I folded my arms. "Blackmail seems to be something you understand, though. So how about this? You tell me everything that's been going on, and then you get the hell out of our lives for good, or—" I paused to think of how to word it, but she took it as a dramatic pause.

"Or what?" she snapped.

"Or I'll have you thrown out of the Crimson Glove Society for filming that ravishment scene with Vanette you showed me. You know, the one where you said she was being raped? I hear it was quite a specialty of hers."

"How do you...?" She stared at me.

"I imagine the society takes very, very poorly to anyone flouting their rules. I heard stories when I was a trainee about how they ruined someone they expelled, financially and socially."

This time when she started to cry I think they were the first real tears I'd seen from her. She struggled to hold them in, and made an ugly snorting sound, nothing like the dramatic weeping she'd shown so many times before. "Well, it hardly matters, since I'm ruined anyway!"

Pascual went and dabbed her nose with a handkerchief and this time I didn't stop him.

"What do you mean, ruined?"

"In the divorce from Huntington. He was an imbecile, wrecked our personal finances first and then looted the company. I inherited a company on the verge of bankruptcy. And then I find out our biggest earner is going to retire? I had no choice. I won't go back to a life of destitution! I'm too old to model now. I've already sold off all the property I could to try to pay off the company's debts, but without continual income from the Lord Lightning franchise, we're sunk."

"And forced marriage was the best plan you could come up with to keep him?"

Her only answer was to cry harder. Pascual put an arm around her.

I looked at him. "You know what? I think you're the one who is actually legally married to her."

"I know," he said, and pulled her close so that she was crying on his shoulder. "That's what Jasper told me."

Ferrara's head snapped up. "Since when are you in cahoots with him?"

"Since he explained what you were trying to do. He knew it had to be me or Ben in the video. He took us both for a long car ride and I spilled the beans. There's only one reason

I made all those videos with you Ferrara, the marriage one, the wedding night one—"

"Why?" She looked up through mascara-damp eyes.

"Because I love you. I've been in love with you since we first met. I mean, sure, I knew you were interested in Jasper, but I had to hope that once you realized he was never going to give in, you'd realize I was waiting to take his place, once again." He hugged her then, and reached behind her and undid the knot in the scarf, and held her while she cried. I took the scarf and handed it back to Becky, who wrapped it around my waist like a sarong.

Someone knocked on the door. I opened it and was relieved to see James standing there. He slipped into the room and closed the door behind him.

"Where have you been?" I demanded.

"Catching Phil Betancourt and delivering him to the police, who want him in connection with a certain hotel camera porn scandal," he said coolly. "I see you've been busy, as well." He nodded to Pascual. "Did you get a confession out of her?"

"Yes, I did," I said, poking him in the ribs. "Thanks to Becky, too. She's got it all on camera."

"Let me see it."

Becky handed him the camera, which had a small screen that stuck out from it like a wing. James took his phone from his pocket and used the headphones to plug into the sound jack. He watched, his face betraying no emotion while he did.

When it was done he said to Pascual, "Are you still interested in the plan we talked about?"

Pascual brightened. "Very much so. More so after hearing what she said about the company."

"Good. Go get into costume. Take her with you. I'll meet

you downstairs by the stage." He ushered them out of the room. "Now, Karina, you and I need to get into costume, too. We're going to do just the first two minutes of 'Balladeer.' Mandinka is waiting in the back room. Becky, you can come too, if you like, or go out and get in a good spot for the show. I really am going to want a lot of good video of this one."

"I'll do that!" She checked the camera. "There's plenty of memory left!"

We went down a set of back stairs and then into the small private dining room that had been turned into an impromptu green room. I changed quickly into my show costume and Mandinka swooped down, surprised me by kissing me on both cheeks, and then redid my makeup.

The stage at the far end of the restaurant was small, so instead of the whole ensemble, it was only seven of us dancing, including James, Ben, Pascual, and Roland. So each woman had a partner for while James was singing. I was used to being paired with Pascual.

But when we took our places, it was James who paired with me. James, in no mask, no special makeup other than the standard stage makeup Mandinka had put on us. I gave him a look, but there was no time to ask what was going on. The prerecorded music began and we moved into the first steps of one of the new songs.

Pascual took center stage with a cordless microphone, his eyes hidden by the half-mask I had seen before in one of the videos. Cheers went up, including some very excited screams from the fangirls scattered throughout the crowd. People pressed against the small stage.

It was only a two-minute version, so the music faded out at one point when the dancers were all on the floor and

Pascual was still on his feet, holding a long note. As the music dropped away, his voice was all that could be heard, and the longer it went on, the more frenzied the cheers became. And then he ended it at last, flung off the mask, took a bow, and then retreated from the stage amid a flurry of flashbulbs. The dancers, myself included, scrambled up to follow him, but someone caught me by the hand and pulled me back.

James led me to the mic stand, took the microphone in his hand, and cleared his throat. "If I could have your attention for a minute, please. Indulge me."

People began to quiet down. Someone clinked the side of their glass the way you do to get attention at banquets and weddings.

He cleared his throat again. "I have a very important announcement to make and I may as well make it in front of you all."

I stood, stunned. Was he going to announce his retirement?

"I love you, Karina," he said. "I love you more than anything. More than dancing, more than art, more than life. So I have one question for you."

Before I was aware of what he was doing, he pulled a small velvet box from inside his costume. It was exactly like the one Phil Betancourt had shown me in my mother's dining room.

No. It *was* the same one. James dropped to one knee and cracked it open. The diamond shone insanely bright in the spotlight.

"Will you marry me?"

I don't know how the audience heard me say "yes!" since I forgot to say it into the microphone. But the way I attacked his face with kisses was probably as good as words, and the way I bowled him over onto the stage, with my mouth locked on his, cleared up any doubt about how I felt. By the time we sat up they were chanting "Yes means yes! Yes means yes!"

The proposal would rate two sentences in the story in *Entertainment Weekly* that bore the headline: *LORD LIGHTNING UNMASKS!* The article read, "The theme of finding one's soul mate that runs throughout LL's previous work even spurred two backup dancers to get engaged onstage at the Vegas publicity gala. Whether they had a Vegas wedding afterward is unknown."

Epilogue

Two hours before opening night I had the worst case of butterflies in my stomach ever. James calmed them completely by blindfolding me in a folding chair in the middle of the green room. He put his hands on my shoulders, standing behind me, and gave me one order. "Breathe."

I don't know how long I sat that way, but it worked. I calmed down immediately. I concentrated on my breathing and I could hear every conversation going on around the room. Someone was looking for Roland, found him, and delivered some flowers. A theater manager came in asking for Ferrara and was told she'd had to return suddenly to England on urgent business. Yes, the urgent business of keeping her promise to us that she would stay away from James. I heard James remark to Chandra that she had better order extra security for Pascual, and her reply was that she already had. "You can be less of a control freak now, can't you?" she complained. "Pascual's my boss now, not you."

From a bit further away I heard Pascual add, "More like you're my boss, Chandra!"

"I merely state my advice to you as a friend," James told her. "Speaking of which, did you get that place on Central Park you wanted? That will make it easy to drop in on me and Karina for dinner."

"Tsk. I would never 'drop in' on you two. I'm too likely to find you swinging from the ceiling buck naked. I'll call first."

In another corner, Mandinka was giving Annika advice on how to treat a cracked callus on her foot. Alicia was chiding Ben for letting Pascual get the prime gig. Ben was saying he much preferred it this way. "Let him be the one to dodge teenyboppers in the streets! I'd rather collect my paycheck and go home. The couple of times I played the part of limo diversion were scary enough."

I could hear Pascual then, as Chandra quizzed him in a practice interview, getting him ready for a quick on-camera segment with *Entertainment Tonight*.

"What gave you the idea for *Bonded*?"

Pascual cleared his throat. "Um, well, as you know, my private life is closely guarded, but I have some familiarity with the worlds of bondage and discipline, and the storyline grew from there."

It was amazing how he adopted James's formal way of speaking. He went into character.

"And you don't have a problem with the subjugation of women in the BDSM lifestyle?"

"BDSM, contrary to some beliefs, is about empowering both partners, and who said the women are always on the bottom? That's certainly not true in any BDSM club I've been to."

"Eh, that might be a bit too wordy and too close to opening a personal can of worms." Chandra advised. "Think about it: You've been to a BDSM club?"

Pascual dropped into his regular voice. "Ah, I see what you mean. Yeah. That's saying a little too much."

"Try another one: And how do you feel about commercializing your sexuality for the sake of the almighty entertainment dollar?"

Pascual cleared his throat and delivered a drop-dead droll James line. "My dear, that's rock and roll."

Chandra laughed. I'd never heard her laugh before.

I don't know how long I sat like that, but when James took the blindfold off and told me to get warmed up, the painful edge of the anticipation was gone. From then, time flew and I knew I would be fine once the performance began. It was the waiting that had been difficult to get through. The performance went by so fast I barely had time to worry. I barely had a moment to glance into the audience, up at the side balcony boxes where our mothers sat together. Jill was there, too. Earlier today she told me she had finally talked to Troy and he would be showing up later in the week. His band had gigs all weekend. They were getting some local notoriety in the Bay Area. Well, I could introduce him to some people in the record business.

The only person whose face I could actually make out when I glanced up at the box, though, was Becky's, because she sat forward in her chair, hanging on the railing, her chin perched on her knuckles, her eyes wide as she took in the spectacle.

James and I met at the center of the stage and then dropped through the trapdoor to quickly get into our flying rig. We had exactly forty-four seconds to do it. We had gotten it down to twenty seconds in rehearsal, though. This time as I stepped into the harness, his hand slid over my buttocks.

He unsnapped the three tiny snaps in the crotch of my bodysuit. I grinned back at him, not at all surprised by this turn of events. His cool smile and the glint in his eye told me all I needed to know. He was getting off on the fact that he was about to fuck me in front of our families and thousands of paying spectators. And none of them would be the wiser.

He didn't have to do much beyond give me that look for me to go wet for him, and in another few seconds he was seated deep inside me. Another few seconds and all buckles were snapped into place. He tested the lines above our heads and gave Barnaby the high sign, and up we went slowly at first until we cleared the parts of the set that didn't move. We hung there, waiting for the musical cue that would send us soaring out over the audience.

"How does that feel?" he asked, his hands on my hips as I stretched out into a full spread eagle.

"Mmm, fantastic. Is this just for tonight? Or every night?"

"Glad you asked. You know, the angle is not quite perfect like this. It would work much better with my cock seated in your ass."

"Oh, would it now?"

"Definitely. Good thing we have ten shows. I know a fabulous technique for stretching out orifices. I bet it'll only take five days until you're ready to take me."

"We'll need lube."

"I'm certain we can get that."

We started to rise again, now only ten seconds from our

cue and hidden from the audience only by a small curtain and billows of dry ice mist.

"Hey," I said, in the moment we had left before we were visible to the crowd, "do you think we should have a Vegas wedding?"

He rocked his hips, driving his cock deeper and sending sparks of pleasure through me. "Sweetness, this *is* our Vegas wedding. And the whole world are our witnesses."

The curtain dropped and out we flew, as weightless as if we were floating on our shared joy.

From the moment she meets him in a New York bar, waitress Karina knows James is different. Awakened by his touch, Karina discovers a wild side she hadn't known existed—and nothing is off-limits.

See where it all began...

Please see the next page for

a preview of **Slow Surrender**.

One

Out of the Blue

The night of Lord Lightning's good-bye concert was a crazy night to say the least. I was doing one last waitress shift at the bar my sister managed in Midtown, the concert having taken place at Madison Square Garden, just a few blocks away. The bar was packed with "Lord's Ladies," who were inconsolable and tearing their hair out (or wigs, actually) while smearing their face paint with tears. My roommate Becky was at home crying about the same thing. Me? I couldn't care less what some self-absorbed rock-star asshole was doing as his latest publicity stunt, but it was all over the big-screen TVs: his masked face projected sixty inches wide along with footage of the screaming fans at his supposedly last public performance. The whole city was turned upside down, and I remember so clearly the Lord's Ladies because they were such a royal pain in the arse! Ordering as little as possible, taking up the best tables all night long, and I could already tell they were going to be lousy tippers.

I'd even had one table dine-and-dash on me. I didn't

think the night could get any worse until I got to the hostess station and caught a glimpse of my thesis advisor walking through the front door. The same advisor I'd told I couldn't meet tonight because I was "too sick to leave my apartment, *cough cough*" when my sister, Jill, had convinced me she was desperate and needed me to work. She had promised a great night for cash tips, which was the only reason I'd agreed to this madness. Even worse, on top of it all was the fact that he'd come in with the man I'd had a job interview with that afternoon, a project manager at a design firm where I hoped to work as soon as I graduated, if not sooner. Theo Renault's approval of my thesis was the main thing standing between me and graduation, and I knew from department talk he wasn't one who would casually accept being lied to.

In other words, I was fucked, and all because I was doing Jill a favor. I forced myself to stop looking at Renault and the guy—Philip Hale was his name—as they fought their way through the crowded room toward the bar. Maybe they would have a quick nightcap and get out of here. I tried to focus on the customer stepping up to the stand now, a tall man in a hat and a bittersweet-chocolate-brown suit that was clearly tailored to perfectly fit his lean frame, like something out of a fashion magazine.

Not the kind of guy who was alone, usually, but I hurried to seat him. If I took him upstairs, maybe Renault wouldn't see me. "Table for one?" I chirped as I thought, *Please don't be waiting for someone.*

"Yes, plea—"

"Great! Follow me!" I practically grabbed him by the arm and led him quickly to the stairs. "Kind of a busy night in here. It's a bit quieter on the second floor. I'll get you away from these crazies." I waved the menu in the general direction of the Lord's Ladies, who were starting a group sing-along of some kind.

"I'd like that," he said, his voice deep. He sounded faintly amused.

Probably because I was acting so flustered. "It's not always like this in here," I assured him, as if it mattered. The second floor, unlike the crowded, chaotic first floor, was devoid of both TVs and singing fans and had only a few customers scattered throughout. A group of four women in one corner had already cashed out but had been lingering for an hour. A couple sat near the top of the stairs.

I led him all the way to a table by the windows, over-looking the street, desperate to kill as much time as possible. I had the funny urge to pull out his chair for him, as if this were a white-tablecloth kind of place, but I hung back until he seated himself. He had a topcoat folded over his arm, and he hung it over the back of his chair, put his hat on the wide sill of the window, then sat. I set the menu down in front of him.

"The kitchen is already closed," I said, going into my automatic "after 10:00 p.m." patter, "but the full list of cocktails is of course available, as are the selections on the dessert menu." I turned the menu over to the list of desserts. "Today's sorbet is passion fruit."

"Passion fruit?" he asked, one eyebrow raised like he was skeptical of it.

"Nah," I joked. "That's the name of my Lord Lightning cover band."

That made him laugh. In the streetlamps that shone through the window, I couldn't tell the color of his eyes, blue, hazel, green? The light from outside was stark and bluish compared to the soft amber lights in the bar, making his cheekbones look impossibly sharp. His hair was dangerously blond, almost white, and cropped close to his head. His age was impossible to gauge; he could've been a young forty or a haunted twenty. He was gorgeous and striking and his voice had a slight British tinge to it as he said, "Oh, just try to work it into every conversation, do you?"

"Yes, exactly." I grinned. Normally, flirting while waitressing was asking for trouble and I avoided it at all costs. I didn't like men thinking just because I was female it was okay to treat me like something on the menu. But I was on a mission to waste as much time as I could. Besides, he was quite attractive and that was an understatement. "Actually, I think the sorbet is lemon with a little orange food color. It all tastes the same."

He chuckled. "So, you don't recommend the sorbet?"

I chewed my lip a moment. "I lied," I said. "I've never actually had it."

"Well, at least one of us should embrace new experiences," he said. "Bring me a dish of the sorbet, and a bourbon. Something better than Maker's Mark." His eyes were on me, very intent, as if he had no intention of actually opening the menu.

I collected it from him.

"Coming right up." I couldn't resist making a fake little curtsy and then hurrying away.

That worked out perfectly, I thought. I punched in the drink order from the upstairs server station, then went down to the kitchen to dish the sorbet myself, completely out of the view of Renault and his friend. I picked up the bourbon from the back station, added it to the round tray with the sorbet, and headed right back upstairs.

"Here you are," I said as I set down the napkin and the drink, then the small metal dish of sorbet and a spoon.

"Thank you," he said, and sounded sincere about it.

I busied myself for a little while, refilling the water glasses for the four-top and checking that the couple didn't want a round of dessert. They didn't, which was just as well, because the sugary sweetness coming from the two of them cooing at each other was enough to hospitalize a diabetic. I guess they were having each other for dessert. It was hard not to feel bitter watching them when I'd never met a guy who could act like that and actually mean it. While I wiped down some of the empty tables, I glanced over at my solo customer. He was sipping the whisky very slowly and looking out the window. Maybe it was that a man drinking alone always looks melancholy, but I got the feeling he was a little sad about something. Wistful, maybe.

I also noticed he wasn't eating the sorbet. I went back to his table. "Was it not to your liking? I can take it away and bring you something else you might like."

He settled back in his chair and gave me a thoughtful look. "Actually, there is something I'd like."

"Name it." I gave him my waitress smile.

"I'd like you to try the sorbet." He picked up the spoon, which was still resting exactly where I'd left it, and cut into the perfect scoop that had clearly been untouched.

"Me?" I asked, as if he could have meant anyone else. "Why? To make sure it's okay?"

"No, no. Because you said you hadn't had it before. I thought, what a shame. She works so hard in a place like this, and she's never tasted the sweetness right in front of her?" He held up the spoon, waving it enticingly.

I glanced behind me to make sure Jill or some other server wasn't watching. Normally one didn't do this sort of thing with customers, but I wanted to see what would happen if I did. "All right."

He held the spoon still, then up toward my chin. I leaned forward, my hands on my apron, and I slowly closed my mouth over it. The spoon was cold and the sorbet tart at first, then sweet as it melted in my mouth. "Mmmm."

His gaze never left my face and he smiled as I straightened up. Attention from guys often felt slimy to me, but from him all I felt was warmth, his eyes like hot spotlights.

I wanted to shine in that light. "Anything else I can get for you?" I asked, one of my standard lines.

He ran his finger along his chin, as if I had proposed a question requiring deep thought.

"Er, you know, I can have the bartender pour you something else, if you don't like this," I blathered.

"Oh, I like this," he said, a half smile coming onto his face, and I felt he wasn't talking about what was in his glass. His neck was long and graceful, and he had not the slightest bit of slouch in his posture, like a male figure skater. Or a model. He seemed more gorgeous the longer I looked at him, with high cheekbones and a luscious-looking mouth. He tilted his face up at me. "Your name tag says *Ashley*. Is that your name?"

"Yes, of course," I answered. It was a lie, actually. Ashley was the girl I was filling in for tonight, the one who was actually too sick to come in. I'd quit working here a few months ago to concentrate on my thesis; the "Karina" name tag had been lost or repurposed by now. For a second I wondered if Ashley was really sick or if she'd lied just like me, while she covered the ass of someone else, and so on and so on. Sadly, there was no one who could cover for me if Professor Renault caught me.

"Ashley, Ashley, gray as a cat, as you drift to the floor from the end of my cigarette," he said, as if reciting a poem. His voice was cultured and smoky like a deep jazz saxophone, making me feel melty inside. There was something charming about him, even if what he said made no sense.

"Ashley, tell me something," he said, angling his head as if to see me better. "Would you like to try something else new?"

"Something else?" I echoed. "What do you mean?"

"Are you bored? Tired of the rat race? Looking for a little adventure?"

"Well, sure. Who isn't?" I said.

He nodded at my automatic response. "Indeed. Ashley, I'm bored. I would like to play a game. And I would like someone to play it with me."

"I bet you say that to all the girls," I joked.

His expression darkened, surprising me. "Actually, it takes a very special person to pique my interest."

He thinks I'm special? I thought.

"If you don't want to play, that's fine," he added. "I'll leave and never come back if you say no."

Right about then, my weirdo meter should have been pinging hard. But my inner alarm bells were silent. Maybe because he wasn't giving off a weird vibe and he seemed sincere about leaving me alone if I didn't want to play along. And maybe because it was hard to say no to such an attractive man. I decided to test him out a little, though. "I'll play if you'll answer a question."

He smiled. "Name it," he said, imitating me perfectly.

"Tell me why a wealthy, well-dressed man like yourself is drinking alone."

"You mean, am I here fleeing a harridan wife or escaping my supermodel girlfriend?"

I shook a finger at him. "No answering a question with a question, mister. That's rude."

He flattened a hand against his lapels. "I beg your pardon. You're right. An honest question deserves an honest answer. The truth is I've come to the end of a very long and tiring episode in my business. I'm at loose ends for the first time in a long time, and to celebrate, I wanted to be alone for a while, something I haven't had a chance to do recently." He glanced out the window, then turned his full attention back to me. "In fact, I was just working myself up to a promise to spend more time by myself"—he paused and swirled the bourbon in his glass—"when you came along. There. Was that a satisfactory answer?"

I smiled. He seemed confident, sophisticated, and eminently reasonable. He seemed real. "Yes, it was. Okay, so what's the game?"

"The game is very simple. I ask you to do something, and you do it."

"Something like what?"

"Something like this: I have a marble in my jacket pocket. I'd like you to reach into the pocket, take out the marble, and put it in your mouth. I'll also have another bourbon and a glass of water, and when you bring me back the drinks, put the marble into the glass of bourbon. That's how you'll return it to me." His voice deepened and it felt like silk sliding over my skin. "Would you do that, Ashley?"

No one had ever said something like that to me before. It was like a dare, like a secret, like something private just the two of us were getting away with, exciting and a little bit illicit. "If this is a game," I said, "what do I win if I play?"

His full smile was like a prize itself. "I'm a genie. I'll grant you a wish," he said with a laugh. His voice was as rich as melted chocolate, even when he lightened it playfully.

"Okay." I gave him a goofy little curtsy. "I get it." Playing the game and sharing a secret *was* the prize.

I stepped closer to him, glanced back to make sure Jill or someone wasn't watching me from the stairs or server station across the room, and then bent over to reach into the pocket nearest to me. The jacket was a surprisingly soft fabric that felt almost like suede, a stylish cut, but it still had pockets like a traditional suit.

The pocket was empty. His eyebrows twitched with amusement. Okay, other pocket. Now I had to lean across him.

As I did so, he probably got an eyeful down my white, button-down shirt and I kind of liked that thought. My nipples tightened as I wondered if he liked the view. I slid my hand into the pocket and found it empty also. "Hey—"

Before I could voice my protest, he spoke. "There is *one* more pocket."

Oh. The exterior breast pocket was clearly a fake one, which meant the real pocket was inside the jacket. The expression on his face was bemused. Well, what did I know? I'd never played this game before. Maybe I should have thought of that first. Whatever. I gave him the old eyebrow right back, and slid my hand inside the jacket.

As I did, I caught a whiff of a spicy, masculine scent, not

quite strong enough to be cologne. It was as if I could feel his body heat with my nose.

Intoxicated by his scent, I finally felt something square and hard. I pulled it free: a ring box? Now I really wondered why he was drinking alone, if this was an engagement ring or something like that...

I glanced at him before I opened the box only to find a marble perched on a bed of velvet. I plucked it free.

The marble felt warm from being kept close to his heart. Just a round, glass marble with a swirl in it.

So, what were the instructions again? Put it in my mouth? I shared a look with him as I held the marble between two fingers. The request was a little bit dirty and a little intimate without being overtly sexual, and I think he knew that. It was a dare.

Did I dare?

I did. I made a show of dropping the marble into the alcohol he had left, swirling the glass around with a clinking sound, and then fishing the marble out and popping it into my mouth.

"Don't swallow," he warned.

I smiled, took up his glass, and went to fill his order.

Thankfully I didn't have to speak to send his drink order to the bar. I typed it on the upstairs order station, and then went down to put the glass in the bus bin.

Then what? I couldn't chance going into the main section of the bar, and I had to keep busy or it'd be obvious I was slacking off.

The ladies' room. I'd take a quick "powder" and then see if the drinks were up.

In the employee restroom, I straightened my hair and my

shirt. Normally I wouldn't give a damn about what a customer thought of my appearance. In fact, normally I hoped they didn't even notice me. But he was so impeccable and smooth! I wished I could seem even half that sophisticated, and since I couldn't, usually being invisible was better. I'd gotten some ketchup on the cuff of one sleeve at some point during the night. Sloppy. And this was my last unstained shirt. I made a note to ask Jill if she could cover that, too, at least a thrift store one. I hated being broke. I needed to get the hell out of grad school and start making some money. I had to find something to do with my life other than staring at pre-Raphaelite art and writing pretentious analyses of it. My mother told me endlessly that grad school was a waste of time, except for the fact that I might meet a well-educated guy to marry. I hadn't even gotten that part right.

A knock on the door jolted me. I hoped it wasn't anyone I would have to say much to. I tucked the marble into my cheek. "One sec!" I ran the water and washed my hands.

When I came out, Jill was standing there, her beefy arms crossed. "You okay in there? I've been waiting."

Well, nothing like the truth at a time like that, right? "I'm hiding because the advisor I blew off tonight to cover your ass is out there right now!" The marble clicked against my teeth as I tried to make myself understandable. Hopefully she would think it was a cough drop or an ice cube.

"What advisor? You didn't tell me you blew someone off!"

"Would it have mattered? 'Karina' "—it came out "Kawina" with the marble in the way—" 'I'm desperate. You're the only one who can do this. I need you,' " I hissed, imitating the way she had wheedled me on the phone.

"Of course it would have mattered."

I shook my head. "Last time I told you I had plans and didn't drop everything to work for you, you got Mom all pissed off at me and made my life a living hell for months."

"You had 'plans' with stupid Brad, who was no good for you anyway! I really did need you, and that night blew chunks without you." Jill had just turned thirty and was a good deal heavier than me. When she smacked the door frame next to my head, I swear the door felt it.

"Well, this is it, the last time. Now, excuse me. My order's up." I pushed past her. I loved Jill, but she thought because she was the oldest that my brother, Troy, and I were her lord- and lady-in-waiting or something. Troy was only a year younger than me, but he might as well have lived on another planet for all I saw of him or understood of him. And that was a cheap shot bringing up Brad. He was a failure in every sense of the word. I had thought dating an older, more distinguished guy was a good idea for someone about to leave grad school. He was thirty-three, seven years older than me, and I'd made the mistake of thinking that meant he was a functioning adult. Instead, he'd bounced between acting like he was fifty-three and in need of a geriatric nurse and acting like he was *three* and in need of a time-out. Worst of all, he was already trying to get a prescription for Viagra.

I meant it when I said failure in every way.

Thankfully, the order was up. I took the glass of water and the bourbon up the stairs, thinking, *So far, so good.*

The four-top of women had left, and the couple was holding hands and had their faces close together. I could see the tatters of wrapping paper on the table from the gifts they'd exchanged. I'm sure they were perfectly nice people, but all I wanted was to tell them to get a room.

As I approached my mystery man's table, I realized I had no idea how I was going to get the marble out of my mouth.

It was too late to go in the back and drop it into the glass there. He'd already seen me, and his gaze seemed to be drawing me toward him. His eyes never left mine as I crossed the floor, feeling like each step was getting heavier and heavier.

At last I stopped in front of his table, drew in a deep breath, and set down the glass of water. I then held up the shot glass of bourbon as if I were smelling it, brought the marble out until I held it with just my lips in an O shape, and let it go, almost like I was blowing him a kiss. The marble fell with a *plop* and I set the bourbon on the table, resisting the urge to wipe my lips. I settled for licking them.

He ignored the glass on the table, his eyes never leaving my face, and I saw his gaze sharpen at the momentary appearance of my tongue. I wondered if he was as turned on as I was. I had never flirted with a customer. Not like this.

He lifted his drink and smelled the bourbon, waving the glass under his nose and then closing his eyes for a moment as if savoring the scent. I nearly sighed when he did, as if I'd been released from a magic spell. A moment later he stared at me again as he took his first sip.

He nodded, as if satisfied, and set the glass down. "How did you choose which bourbon to give me this time? This isn't the same one."

"Well, you seem in the mood to try new things tonight," I explained. "Plus I figured you for the type that wouldn't go down in quality, so I went up."

He nodded again, approvingly, as if I'd answered a particularly tricky test question.

"Do I get my wish now?" I asked jokingly.

His face remained stern as he laid his hand on the table-top, fingers curled as if he were holding a live moth. "Think very hard about what you want, then close your eyes."

I did as he asked, without hesitating. Well, I closed my eyes, anyway. But what did I want? What should I wish for? I supposed this was like making a birthday wish before blowing out the candles. Wishing for happiness seemed way too general. Wishing for money felt wrong. Wishing to gradu-ate... *I shouldn't have to wish for that, damn it.* I deserved to finish and move on with my life. Wishing for that job I'd interviewed for? That was like wishing for money. And I wasn't even sure I wanted to work for Philip Hale. Something about him creeped me out a little.

"Make your wish," he whispered, and yet I heard him per-fectly clearly. "Then take the wish out of my hand."

I want to know what love is, I thought, and opened my eyes. He was grinning as he opened his hand and there was nothing there, but I played along by snatching up a bit of air and pretending to shove it into the breast pocket on my button-down shirt.

He startled me then by standing up, very close to me. I didn't back away. Instead, I looked up at him, wondering if he was feeling the effects of the alcohol. He was tall and he looked down to meet my eyes, his now shadowed, hawkish and intense.

"Thank you for playing this game with me," he said, voice low. I heard glass clink as he held up the marble, glistening with booze. He licked it clean, his tongue long and sinuous like a cat's, and I imagined what it would feel like licking me instead of the piece of glass. "You're very rare, Ashley. I would like to play another round with you sometime."

"I, um, okay," I said, hardly able to speak. I felt more like I was the one who had downed a shot, fueled with liquid courage.

He handed me a card with his other hand. "Call the number on that card if you're interested."

"Could we, um, play another round right now?" I heard myself ask. He was mesmerizing. He was different. I'd never met a man who made me feel like this: turned on and intrigued and challenged, and yet I felt safe, like he was someone I could trust.

He chuckled very low in his throat. "Desire is good," he said. "Being pushy is not."

"Oh. I'm sorry."

He closed his eyes a moment, as if he were thinking it over, and that helped. We were still standing far too close for far too long in a public place. I wanted to lick the shine of bourbon from the edge of his lip. He'd used the word *desire*, which made it clear what we were talking about, didn't it?

What he said next surely did. "Very well. One more round. Take the marble, and put it into your panties. You'll keep it there the rest of your shift. When you get off, call the number on the card to get your next instructions."

My heart was beating in triple time. "Okay," I said, sounding a bit breathless.

He handed me the marble and then raised his eyebrow.

"Right now?" I squeaked.

He nodded. The couple had stood to leave and were paying us no mind.

Under the front knot of my apron, I reached inside the waistband of my jeans, sucking in my stomach to make room for my hand. From there I dug my fingertips under the elastic of my panties and let the marble drop. I held in a gasp as it slid straight down the seam of my body, to where it found a pool of dampness I hadn't realized had gathered there.

I hadn't been this turned on in months. Possibly I hadn't been this turned on *ever.*

He leaned in to whisper, "Good girl," and I felt like I had won another prize. The feeling only deepened when he ran one finger along my jaw, such a light touch I barely felt it. "If you don't call, I'll know you decided you didn't want to play after all. I won't be— No, that's a lie. I *will* be disappointed if you don't. However, I'll respect your wishes."

"I'll earn another wish from you," I said in return. In the back of my head I was already thinking that if I wanted to back out, it would be easy. My name wasn't even Ashley, and this wasn't my actual job. But in the front of my mind all I could think of was how much I wanted to keep playing... with him.

He grinned. "Excellent." He nodded, then stepped back to put his topcoat on and walked out without looking back at me.

I stood there for a few more breathless seconds, until he was out of sight. Then I looked down and saw that the two twenty-dollar bills I thought he'd left on the table to cover his tab were actually fifties.

I shoved them into my apron pocket and collected the glasses from all the tables before heading down the stairs, carrying the tray over my shoulder. With each step I took, the marble rubbed back and forth in my panties, inflaming me. I wondered if anyone would be able to tell how turned on I was and was thankful for the amber and red lights in the place.

This was by far the kinkiest thing I had ever done. If Jill knew I had flirted with a customer like that, or with *anyone* for that matter, she'd freak. So it was imperative that I keep our secret. I suddenly realized I didn't even know his name. I looked at the card. All it had on it was a phone number. I slipped it into the back pocket of my jeans, wondering what his hand would feel like there.

I was so wrapped up in thinking about him that I almost dropped the glasses I was holding when someone grabbed me by the arm.

"Karina Casper! You told me you were too sick to get out of bed! What do you have to say for yourself?"

It was Professor Renault. And I was plain caught.

About the Author

Cecilia Tan is a writer, editor, and sexuality activist. She is the author of *Mind Games, The Hot Streak, White Flames, Edge Plays, Black Feathers, The Velderet,* and *Telepaths Don't Need Safewords,* as well as the Magic University series of paranormal erotic romances. She has the distinction of being perhaps the only writer to have erotic fiction published in both *Penthouse* and *Ms.* magazine, as well as in scores of other magazines and anthologies including *Asimov's, Best American Erotica,* and *Nerve.* She is the founder and editor of Circlet Press, publishers of erotic science fiction and fantasy. Her novel *Slow Surrender* won the RT Reviewers' Choice Award for Best Erotic Romance of 2013.

You can learn more at:

CeciliaTan.com

Twitter @ceciliatan

Facebook.com/thececiliatan